A Distant Voice in the Darkness

A CIP catalogue record for this book
is available from the British Library

ISBN 978-1-7397814-1-5

Published by 186 Publishing Limited 2022

186publishing.co.uk

To my father
Shambhu Nath Dutt
1900 – 1969

and to his great-granddaughter Bethan Beatrix Long
2001 – 2006

A Distant Voice
in the Darkness

Leela Dutt

Ships that pass in the night, and speak each other in passing,

Only a signal shown, and a distant voice in the darkness;

So on the ocean of life we pass and speak one another,

Only a look and a voice, then darkness again and a silence.

Henry Wadsworth Longfellow

Chapter One

Eleanor

What the hell is that hideous smell? Overpowering – burning, surely. But a hint of orange in it - or am I imagining that?

Pause to get my breath back at the top of the stairs. I'm here in this hall of residence to return a book I borrowed, but the pesky girl isn't in; it's Friday night, she's probably out clubbing. All right for some.

I can see smoke in the corridor now. Must be a fire. Let's see, kitchen at far end. Hurry, there's someone coughing!

Open the door carefully – oh God a fog!

There's someone in here; a very young man, peering at me through the mist. He must be a First Year student, like me, but eons younger than me. Tall, with an untidy mass of black hair that sticks straight up like a cartoon. And the most peculiar eyebrows, like a gable. He's taken off a large pair of NHS glasses, all steamed up, and put them on the work top.

'Oh hi,' he says. 'I'm not sure what's gone wrong. I was only trying to cook a chicken for my mates...'

I barge past him and open the oven door gingerly. Yes he's right, that blackened corpse must have been a chicken once. I grab a couple of cloths that someone's conveniently left next to the stove and lift the dish out gently.

'Oh, thanks! I wasn't sure what... My name's Alec Jenkins, by the way.'

'Enchanted to meet you, Alec Jenkins.' Sarcasm is a bad habit of mine, people say, but I don't think he's noticed. 'I'm Eleanor Larsen-Bruun.' I smile; I mustn't be unkind. It would feel like kicking a kitten.

'Hi, Eleanor! Do you think it was the marmalade I put on top of it? My Mum puts marmalade on chicken when she cooks it...'

There's a half empty jar of marmalade by his glasses on the work top.

'Well maybe she doesn't put quite so much... Could you open the window, Alec, do you think?' I feel round the underside of the bird.

1

'What have you got here? Oh no!' Inside the wretched thing is a melted plastic bag. 'Actually I think you're supposed to take the giblets out first. You can make gravy with them,' I explain. What is this, a cookery programme?

I pull at the outside skin. 'It's not that bad, Alec. You can eat most of it, look.' We are beginning to get a whiff of not altogether unpleasant roast chicken, and it's several hours since I ate anything. I've been in the lab all day, with no time – or money – for lunch. 'There should be enough here for your mates, if you cut it carefully.'

'Well actually I don't think any of them are free tonight. There's a match - I didn't realise.' He looks at me sadly. 'But it seems a shame to waste it. I don't suppose you'd like some, Eleanor?'

Which is how I now find myself curled up on his bed tucking into roast chicken, mopped up with some slices of bread I liberated from the communal kitchen.

'These black bits of skin are nice, you know,' I tell him. 'I've always loved burnt toast, too. My mother thinks I'm mad. But then she thinks I'm mad whatever I do. So does my sister.'

He's got a nice tidy room, this Alec Jenkins. Neat piles of books on the table. Bed already made when we came in, for goodness sake. He's even got family photos on the wall, at least I assume they are family. A portrait of a pretty young girl with long blonde hair – maybe his girlfriend? Shame, but there you go. He was bound to have a girlfriend, wasn't he?

I'm attacking the chicken with cheerful abandon; who cares about getting your fingers sticky? 'My father always said that if it has wings, you are allowed to pick it up in your fingers and eat it. That's a Danish rule, he said...' I tell Alec now.

'He sounds nice, your father. Is he...?'

'He's dead now.'

'Oh I'm so sorry.'

'He died when I was fifteen. I loved him very, very much but he died anyway.'

Wow! Where did that come from? I never talk about my Dad. Certainly not to some random person I've just met. But there's something about this Alec that makes it OK to say anything to him.

'My mother's Italian,' I add. 'She's a lot older than me – she was forty-three by the time she had me, but she tries gamely to keep up. We live in London.'

'Italian, is she? That's where you get your looks from, then.' Alec is getting out a hanky to wipe his chin.

That's what they all say. Bugger. I think he's going to offer me a drink of pop now. What to say? I hate fizzy drinks.

*

The rain is dripping down my neck and making its way to my bra, which was clean on today, because you never know. I can't feel my feet any more – my socks got soaked, then froze solid around the time we left the museum.

So this is Caerleon. We are squelching our way across the Roman amphitheatre, and Alec is telling me scintillating facts about it. I can't hear what he's saying over his shoulder because it's blowing a gale. I think it's something to do with the Romans.

I wonder how soon we can go and look for a café for lunch. I assume lunch is part of the plan for the day?

We came here on three buses; Alec usually borrows his father's car to go anywhere but his brother Charlie crashed it last weekend. Wrapped it round a lamppost, apparently. He was taking someone called Milly to the cinema. How fast was the lamppost going? Their Dad Norman was incandescent, and refuses to let anyone use the courtesy car.

I asked if Milly is Charlie's girlfriend, but Alec said not really, Charlie has a string of girls, but Milly poor thing is smitten with Charlie. She's the daughter of an old school-friend of their mother's, and Barbara is determined that she will marry one or other of her sons. 'Charlie just uses Milly. He uses everyone,' Alec told me with surprising venom.

I haven't met any of his family, of course, though they live quite near, in Lisvane, the posh bit of north Cardiff. They sound fierce, and I don't think he wants to let them near me. For the time being. Which is odd, considering that we've seen each other pretty well every day since that weird marmalade-roast-chicken evening. He turned up the very

3

next morning when I was just off to the lab, to tell me that a mate of his was having a party that night and he wondered if I would like to go. That girlfriend I had imagined turned out after all to be just his little sister Roz. I expect I'll like her.

I hate parties. I have nothing to wear which doesn't make me look like a short dumpy woman with too many cardigans. And I specially hate parties where you don't know anyone.

There was a hopeless squash round the food, and he put his arm around my waist to guide me to where we might grab some. That's when I first thought, YES! That's NICE, do keep doing that...

He took a couple of plates and began to pile them high with a bit of everything. 'Don't know what this is, do you? Never mind, we'll try it.' There was quite a lot of not altogether unpleasant wine.

Eventually we noticed that we hadn't actually spoken to anyone else since we arrived, and he suggested that we went elsewhere. 'Sorry Eleanor – when you've taken so much trouble. Getting dressed, I mean. I like that green thingy, by the way – what would you call it? Your blouse, is it? Whatever. We can stay if you want...'

'I do normally, you know. Get dressed. Before I go out anywhere.' I giggled inanely – I think the wine was getting to me. 'But I don't mind leaving. We can go back to my place if you like.'

My place was mercifully empty, it being the middle of the evening. There was a smell of stale baked beans, and someone – Her Upstairs probably – had left the cheese and its dirty grater out on the table as usual.

But he didn't appear to see the clutter in my room. Swiftly I swept up the jumble of stuff on the bed – lecture notes, mainly, and a recent letter from my sister, a dirty bra and a couple of half-eaten apples – and made a space.

Well at least he can't have thought I'd planned all along to bring him here.

He looked round for a chair to sit on. There was only the one, so very carefully he lifted up the papers and a couple of books, straightened them into a neat pile, and placed them on the desk. He sat on the chair while I curled up on the bed.

'Why don't you come onto the bed too? There's plenty of room.'

4

'Oh! Well, all right, then.' I shifted along and he squatted gingerly on the edge of the bed.

I smiled encouragingly, but he didn't quite seem to know what to do next. 'Well...this is nice. Have you lived here long?' he said after a moment.

Don't ask me why on earth he said that.

'Long enough,' I laughed, taking his hand. Then I leant forwards and kissed him on the mouth. For a fraction of a second he looked startled.

*

So here we are – the long-dreaded Visit to Lisvane. Alec says we can't put it off any longer.

It's early December, Christmas is looming, and Alec's mother Barbara - or should I call her Mrs Jenkins? – is decorating an enormous Christmas tree. They live in a large house set back from the road, big garden at the front and a bigger one at the back. Tomorrow I'm going to have to get out my sketch pad and do some drawings – I always do that when I want to remember what I've seen.

Barbara pauses briefly, and pushes the hair back from her face. 'Oh hallo there. You must be...?'

'This is Eleanor, Mum. I did tell you.'

'So sorry. I'm good with names, but Charlie, that's my other son,' she went on, sticking her hand out briefly. 'Charlie brings back a different girl every fortnight; I simply can't keep up with them!'

'Is Charlie around?' There's a distinct note of hesitation in Alec's question.

'Oh yes, he's here somewhere. Supposed to be revising for his Mock A Levels but you know Charlie. Probably playing the guitar.'

Charlie is her favourite, obviously.

As Barbara stretches up to hang a big golden globe near the top of the tree, her foot slips. 'Damn!' She clutches at Alec's arm. 'I can't quite reach. Could you be a brick...'

Alec takes the bauble off her and hangs it as high as possible. 'Chin up, old bean!' he cries with a grin, and Barbara gives a great guffaw.

This is some obscure Jenkins family joke, strictly private. Some families do that to you, don't they?

'Now look, darlings,' Barbara says, getting her breath back. 'Do you mind leaving me in peace for half an hour? I must get these blooming decorations finished while Norman is out, else he'll come back and want it done differently.'

'I doubt that very much,' Alec mutters to me under his breath.

*

Norman appears at dinner time and greets me warmly. He seems friendly, and he's got a wonderful smell of vanilla from his pipe. He asks me where I live, what I'm studying, which isn't my favourite topic of conversation; it's so much more interesting when you can get other people to talk, don't you find?

I've heard a lot about Norman. Alec says he gets terrible nightmares because he was at Monte Cassino during the war, but he never brings it up.

'No one is allowed to mention it, ever,' Alec told me. 'I mean, seriously, ever. My little sister Roz tried to, once. He exploded!'

'Did he really?'

'We didn't know what hit us. Mum rushed him away upstairs, and he didn't speak to any of us for a week. Oh and I've got a mysterious uncle that we never talk about either.'

Well we've got through dinner all right, more or less. Roz the younger sister is here - she seems friendly. Charlie turned up late for the meal, dashing in as Barbara was dishing out potatoes, pulling on a jersey and explaining that he had to go out in half an hour because he had a hot date. He's shorter than Alec, with thick blond hair, and he's got the same gable-end eyebrows as his brother. Where do they come from? Norman's got them too, but not so prominently. Charlie grinned cheerfully at me and squeezed into a place next to me. 'Mind if I sit here, my Sunshine?'

Alec's mother is what she calls a "good plain cook". No marmalade in sight this time - she produced a leg of lamb with all the trimmings. Barbara Jenkins is the kind of British woman against whom

I'm afraid I've always nursed an irrational prejudice. She conveys effortless superiority.

I'd better try to help clear away. We're standing in the kitchen, and Barbara remarks casually, 'I hear that you are of mixed parentage.' She makes it sound like an unfortunate disease.

'Er...'

'I don't really approve of mixed marriages, although my younger brother Ian did marry...' She snatches a saucepan which I'm trying to put away on a shelf. 'No, no – that doesn't go there. Here, you'd better wash – I'll never find anything if you put things in the wrong place! But at least both your parents are European, I gather – which is more than can be said for my poor sister-in-law,' she went on. 'Are your parents happy together?'

'They were happy, for twenty-five years. Then my father died.'

'Oh I see.' Barbara sniffed. 'Well, there's exceptions to every rule.'

Next day I'm sketching the Jenkins house, isolated from the outside world it seems to me. I'll make the ivy cover the whole house, not just the corner where Barbara has trained it. I'm going to put Charlie's music certificates hanging over the fireplace in the living room, lovingly placed there by his mother. Then the individual bedrooms, each with its separate occupant, oblivious of the other members of the family.

A curious thing strikes me now: on the walls and shelves of Barbara's home there are dozens of photos of the three children at various stages of their life, as you would expect. There are also a few of Barbara's family – younger brother Ian, parents and so on, even one of her parents' wedding in 1924. But there's not one single picture anywhere in the house of Norman's youth or the family he came from.

I'm sketching Norman, smoking that large brown pipe which smells of vanilla – heavenly! He's a quiet man, not given to interrupting – but then he's been married to Barbara for so long he's probably forgotten how to; he quaintly refers to her as the Duchess. Barbara's got a useful habit of never quite finishing a sentence so that you don't know when it's all right to put your own thoughts into the conversation.

It was Norman who explained to me why Barbara's brother Ian was a significant family member. 'The wife's brother had to live with us when we married,' he said, puffing on his pipe. 'He was only eleven at the time. Father died at Dunkirk, mother copped a V2 bomb right at the end of the war. The Duchess is very good with him.'

'Is Ian still around?' I asked him, hoping the conversation would last so I could enjoy the smell of vanilla.

'Oh no, he upped and went off to Nigeria to lecture in economics. Married a half-Indian lass from Cardiff – Val, they call her. Pleasant girl I've always thought, though Barbara didn't take to her for some reason.'

'Why was that?'

'Never fathomed out why. This Valerie already had a boy before she married Ian, nice little lad called Matt, same age as our Roz. Maybe that was the problem. Then they had another boy.'

'Though why they wanted to go off and live in Nigeria, for goodness sake...' Barbara came into the room with a tray of coffee and caught the end of her husband's remarks. 'I shall never know. I've always thought there are plenty of beautiful places in our own country that we haven't seen yet – no need to go to the ends of the earth! Milk, Eleanor? Oh I do hope you don't take sugar – I'm afraid we're clean out.'

She poured out the coffee carefully – I can't imagine Barbara ever spilling anything. 'No we've never been to Nigeria, Norman and I,' Barbara went on. 'Norman doesn't travel.' She made her husband sound like a delicate type of wine. 'But Alec, now, I believe he's thinking of going next year some time.'

*

Term's over at last and I'm relaxing, staying up a few days in Cardiff.

'My poor brother – he'll be so disappointed that you're off to Italy for Christmas. I don't suppose he's even got inside your knickers yet,' Charlie says cheerfully. He's strumming on his guitar upstairs while his brother and sister are fetching mistletoe from the garden centre for Barbara. 'Bit backward, is young Alec.'

There's nothing to say to that.

'Sorry, sorry! None of my business! But you do look extra gorgeous when you blush, my Sunshine.' He reaches across to pick up

8

another book of music. 'Suppose we ought to have something Christmassy now... Have you met our Milly, by the way?'

'Not yet. Alec mentioned her.'

'Mousy girl. Wears beige a lot.' Charlie plays a falling series of chords, ending with a dull thud. 'Goes to Howells School for Young Ladies, where they have to wear posh gloves. It's her eighteenth birthday just before Christmas.'

Barbara is most insistent that the whole family should go to Milly's birthday party, which is to be held in the local community hall. 'Such a shame you are going away, dear,' she said to me this morning with a brief smile.

'Oh no she isn't – your flight's not 'til the twenty-second, Ellie!' Alec remembered. 'You can still come to the party.'

'Well I'm not sure...' The thought horrified me.

Charlie groaned. 'It'll go on 'til all hours, if I know Milly's friends. The Hooray Henriettas. You'll have to stay the night here, Sunshine. You can't possibly go back into town in the middle of the night. Eleanor can have the spare room, can't she, Mum?'

Barbara breathed in. 'Yes I suppose so, if I move out all the Christmas presents I'm storing there. Give me time – I'll find somewhere. It's not as if I've got anything else to occupy me, the week before Christmas. Fifty Russians arriving first week of January, all needing me to find them accommodation, but worry ye not.'

*

Charlie's brought his guitar to Milly's birthday party and he clearly intends to spend most of the evening in the kitchen of the community hall entertaining the hired teenagers who are here to serve food and wash up. Obviously I don't know anyone else here, so I'm finding the kitchen the most comfortable place to be. Norman has gravitated here too.

'Far too many people,' he grumbles, perching himself on a stool by the oven and lighting his pipe. 'Who the hell are they all?' The pipe's familiar vanilla smell fills the kitchen, mingling with other smells of cocktail sausages in the oven and melted cheese on spicy pizzas.

Through the hatch there's a swirling mass of party-goers. In the middle of the room I can see the Birthday Girl herself: Milly Pryce-Roberts, eighteen today, small and pale, in a light brown dress which as Charlie pointed out, really doesn't do very much for her. She seems overwhelmed by all the attention and fuss – poor kid. I wonder if she hates parties, like I do? I feel really sorry for her. Everyone keeps piling gifts into her arms as they arrive, elaborately wrapped, and no one gives her time to unwrap them.

Alec is over there with Milly, smiling, trying to help with the presents, offering to put some of them on the table by the window. He can see how embarrassed she is by the concentration of interest in her.

Eventually he comes out to the kitchen to fetch me. 'You must come and say hallo properly to Milly,' Alec says, and takes me by the hand.

'Oh, hi,' Milly says shyly when we pin her down. 'I've heard about you. You're at the university, right?'

I nod. 'Great party you're having,' I tell her, trying to sound encouraging.

Milly grimaces. 'My parents organised it all.'

*

It's all over at last - as Charlie predicted, it's well after midnight - and here I am in Blessed Barbara's spare room, which has been stripped for my benefit of all the Christmas presents she was storing here.

I'm cold, and I've put on a thick sweater. I'm trying to sleep. Obviously.

No chance.

One of those nights when the events of the day crowd in on you, chasing each other round and round in your head. No point just lying there letting them, might as well commit them to paper.

Let's start with a neat little sketch of Milly herself, her pale thin hair swept back in an old-fashioned bun. How many of Milly's own friends had come? Or does she have friends? She strikes me as a solitary, shy person.

And where was Charlie in all this? Why had he stayed so long in the kitchen – did Milly mind that? Later in the evening when the live band arrived on the stage and people began to dance, Charlie emerged and grabbed Milly's hand to persuade her onto the floor, but after a while he went on to some of the other girls. He danced with me too, a solid chunky figure, calling me his Sunshine.

I'm sketching the dance floor with assorted couples strewn across it.

Suddenly there's a crash from outside the room – what the hell is that? Much too loud for a door being banged, surely?

I'm holding my breath.

I put down the pad and tiptoe to the door, opening it cautiously. The landing is completely dark – thick curtains drawn, and no light left on.

There's a blood-curdling shout from a room at the far end of the landing.

'Oh my God, the planes... They're coming in early! I can't... Stanley, can't you see? The bombs, they're huge. Look, they're dropping on the mountain! Stop them, Stan, must stop them... The bomb doors – opening – dozens of them... Early!'

Someone is screaming, and I realise that it's Norman.

'Get the refugees out for God's sake! They promised. They're going straight for the Abbey... They promised they wouldn't...'

Is he all right?

'Listen, can't you hear? Stan, what shall I do? I don't know... The ground, it's shaking. Can't you feel it? Hundreds of people trying... Choking in the dust. That man, look, with the child. Stop! Oh God, that wall is coming down...' And he screams again.

I'm frozen to the spot, the flesh on the back of my neck tingling.

Where's Alec?

The door at the end of the landing opens and a crack of light appears. It must be Barbara – and at once I close my own door as silently as possible and creep back to bed, extinguishing the table lamp. The woman is obviously in control, whatever is going on, and I'm quite certain that she would not want to encounter a visitor on her travels around the darkened house.

*

Rome at last. Christmas with Mum and Gabriella and her family.

Relaxing – and playing with the baby. And lots of lovely food, prepared by everyone else. Life back to normal.

Alec has phoned a few times.

'He seems quite keen, this boy,' Gabriella remarks after the third call. We're shopping in the market for some fish, and I'm pushing the pram. 'Mum was wondering...'

'Typical!' I turn and glare at my sister. 'You and Mum have been gossiping about me as usual, haven't you?'

'Us? Gossip? We wouldn't dream of it... But you have, you know, happened to bring him into the conversation once or twice while you've been here.'

'No I haven't! Well only when we took the children to the Colosseum on Friday. I may have told you that Alec and I went to the amphitheatre at Caerleon a few weeks ago. It reminded me, seeing the Colosseum again, so obviously I mentioned it.'

Gabriella laughs and leans across to pull the hood up over her baby's pushchair; it looks like rain. 'Yes, and when I decided to do a roast chicken the day you and Mum arrived, you told us how this wonderful Alec of yours puts marmalade on chicken when he roasts it!'

'Did I?'

'You know you did.' Gabriella takes my arm. 'I've never heard you talk about a boy like this before. You've always been so casual. When we were at school, there was that lad – what was his name? I forget. Anyway, that other one, the one with the horrendous hair. And a few more. Oh, and the one whose mother collected stamps.'

My sister is an elephant – she remembers things.

'Oh, him! We only went out three times.'

'That's what I mean. So the amazing new Alec, how long have you known him?'

'Ten weeks and three days. Roughly.'

Gabriella looks at me. 'It's serious, isn't it?'

Watch out! I'm not sure about admitting to this.

'I don't know, Gabby. It feels kind of right.'

'Yes? Mum thinks he sounds terribly young.'

'Oh for God's sake! He's the same age as me. I don't feel young. Anyway, what about you – you were twenty when you married Giulio: I don't seem to remember Mum worrying about how young you were.'

'That's different – Giulio's Italian. Of course Mum wanted me to marry a nice Italian boy from a family she knew! This is quite different.'

We stop by a fish stall.

'Little Sister...' She turns to look at me with a frown.

'What?'

'You will be careful, won't you?'

*

I'm travelling back alone, for Mum's arranged to stay on another fortnight with Gab's family. My flight has been delayed for six hours, and I'm quite exhausted. The food on the flight was distinctly disappointing - I'd been hoping that prosciutto e melone would make up for the delay, but prosciutto was apparently off.

I'd better pick myself up and go and look for a bus.

'Eleanor! Over here...'

Oh good heavens - there's Alec running across the arrivals terminal.

He flings his arms round me and kisses me. 'I've missed you so much. And I want to tell you this great idea I've had.'

Careful, it probably won't work, whatever it is.

'What's that?'

He picks up my suitcase. 'You know my Uncle Ian lives in Nigeria with his family? I'm going out to see them in the Easter vacation.'

'Yes, you said.'

Presumably Barbara will be paying for Alec to go out to see her brother.

'My Dad says he'll pay for both of us to go, if you want to!'

I stare at him.

'You don't mean both as in you and me?'

'Certainly do! Won't cost much, only the flights – we'll be staying with Ian and Val. They've got this huge house on campus. Say you'll come, my darling!'

'Oh no, Alec – I couldn't possibly. I haven't got any spare money.'

'Not a problem – I told you, Dad'll pay for the flights, and then like I say we just stay with Ian and Val. I've got a bit of money saved for trips and stuff, you don't need to worry. Please come! At least think about it...'

Chapter Two

Nigeria, 1973

Alec was sick on the steps outside the University of Ife Health Centre the day they touched down in Nigeria. As it turned out, that considerably shortened the time it took Val Beynon to get them registered as visitors.

He rested hunched up against a palm tree, while Matt and his Nigerian friends looked down at him sympathetically. The boys were out for a Saturday bike ride together.

It really was blisteringly hot – pushing thirty-five. Even Eleanor felt it.

Alec was dripping green streaks of bile onto the ground, but the boys didn't seem to mind. The tallest one offered him a sip of coke from a plastic bottle, which Eleanor thought was a sign of real generosity, but Val was quick to stop him.

'That's big-hearted of you, Seretse, but Alec will be fine.' Val put her arm around her nephew. 'You'll feel better now, dear. Better out than in, we always say.'

Alec glanced round at Eleanor, who was looking anxious. It was wonderful to have her here - he'd thought she wouldn't come.

It took Eleanor till the next day to get out her sketch pad, but then she drew everything – the compound where the Beynons lived: House G15 at the far end of Road 13, just next door to Mrs Adejuyigbe, whose husband was a professor. All the houses had extensive grounds with trees that she'd never seen before – there was a paw-paw tree outside her bedroom, and at the back of the gardens was a clump of trees where Ian told the children that the black fruit bats lived. They heard their screeches at dusk. Mrs Adejuyigbe kept chickens in a coop at the back of her house, and they could hear them clucking merrily all day.

Towards the back of all the compounds were what were called the boys' quarters: concrete huts for the servants. Val said that when they were first shown round their house, Ian had asked if these quarters had fans, since their own house had several. The Nigerian official had smiled indulgently as if Ian was making a feeble jest – but Val knew he was serious.

'What are you drawing? Show me.' Alec went into Eleanor's bedroom the next day. His navy tee shirt was already stained under the arms and his shorts were sticking to his legs.

He climbed up onto her bed and kissed her briefly.

'Oh, I'm just trying to sketch the hens in the next-door garden. I love the way they rush around squawking when the gardener goes into the coop to catch one of them. Val says they do a brisk trade in chickens for campus dinner parties.'

'This is good, this drawing, Eleanor. You ought to publish it or something.'

'It's just a hobby, Alec. Not much use for it in the lab!'

He took off his glasses and put a damp, sweaty arm around her. 'What do you want to do next? Down to the staff club for a swim, or...'

'Mmmm...' She folded away her sketchpad on the bedside table. 'Maybe a swim afterwards?' And she helped him tug at the button at the back of her frock. It really was ridiculously hot.

*

The staff swimming pool was a major focus of social life, they noticed in the coming days. It was a kidney-shaped pool, deep at one end, and surrounded by a well-kept lawn; a noisy place, for thousands of frogs lived just inside the rim of the pool and they'd croak away to each other without taking any notice of the humans.

Matt and his friends often met at the pool. Eleanor saw Seretse again, helping Matt's little brother Owen on with his arm bands. He was learning to swim, and Seretse was teaching him. He really was an unusually kind young lad, was Seretse.

One afternoon Eleanor and Val lay sprawled on deckchairs by the pool, under large straw hats; Val had lent one to Eleanor who was making a sketch of the pool to send to her Danish cousin Kirsten.

'How do you get on with Alec's parents, Eleanor? See much of them?' Val asked now.

Eleanor hesitated. 'Not if I can help it!'

Val grinned.

'I don't think Barbara really approves of me,' Eleanor went on. 'Does she, Alec?'

Alec was stretched out on the grass next to the chairs with his eyes closed.

'Oh I wouldn't say that...' he muttered without too much conviction.

'Join the club!' Val exclaimed with surprising force. 'She never liked me... Well not in the beginning, anyway. Thought I wasn't good enough for her wonderful brother. But she's got a heart of gold, underneath – it's just that you have to be around for long enough to find it.'

There was a sudden splash as one of Matt's friends picked him up and chucked him into the water. Val scolded them for drenching everyone sitting by the pool. 'Neo and Matt – you're a pair of menaces! Go away and leave us alone.'

'Norman's all right, when he's feeling sociable,' Eleanor went on. 'He pretends to be interested in what I'm doing. Sometimes I wish he wouldn't – I don't really want to talk about physics when I'm away from college! I'd much rather ask him about himself.'

'Ah now that's difficult, Eleanor. Norman hates talking about himself, I've always thought.'

'I don't think I've found Barbara's heart of gold yet! She always makes me feel that I've forgotten to wash the sleep out of my eyes...'

Val laughed. 'Oh yes! I know exactly what you mean.'

'The first time I went to her house, she told me she didn't approve of mixed marriages!' Eleanor said.

'Oh dear. Yes that is one of Barbara's things. You mustn't take it personally...'

There was no reply to that, Eleanor thought. She leant back in her deckchair as they watched the waiter bringing a tray of iced drinks to a family across the pool.

'You must have known Barbara for a long time?' she said in the end.

'Uh-huh.' Val paused to shout at Matt to go and find out what his younger brother Owen was up to – and make sure he wasn't drowning. 'I've never forgotten the first time Ian ever took me to visit the

Jenkinses, soon after we met. I'd already got Matt then, he was just a year, and their Roz was two months older than him.'

Val made a face. 'You remember, don't you, Alec? You were exasperated by Charlie! As usual, I discovered later. That first visit, my main impression of the boys was of demented babble. Charlie was seven at the time, and pretty uncontrollable. Alec was quieter – he would retreat to his bedroom, closing the door with a deep sigh, Barbara told me, and read his comics or do his jigsaws just to get away from everyone else.'

Alec grinned. 'Sounds about right.'

'But on our second visit you were much more forthcoming, weren't you, Alec, because you'd had a birthday and been given a spanking new black and gold bike which you were most anxious to show me.'

He groaned and opened his eyes - he knew what was coming.

Val went on, 'I lifted Matt up and we watched Alec riding up and down the pavement.'

'Sounds fun,' Eleanor said. 'I had a bike around that age too. My big sister Gabby taught me to ride it.'

'Nothing as co-operative as that in the Jenkins family! Later in the afternoon Charlie vanishes for about half an hour, doesn't he, and suddenly we hear an almighty crash outside. We all rush out and find Charlie lying in a heap on the road. He and three of his friends had been competing to see who could get a bicycle to mount up onto the low brick wall around the Jenkins' front garden and leap over it. Charlie had almost made it, but the bike he was riding hadn't, quite. It lay in a mangled heap underneath him.'

'Oh no!' cried Eleanor.

'Oh yes – I knew instantly: it was Alec's bike. Typical. Anything Alec has, Charlie always has to wreck, doesn't he?'

Well, you said it, Val, Alec thought – but he made no comment himself.

Back at the house they found that the cook steward was preparing a dinner party for some of the Beynons' friends. He was a short stocky man, an Ibo named Mbibi, dressed neatly in cotton trousers and a white tee shirt; he was older than the Beynons, and they sensed that Val was in awe of him. Eleanor simply could not imagine having to tell a man like Mbibi what you wanted him to do for you. Val said that she'd never wanted to have servants, and certainly didn't want anyone to help with the children, but a Black American friend of hers on campus had urged her that she ought to hire someone because local people depended on the university staff for employment. Mbibi in particular needed the money: it was only three or four years since the civil war had ended, and he was supporting a family of six back home in Umuahia, in what had been Biafra. The Beynons paid him fifteen pounds a month, which was a good wage for the time.

'What are you cooking tonight, Mbibi?' Eleanor asked. She hoped he wouldn't be offended if she did a sketch of him at work. He was so deft and quick, the way he cut up the vegetables. There was a wonderful smell of freshly sliced peppers.

'Madam asked for chicken tonight. I bought a couple from Mrs Adejuyigbe this morning. The gardener recommended this big one – look, plenty of meat on it.' He was proud of his work, and he certainly didn't cook the giblets in a little plastic bag inside the bird – as Eleanor pointed out later to Alec; ouch.

Val came into the kitchen. 'Oh yes, those two will be quite big enough. I'm so glad Mbibi gets the chickens for us, you know, Eleanor. I can't stand the thought of going over to that garden and making them catch me one of those poor creatures. They are all so alive, clucking and rushing round happily. Then they kill one just for me.'

Eleanor looked at her.

'You think I'm soft, I can see, Eleanor...'

'No, not at all, Val! I'd be just the same.'

'To be honest, Eleanor, I wish I could just pick up a dead chicken from a shelf in Sainsbury's: then I'd know it was dead already, whether I chose it or not!' She turned with a grin and went off to see if Owen was ready for bed.

It seemed to Eleanor that Val was making a good fist of living this life of hers, the Expatriate Wife. She taught literacy classes to domestic staff from all over the campus, she had a wide network of friends, both Nigerian and indeed from every continent. She coped effortlessly with emergencies such as power cuts and water shortages. She knew why you sometimes had to keep the bath full of water. In short, she seemed happy. But it was not at all a life that Eleanor would ever want for herself, she was certain.

'You see, Eleanor, when you marry someone,' Val said to her one day at the pool, 'you marry their dreams.'

'Do you?' Eleanor stared at her.

'Oh yes. Ian loves his job here. It gives him far more scope than he would ever get at home. More responsibility. More satisfaction. He thrives on this life.'

Eleanor could see that was true.

'And so I could never turn round and say, that's enough – I want to go home. I just couldn't do it.' Val smiled sadly at her.

Eleanor thought for a moment. 'So what are your dreams, Val?'

'Ah now that's a question, Eleanor. I don't know; maybe I shall find out one day?'

*

The university was on the edge of an ancient Yoruba town called Ile-Ife, a thriving, bustling place with a market where you haggled for everything from steak to colourful bales of cloth. Alec was keen to visit the National Museum, which had not long been open, and he took Eleanor there early one morning, before the heat got too oppressive.

'I want to see the famous terracotta heads,' Alec said, taking her hand. 'I've come across amazing pictures of them. Ife was a big city between the ninth and twelfth centuries, you know. It was a major artistic centre.'

'Really?'

They stood and looked at the terracotta heads, big impressive carvings which made Eleanor want to sketch them.

'It's funny how some people are surprised these days that there was so much going on here centuries ago,' Alec said. 'Down in Rhodesia there's a huge stone city called Great Zimbabwe, obviously built by Africans hundreds of years ago, but Ian Smith has a theory that Arabs must have been there because Africans couldn't have done it!'

They turned and walked back towards the entrance, where they paused to take sips from the water bottle Val had provided, and Eleanor bought some postcards of the terracotta heads.

'I'd love to go and see Great Zimbabwe for myself one day,' Alec said, his eyes shining. 'We could go together, couldn't we?'

Eleanor smiled. 'Maybe...'

Later that afternoon she lay on her bed with nothing on at all, wondering if the heat was going to let off enough for her to get any sleep that night. Ian had told her the rains would come eventually, but probably not before the end of their holiday.

'I like your Auntie Val a lot,' she said to Alec. 'She doesn't let the grass grow under her feet, does she? The other day she was describing all the novels she's read while she's been here, from the university bookshop. Everything that Conan Doyle and John Wyndham ever wrote. And these English classes that she teaches...'

'We'll have to check out the bookshop. Bound to find something on the Ife bronzes.' He stretched out next to her and put his arm across her stomach. 'OK?'

'Oh, Alec it's too hot!' she said, but he knew she didn't mean it. She sat up and nuzzled his ear.

'I love the way you do that,' he said, taking off his glasses.

*

In the early days of their visit, they explored the campus, which was set in thirteen hundred acres of dense tropical forest. It contained three hills – named with ruthless logic to match the road and house names: Hill One, Hill Two and Hill Three, though as Ian told them, it was very unlikely that the local Yoruba villagers knew them by those names. Rumour had it that a priestess lived at the top of Hill Two, the nearest to the Beynons' house, but no one ever saw any sign of her.

'Are there any wild creatures on the hills?' Eleanor asked.

'Oh no,' Ian told her. 'It's hardly the Kruger National Park round by here. A colleague of mine thought he saw a small leopard five years ago.'

Ian took Alec for a walk up Hill Two early one morning. He'd asked Eleanor too of course, but she'd groaned at the thought of getting up at a ridiculous hour, and the men set off on their own. The hill was an inselberg, a core of bare rock above the plain, and an easy climb with good paths.

There was no sign of the elusive priestess, as they ambled along in easy companionship.

'Glad you brought Eleanor with you,' Ian said as they paused on a bend in the path. 'We weren't sure if...'

'She's great, isn't she?' Alec grinned.

'Oh yes - and Val likes her a lot, too.' Ian looked at his nephew. 'Have you made any plans? You've got another two years before you finish your degree, of course.'

'Yes we both have. I'm hoping we can get married as soon as we finish. You'll have to come home that summer!'

'And then what, have you thought?'

'There's so much I want to do, Ian! I want to travel, of course, like you have... Take Eleanor all over the world, if we can.'

'Well Val and I certainly enjoy living in Ife. I suppose Eleanor will go on sketching wherever you end up, won't she?'

*

One morning they joined Val on the school run, dropping the boys and their friends off at the staff school.

'Owen's got a really nice teacher this year,' Val told them. 'She and her husband are political exiles from South Africa.'

Val pointed out a short cut that Alec and Eleanor could take through the forest to the university's teaching blocks, so they left her at the school and set off.

'I suppose there aren't any snakes here, are there?' Eleanor said. 'My mother's terrified of snakes.'

Alec laughed and put his arm around her waist. 'No, you're all right: Ian says they slide away if they hear you coming! They are only small ones.'

As they walked, they suddenly came across a clearing in the forest where someone seemed to have made a garden. It was completely deserted, but there were obvious signs of human life: someone had planted dozens of rows of different plants and flowers.

'Isn't it wonderful – what is it?' Eleanor said.

'The Garden of Eden! No, it looks like some sort of nursery. Probably some university department experimenting with crops that grow in the forest.'

They looked around, and noticed a shed over in the far corner, perhaps where the gardener kept tools.

'Let's sit down a minute,' Eleanor suggested. The day was beginning to warm up, although it was not yet nine o'clock. 'I'm out of breath.'

So they stretched out on the forest floor, looking up at the great green canopy at the top of the trees. 'It's miles and miles above us, isn't it?' said Alec, taking her hand. 'Imagine if we could go up there!'

Alec always wants to go and see things. He's got to find out what's happening. So do I, in a way, but perhaps not the same things.

'Eleanor?'

'What?'

'I love you, you know.' He rolled over and put his arm across her chest.

Sweat was already running down her neck into her blouse, making her smell of exertion. 'I know,' she said. 'I love you, too...'

I really do. It's just I don't know if I can love your dreams.

He began to kiss her, tugging at her shorts. He didn't seem to mind the sweat.

'Here, Alec...? Are you sure it's safe?'

'Told you, the snakes all slip away...'

*

Early one morning Eleanor came into the dining room to find Alec deep in conversation with Owen. The child was showing him a picture he'd drawn at school, which no one else had taken much notice of – just my baby brother's usual scribble, Matt had said.

'That's lovely, Owen,' Alec said. 'It's a story, is it? That your teacher told you? What's this bit, here?'

'It's the exes,' Owen declared proudly.

'Oh I see. Exes.' Alec looked up at Eleanor. 'Do you think they start algebra at five?' he murmured.

Eleanor smiled and sat down on the other side of Owen.

'Er... what exactly are exes, Owen?' Alec asked him at last.

'Exes!' Owen could not believe that anyone as big and important and clever as his cousin Alec could be so stupid. 'These are the Big Bad Robbers cutting down the trees, look,' he said patiently. 'And those are their exes. You have to have exes to cut down trees!'

'Ah, I see. Yes of course.' Alec turned to Eleanor. 'Val did say his teacher was South African, didn't she?'

Eleanor laughed. 'So she did.' She wondered then how many other nineteen-year-olds would be interested in a five-year-old kid. It struck her that Alec was an immensely kind man, in dozens of small hidden ways.

Is it the small kindnesses that matter?

*

After the first week Eleanor and Alec left Ife and set out on the open road to the north. Only Val was free to accompany them; she drove them in the family's little white Volkswagen Beetle, their sparse luggage stowed under the bonnet in front.

Eleanor thought the travellers were amazing. The roads were open to anyone and everyone. All drivers sported comforting stickers proclaiming 'Nigeria drives right' for they had only recently changed from the left.

'Look at that lorry!' Alec clutched Eleanor's hand and pointed at a huge vehicle with a couple of dozen passengers perched on top of it. At the front was a sign which read 'GOD BLESS.'

'You'll see plenty of those,' said Val, deftly driving across the road to avoid a pothole. There was a well-beaten track round it. 'I do normally stick to the right. If there's anything coming I can always flash at the driver to let them know there's a pothole the size of Ibadan for them to look out for...'

There were people everywhere: roads were clearly meant for walking. They saw groups of women in colourful clothes carrying stacks of sticks or sometimes great baskets on their heads, on their way to market. Eleanor wanted to stop and find out what was in the baskets, but Val said there wasn't time. 'We'll stop at plenty of markets, Eleanor, but we mustn't hang around – we have to be off the road before dark. Only the suicidal drive at night.'

There was a great deal of difference in people's speed. If Val saw something coming along behind her much faster than she was going, she got over to the side to let it past: which was perhaps wise when it turned out to be a cavalcade belonging to some important government official or military chief on his way to a meeting. She in turn overtook pedestrians and carefully negotiated her way around a motor-bike rider with three metre lengths of sugar cane strapped sideways across his bike, taking up a good deal of the road. The sugar farmer was putting along much slower than Val, even before he spotted a friend across the road and stopped for a chat.

The most comfortable place they stayed was the city of Jos. It was much cooler there, temperatures in the low twenties, for the capital of Benue-Plateau State was in Nigeria's middle belt, on a plateau four thousand feet high. Wild poinsettias dotted the surrounding landscape, and driving into town they passed Fulani boys tending their cattle.

Val had booked three rooms in a guest house run by missionaries. As they signed the visitors' book before dinner, she told Eleanor about friends of hers at Ife whose four-year-old daughter Josephine had insisted on signing this book 'Jos' since that was patently the right name to use in this place.

'We'll be quite safe here,' Alec said later in Eleanor's room. He was looking out of the window at the night guard's hut, which was a round brick edifice with a pointed straw roof.

I never feel anything but safe when you are around – but is safety all that matters?

He turned round and grinned at her. 'And we'll sleep well tonight – it's so much cooler than down in Ife.'

She always did sleep well afterwards. Alec had once shown her a notice pinned to the door next to his in halls, which read: 'If blessed be the sleep of the just, then yet more blessed is the sleep just after.'

Of course Alec was excited by the archaeology. 'The earliest known Nigerians lived around here,' he said to Eleanor as they explored the museum next morning. He told her about the Nok people, who were skilled artisans from around 3000 BC, who vanished before 1000 AD but left behind their terracotta heads and artefacts.

More terracotta heads. More artefacts.

Eleanor stood in front of one especially beautiful head. Alec was holding her hand and reading the inscription, and she began to wonder what sort of person had made this head. A man or a woman? Were they looking at a real person when they did it? How did they live – what food did they have, what animals? Did they have children who would one day make carvings of their own?

This is Alec's life. He's going to discover things like this and tell people about them – but what about me? What am I going to tell people about? Will I explain to hordes of children how heat is transferred? Why electrical devices are so useful? I doubt it somehow.

On the way out she bought several postcards of the terracotta heads.

Temperatures shot up again when they set off for Kano, which was way up on the fringes of the Sahara, surrounded by Sahel savannah. There should have been irrigated farmlands but there had been a worrying drought since 1970.

They stopped at a roadside market to pick up some fresh tomatoes and peppers to take to Kano, since Val had arranged to stay with friends there, but Eleanor didn't even have the energy to sketch the scene. It was a large market, with some traders displaying their produce on trestle tables, while others had huge heaps of food on the ground. They were doing a brisk trade. Val haggled over the price of some onions, but even she gave up sooner than usual.

'I hope you are keeping all your sketches, Eleanor,' Val said as they got back into the car.

'Course she is,' said Alec, and you could hear the pride in his voice.

Val swerved carefully round a couple of lads on mopeds who were balancing an eight-foot pane of glass between them and gave them a friendly wave and a hoot. With amazing poise one of the boys waved back.

Kano was worth the effort: Eleanor had never seen a place like it before. The old walled city was full of ancient flat-roofed clay houses. Alec told her it had been founded in 1000 AD as an independent Hausa city state.

'Shall we ever come back here, do you think?' he asked her as they stood hand in hand in front of the fifteenth century Emir's palace.

'Who knows?' she said after a pause.

She could imagine him coming back, perhaps digging up some artefacts or whatever it was that archaeologists did. But as for herself: no, she couldn't imagine coming back here with him, another expatriate wife like Val, supervising dinner parties and giving English classes to domestic staff. No, whatever there was ahead of them, it certainly wasn't that.

By the time they returned from up country, their holiday was almost over, and in no time they were packing to set off for Ibadan airport. Eleanor struggled to shut her suitcase, because she'd bought cloth from the market for her sister and her mother. Alec had bought his parents a wooden carving of a boy climbing a sloping palm tree to fetch down some coconuts, and he had bought another carving by the same artist to present to Val and Ian. Eleanor was fazed by this - she hadn't any money left to buy a present for their hosts. She always had much less money than Alec did.

'Oh that doesn't matter!' Alec exclaimed. 'This carving is a present from both of us, obviously.'

Obviously? Are we joined at the hip?

'Thank you so much for having me to stay,' Eleanor said to the Beynons with a smile. 'It's so kind of you - you've taken such a lot of trouble.'

'Oh that's nothing. We've enjoyed -' Val began.

Ian interrupted. 'What Val really wants to ask you, only she's too embarrassed to say: Eleanor, would you give us one of your sketches? Please!'

'Oh!' Eleanor was startled. 'Why yes, of course. Which one would you like?'

*

Eleanor couldn't settle when they went back to Cardiff.

'I feel as though I'm waiting for something to happen, but I don't know what,' she said to Charlie one afternoon in early May. She'd gone up to his room to see if he fancied some of his mother's walnut cake,

27

just out of the oven. He was supposed to be revising for another A Level exam the next day, but Barbara had sent Eleanor up to find out if he needed a break: a short one, Barbara emphasised.

'Yes! I know what you mean, Sunshine,' Charlie gave his guitar a little strum and his textbook fell to the floor. 'There's got to be more to life than this boring, boring stuff!'

Eleanor was perched on the windowsill. Outside Norman was mowing the lawn, while Roz and her school friend lay stretched out on a rug on the grass soaking up the sunshine. Suddenly Eleanor saw a cartoon in which Norman mopped his brow and struggled with a heavy lawnmower, unaware that next door the entire garden had been turned into a swimming pool where two young schoolgirls lay floating on inflatable lilos.

'I suppose my brother is working flat out as usual? He always was the Swot of the Class.'

'He's pretty busy, yes,' Eleanor admitted. 'He needs to be, just now. Come to that, I need to be, but...'

Charlie sat up. 'Hey, why don't you give it all up and go and live with your sister in Rome?'

She stared at him.

'Your heart's not in it, is it? You're not going to be whatever it was you thought you were going to be, Eleanor. Why prolong the agony – give up now!'

'Charlie, that's... ridiculous. What on earth would I do in Rome?'

He looked at her shrewdly. 'Draw pictures of all those fancy buildings? And the fountains, the trees. Ancient ruins. The Vatican.'

True, she'd done that often enough, since Gabriella had gone to live in Rome.

'You could sell them. You don't realise how good they are.'

'But...'

'In the meantime, you can get a job on a newspaper. Your sister's married to a journalist, isn't she? He'll have contacts, no sweat. And your mother's family is Italian, right?'

The door opened and Alec put his head round. 'Mum wondered if you were coming down, brother dear.' He glanced across at Eleanor and raised his eyebrows.

*

They sat in silence together far above Cardiff, on the very summit of Garth Mountain, a cool breeze blowing away the stuffiness of the warm July day. Some sheep were nibbling the grass a long way below.

'But why, why are you leaving me?' he said again. 'I just don't understand!'

'It's not you,' she said.

Oh God, for sure it isn't you!

'It's me,' she went on. This came out as such a cliché, but it was only the truth. 'I told you, I can't stay here any longer studying something that doesn't mean anything to me any more. I've got to get away, try something else...'

'But what?'

They were going round in circles – she had already told him that she was going to stay with her sister Gabriella in Rome until she got on her feet, whatever that meant.

'What are you going to do in Rome?'

How can I be expected to know that, before I get there?

She took his hand again. 'It's just something I've got to do.'

He pulled his hand away and glared at her. She had desperately wanted Alec to understand. She had even wondered if he might offer to come with her. No, no, she knew that was ridiculous, impossible: he could never give up his own career. But she longed for his sympathy. Surely if he really loved her he would support her, accept her decision, take it for granted that they would keep in touch? Rome was hardly the ends of the earth. But she could not bring herself to say that: it would sound childish, like an infant howling to its mother, 'If you really loved me you would buy me the earth... Or an ice-cream.'

She said nothing.

All she could see in his eyes was a blank sadness, a deep hurt. It did not enter his head that she could still be his girlfriend a mere thousand miles away.

'But I love you,' he said in the end.

'Yes, I know.'

She sniffed as the wind blew about her face, and she took out a soggy hanky and began to blow her nose.

'Oh, don't cry, Eleanor!'

'Why not, Alec? You are!'

'I wanted to...to marry you, when I've finished here. We're so good together, Eleanor. At least, I thought we were.'

'Yes we... We were.'

He took a deep breath. 'What if... How about if we get married now, not wait 'til we finish at uni? Is that the problem, you don't think I'm committed enough?'

She stared at him.

'I know I haven't got much money at the moment, but we could manage! I've got my grant. My parents would help – we could find a flat to live in. Is that what you want?'

He had a touching faith in his parents, she thought. Barbara would certainly not lend her blessing to a marriage at nineteen, and to the wrong woman for God's sake! But in any case it was not what Eleanor herself wanted.

'No, listen Alec – we can't get married now. We really can't. I'm not ready to settle down. I've got to go to Rome and...and find out where it leads me. I need the space. Please, please understand what I'm saying!'

He didn't understand, of course he didn't – she could see that.

The day was clouding over and a wind began to rustle in the grass. She shivered and put on a dark green sweater she'd been carrying around her waist.

He stood up abruptly. 'I guess we'd better be getting back, then,' he said.

'Yes, I suppose we had.' She had been sitting rather awkwardly with one leg bent under her, and she struggled to get to her feet.

He did not put out his hand to help her, but instead began to walk briskly down the mountain, his feet pointing outwards and his back hunched forwards against the wind.

Chapter Three

Rome, 1977

Eleanor

Looks like rain again, and the light is fading. God this is uncomfortable - I'm crouching down against the wall around another of these Roman fountains. Sucking the end of my pencil, and wondering how long I've got to stay here. I'm trying to sketch a pair of feral cats fighting over the carcass of a fish. It was chucked to them by one of the gattare, the cat women. The older cat growls and snatches the last of the fish away from the other one. What's it going to do next?

It turns and flees, followed half-heartedly by the younger one. 'Don't go moggy!' Look, I'm actually talking to the creature now; maybe I should get out more. 'Here, see what I've got...' There should be a raw sardine somewhere under the papers in my bag - maybe I'm turning into a cat woman myself. I chuck the sardine at the remaining cat. It's hesitating; it's mildly interested. It looks around nervously. 'Well this sardine thing is all very well for the time being, but I'll have to be off in a minute...' Now I'm actually listening to it talk to me; yes I definitely should get out more.

It was one of Gabriella's twins who suggested adding the feral cats to my sketches. There are thousands of them in and around Rome – everybody knows them. They've been here since ancient Roman times – they are even said to have warded off the Bubonic Plague by killing the rats. The children are enchanted by the cats everywhere, and they always want to chase them and catch them – which is impossible, and give them scraps – which is expressly forbidden by Gabriella. I'm looking for something unusual, original, to add to my already large collection of sketches of the regular tourist round of ancient ruins, churches and palaces.

Four years I've been here. Four years since that hideous evening on Garth Mountain when I walked out on one life and – and what? Into another? No, there's not a lot of progress to report; I'm still living with Gabriella and Giulio in Vitinia, in their spacious house in the suburbs. I've sent my Roman sketches to over ten publishers – no, let's

31

be honest now, closer to twenty, if not more, here in Rome, as well as about thirty back in London. Several of them were quite polite, expressed an interest, complimented me on the fine lines of the drawings – but ended up with the same verdict: not commercially viable. 'No, thank you,' was the message.

Yes it definitely is going to rain. Quite heavily.

Damn – there's the paper's chief photographer dashing round the corner into the square. I'm supposed to be out interviewing some minor government minister with this guy today. We couldn't track him down this morning, and so we agreed to meet up later. I'll have to go.

'There you are!' the photographer calls out, hurrying over to the fountain. 'Have you looked up that info about the man we are interviewing?'

'Oh, no, sorry,' I tell the wretched man. 'I haven't had time.'

He frowns. 'Why, what have you been up to? You're quite useless! You must have the facts at your fingertips, else it's a waste of my time coming with you to take photos.'

'Sorry.'

'Then we'll have to give up for now,' he snarls. 'I've got some other photos to take – I might be free Thursday. Or maybe next week... Ciao!' With that he turns and hurries away.

I can take a hint – time to head off for the nearest metro station. It's raining strongly now.

*

Giulio pours me a Cinzano as I walk through the front door. That's typical of Giulio – he's rather a dear, my brother-in-law.

'Thanks, I could do with this. I've had a hell of a day!'

He frowns sympathetically.

I kick off my shoes and head for the kitchen to find out what Gabriella is cooking for dinner. 'That man phoned for you again,' my sister tells me. She's mixing some salad dressing. 'Just before you got in. He's desperately keen to talk to you. They are like bees round a honey pot, these men of yours. I wrote his number down somewhere... Where is it? Oh, no!' Looks like my youngest nephew has snatched the piece of paper to use for a back of a model he's making of a Roman chariot.

'Oh it doesn't matter, Gabby! He'll ring again if he wants.' I perch on the stool by the stove and nurse my drink.

'I thought he was rather nice,' Gabriella offers me her opinion as usual. 'Much nicer than that Frenchman you went out with last year – he gave me the creeps!'

Who cares?

'I wonder what happened to the guy you were with when you were at university – do you ever hear from him?'

'No, of course not.' I finish my drink in one gulp and poured myself another.

No of course I don't hear from Alec. I haven't spoken to him since Garth Mountain. I've composed endless letters to him in my head but not sent any of them.

'I suppose he has finished at university by now,' Gabriella said. 'Do you know what he is doing? You hear from his brother sometimes, don't you?'

I pick up an olive from a tub and pop it in my mouth. 'Very occasionally. Charlie sent me a postcard a bit back, when...when Alec got his degree. He said Alec was going to do a PhD.'

'Oh, I see. There, can you give the kids a shout and say time to wash their hands? We can eat in ten minutes.'

I shift myself from the stool and go to the bottom of the stairs to shout up to the children.

What Charlie had also said was that Alec was now going out with Milly Pryce-Roberts. His mother Barbara must have been in heaven.

Chapter Four

Eleanor

The Romans were here too. Those long-dead people with their determination, their technology, their straight lines.

It was the Romans who built the immense grey three-tiered bridge across the wide flat river valley to carry a water supply down to the population of sixty thousand in the city which now bears the name Nîmes. Astonishingly, the bridge was still standing, forty-nine metres high, almost twenty centuries later: the Pont du Gard. Today I'm sitting curled up on a rock on the river bank, trying to capture its essence on my sketchpad. I wonder if I ought to add a legion of Roman soldiers marching along the road on the lowest of the three tiers?

'Hurry up, Auntie Eleanor – you promised you were going to swim with us!'

The kids are splashing in the broad shallow river below, and my oldest niece shouts up at me.

'Won't be long now! Nearly finished...'

Look, there's Gabriella in the water, throwing a plastic ball at Giulio and making all the children laugh. A tempting family scene, but it can wait.

I'm writing a book about the Languedoc region of southern France, a book which has been commissioned - yes, actually commissioned! I still pinch myself when I remember. Oh yes, it's a small publisher in an unfashionable part of London - well, rather outside London to be totally accurate - and he liked the feral cats and bought the set of sketches of the sights and people of modern Rome. He's got a young ginger-haired assistant called Patrick who comes on pretty strong with me; he's OK I suppose.

The book about Rome came out last year and I've finally moved out from Gabby's home into a small flat of my own. A very small flat.

Sales so far have been modest – a lot of old friends bought it, of course, but at least it led the publishers to ask for a follow-up book about Languedoc.

This is a good place to be, camping here with Gabriella and the family. In a little while there will be another of Gabby's glorious picnics: fresh French baguettes and butter, bought that morning in Remoulins on the way there, with some brie perhaps, ham, salad and some lovely ripe fresh-smelling peaches and a glass of wine. Perfect.

We went to Avignon yesterday. My sister and I explored the old Papal palace while Giulio took the children on a boat trip and taught them to sing Sur Le Pont D'Avignon. This afternoon we'll be heading for the coast to swim in the Mediterranean at La Grande Motte.

There has been some news of the Jenkins family, from Charlie, as it happens. A short note arrived just before we came away on holiday. It's months since I last heard from Charlie - apparently he's still in Australia. Last year he turned up on my doorstep in Rome - my very new, independent doorstep - to beg a bed for the night for himself and an elegant Australian girlfriend he was showing round Europe. They stayed a month in the end, which was a bit of a squeeze to be honest. Nice girl, though; friendly. Maybe he is still with her; he doesn't say. It's just a short scribble of a letter, its main purpose being presumably to send me a couple of press cuttings about Alec. And a small photograph with a torn corner.

I pack up my sketch pad, and look at these press cuttings before I go down to the river. Yes, all right, of course I've already read them. Once or twice.

I'm not quite sure that I want to read press coverage of Alec. But on the other hand - Charlie guessed right there - I don't want not to know either. They were both from British newspapers, The Telegraph and The Financial Times, and had been lovingly cut out by Barbara Jenkins and posted to Charlie in Australia.

Alec has done well so far. He got his doctorate - that was predictable - and he's been appointed to a lectureship in archaeology. I knew that much because Charlie had kept me pretty well informed before. But these cuttings are about Alec's involvement in a highly popular British television series about the Vikings. The programmes are hosted by an older, better known man, but there is plenty of Alec in them too. The Telegraph shows Alec standing next to a replica of a Viking ship, talking enthusiastically about how the Vikings set out on their epic voyages, what they'd carried in their boats, what they smelt like. He caused a minor sensation by coming on in one shot dressed as a Viking himself, complete with helmet and horns – and a large pair of brown NHS glasses. I remember the glasses.

I've managed to avoid actually watching any of his programmes on my visits back to the UK. I don't think I can cope with that, not yet.

Alec married Milly as soon as he finished his PhD. Charlie tactfully sent me a note afterwards stressing what an ordeal the whole wedding had been – his father not speaking to anyone, Barbara rushing round organising everything in competition with her old school-friend, Milly's mother. Quite savage competition, Charlie thought. The guest list of Hooray Henriettas, old school chums of Milly, if indeed she had had any genuine chums. Milly hopelessly shy and hating the attention. Alec embarrassed, not coping well with Milly's shyness. Charlie managed to write a wry account which made me laugh, in spite of myself, and I'm grateful to him.

And now here's Charlie enclosing, along with the press cuttings, a little photograph. The name on the back of the photo is almost too long to fit on: Tamsin Barbara Millicent Jenkins, born May 20th 1980. The picture is too small and blurred for it to be possible to tell whether the infant has inherited the Jenkins eyebrows, and whether her eyes are a piercing brown like her father's.

'Hurry up, Eleanor – we're moving on in half an hour!' Gabriella is calling me now. 'This is your last chance to swim in the river if you want to...'

'Coming!' I shove Charlie's letter and its contents into my bag, and run down to the river. 'Race you over to that branch sticking up in the middle!' I call out to my two oldest nephews as I strip down to my bathers.

*

At La Grande Motte, I dive into the Mediterranean and strike confidently away from the shore. Odd how Alec has changed when I wasn't looking.

He's suddenly become one of the grownups: he's no longer that shy and incredibly young lad I rescued from burnt marmalade so long ago. He's responsible for someone else's life now! I wish I could reach out to him – to say, somehow, that I understand, that I admire him for the new life he has chosen, that I...well, simply that I wish him well.

An idle thought occurs to me as I turn and swim back towards the shore: would it be wildly inappropriate to buy one of those pretty embroidered Italian baby outfits that Gabby is so keen on, and post it to Ms T.B.M. Jenkins?

'No, absolutely not. You must be crazy!'

Gabriella sits up suddenly and glares at me. She has been lying flat on her back in the sun, on a towel.

'Just a little thing, like that lovely pale peach top Mum bought you last year for –'

'No! Whatever are you thinking of? What would it look like, for God's sake?'

'What do you mean, what would it look like? Nothing. It wouldn't look like anything, just a casual gift. Mum's always sending people cute little dresses and stuff when they have babies, you know she is.'

'Not to people she used to go out with, she isn't!'

We both laugh at the absurdity of this; Mum is nearly seventy by now, and she married Daddy during the Dark Ages.

'Seriously, woman – what are you trying to say? That you want to get back with the man, when he's just become a father?'

'No of course not!'

I'm quite sure of that, at any rate. I must hang onto something that I'm sure of.

'But it would look as if you did!'

'Would it?'

'And they wouldn't accept it, anyway. I tell you, if one of Guilio's old girlfriends ever sent us a present for our baby, I'd chuck it away in the biggest dustbin I could find!'

Surprised by the vehemence of this, I don't know what to say.

'You've got to walk away from this, Eleanor. You really have. It's time to let go.'

'I suppose you're right. You usually are.'

'He's making a life for himself, obviously. TV career beginning – who knows where that is going to lead? And the start of a young family. You've got to leave him alone, and make your own life. I'm sure Mum would say the same...'

'Oh don't say anything to Mum!'

'Heavens no, as if I would! But I'm right, aren't I, she would say the same, wouldn't she?'

I stretch out on the dry sand and wiggle my toes in it. I'm beginning to feel that life is ganging up on me, and I don't have the strength to fight it. Maybe it's time for another dip in the sea, where Giulio is splashing the youngest on a lilo in the shallow water.

'OK, you win.'

I stand up and run down to the sea.

Chapter Five

Copenhagen, 1985

Eleanor

The Little Mermaid - den Lille Havfrue - sits curled on the stone by the harbour, hair twisted at her neck and falling onto her back, tail tucked in below. There's a haunted expression upon her face, as though she doesn't quite belong up here in the open air and she knows it. She isn't even surrounded by sea as she should be.

Look, the sea's frozen clean over, all the way to Sweden: a once-in-twenty-years event, the man in the hotel said. The air temperature feels like minus a hundred and three.

So here I am back in Copenhagen, Daddy's home town, gazing at the site of umpteen thousands of his holiday photographs. Usually with me and Gabriella poised uncomfortably on the rocks next to the statue. His own two little mermaids.

I'm still with the same publisher, the one who liked the feral cats in Rome; he's doing rather better now, moved to premises in central London, don't-cha know. Now he's sent me to Copenhagen, to find out how much Denmark has changed since I was a child. A different kind of book this time, he suggested: more personal, more intimate. Some childhood memories. Look up the family if you can, he told me. And plenty of drawings, of course - they are what sell my books, he is certain. Whatever would Daddy have thought? Drawings, then. Well if the publisher thinks I'm going to stand here today, long enough to sketch anything at all, he is severely mistaken. My hands don't even work in this temperature.

My cousin Kirsten is with me today, another of the Larsen-Bruuns. She is doing rather better than me - she's a professional freelance photographer, and she's busy with the amazing ice on the sea. She works rapidly.

I turn to her now. 'Let's go back to that restaurant we passed and get our blood circulating again, Kirsten. I'll treat you to some wienerbrød.' She likes this idea.

So we push our way past the hordes of German and Japanese tourists and at last enter the restaurant. The warmth hits us like a blanket. The Danes certainly understand central heating, but it does mean you have to strip off practically all your clothes the moment you step indoors. There's a wonderful smell to the place, the scent of freshly baked bread and pastry.

My cousin Kirsten has changed a good deal since we last met; I've hardly been back since Daddy died. Kirsten is two or three years older than me, a competent woman in her mid-thirties, with a successful business and a young family in Copenhagen. 'So how's the photography trade going?' I ask her now asked as we look at the menu. Hot chocolate would be the quickest way to warm up, and perhaps the apple cake, or maybe the vanilla cream – or even both. We were very close as little girls, when the two of us spent several summer holidays together on the farm of one of our uncles, and so it was good to discover that Kirsten spends her professional life looking for suitable scenes and people to photograph – much as I do myself with my sketchpad.

'Doing well!' Kirsten tells me. 'Yes, plenty of commissions at the moment. I can afford to take a few days off to spend with you, but I just need one shot at Rådhuspladsen for the tourist board.'

'Oh, I love Rådhuspladsen!' I remember childhood trips to the Town Hall Square, usually the terminus of any tram journey with Daddy. It's a large bustling place, restaurants and shops around the edge, full of so many different kinds of people meeting each other.

'You know that big statue of Hans Andersen opposite Tivoli?' Kirsten continues. 'The tourist board has an idea that I should get some children to climb up onto it and then photograph them for one of their brochures. Maybe we can do that next week?'

'OK. But where shall we go today, Kirsten? If we can bear to walk out into the cold again...'

'I thought the Round Tower next. You said you wanted to go to places you went to as a child – surely you remember that day your father took us there and his hat blew away? Your sister Gabriella was with us. Uncle Svend always made me laugh so much!'

This sets me off giggling, and Kirsten too of course. Rather enthusiastically, I have to say.

Oh dear - there's a shocked look of disapproval on the face of the elderly starched waiter who has just produced our pastries and hot chocolate. He doesn't like me because I tried ordering in my limited Danish, and he pointedly answered me in perfect English.

So – the Round Tower. It really wasn't that funny, we can both see that now, but when we were children Daddy had the knack of making us laugh uncontrollably until we pleaded with him to stop. He could also wiggle his ears without touching them, a trick we could never learn, hard as we tried. Suddenly there's nowhere I'd rather go than the Round Tower.

A blast of freezing air hits us again as we hurry across Kongens Nytorv and through the pedestrian streets straight to the Tower, and we go in. It's so wide that you could drive a carriage and horses up the cobbled path round to the top. It was built by some king in 1642 for a Danish astronomer who wanted an observatory, Kirsten reminds me – she's brought the guide book along today; typical Kirsten.

It's blowing a gale when we finally emerge at the top, out of breath from the long climb. We stand in the open air looking out over the roofs of the old quarter of Copenhagen, protected by a double row of railings. I close my eyes. Somewhere deep in the past a man allows his hat to blow off in a sudden burst of wind and it gets stuck between the two rows of railings. He stretches out his hands but he can't squeeze through. Two little girls beside him are laughing till they cry, while a teenage girl stands by, looking bored. Then an old gentleman appears beside them, a gentleman with a stick, and the hat is hooked in and rescued; that's all. Not much of a story, to be remembered for twenty years.

Are they still there, somewhere – those faraway people? Lost somewhere in time. What happens to people? Why do they disappear, when they have been so alive?

'Eleanor, you're crying! What is it?' Kirsten puts her arm round me.

'No, no I'm not! It's just the wind.'

'I always think of Uncle Svend when I come anywhere near this tower, you know,' Kirsten tells me. 'I'm sorry, I shouldn't have brought you...'

But I smile. 'No, it's all right, Kirsten. It was funny, wasn't it?' I pick up my bag and turn towards the exit. 'Look, I think it's going to snow again – let's go somewhere indoors next.'

We decide to head for Thorvaldsen's museum next, because it was always one of my favourite places.

'You know we have all your books at home,' Kirsten tells me as we hurry along the street. 'We read them to our children.'

I'm surprised; I still think that only a few friends in Rome and Britain can have bought the books, though sales figures seemed to belie that impression.

'And Bedstemor too, naturally. She's so proud of you, she bought every book the minute it came out.'

Our grandmother can't read English, but apparently she loves my drawings anyway. We're having dinner with her tomorrow.

'I wish I'd got in touch with her sooner.'

'Yes, why didn't you?'

Hard to answer that one.

'She's a wonderful woman, our grandmother, you know,' Kirsten continues. 'I love hearing about how she lived through the war. She shows us photos sometimes.'

That's an idea. Maybe as well as sketches I could write a few brief stories about some of the people.

'Oh yes – I remember Daddy telling me once: didn't she have a young German soldier posted outside her front door?' I ask now.

'Yes that's right – a teenager, probably. During the Occupation. Every morning the poor young chap said good morning to our grandfather, but Bedstefar never ever replied. He held his head up high and just walked on as though no one had spoken, as though there was no one there!'

Ah, here's Thorvaldsen: an impressive building, freestanding with huge Greek columns, set grandly by the frozen canal. Outside it's like a full-scale Brueghel scene from the Little Ice Age of 1565; dozens of Danish kids skating on the canal, bright woolly scarves flying, yelling at each other, laughing when they fell over. Rapidly Kirsten takes several snaps, telling me that you never know when you might be able to sell them, but I'm not tempted to hang about with my sketchpad. No way.

'Let's go in!' The famous statues of the twelve apostles are still there in the great hall. This is the bit I used to love – they are magnificent.

'You know we had a furious row here once, you and I,' Kirsten says.

'Did we? Why?'

'Oh, I wanted to go shopping in Strøget because Bedstemor had promised to buy me a new pair of jeans and I couldn't wait. But you wanted to stay here drawing pictures of all these boring old statues, using up valuable shopping time. "Oh du er so vanskelig!" I screamed at you.'

'You called me difficult!'

Kirsten laughs and we sit down on a bench in the great hall.

'Do you remember Uncle's farm? Those wonderful holidays we had there!' Kirsten changes the subject.

'You were older than me, Kirsten – I was a bit scared by some of it. Those wild horses that chased us through the field, and made me run through all that mud and squelch and get my socks and sandals filthy... I've never forgotten that terrifying smell of – I don't know, horse sweat I suppose.'

'They weren't really wild horses, Eleanor – they belonged to the next farm! What I remember is how we used to sit next to each other on those old wooden box toilets in the outhouse and talk for hours. Now that was really smelly!'

'Oh yes. We talked about everything and everybody...and what we were going to do when we grew up.'

'Yes, Eleanor – and look at us now! I don't know what my kids would think of the whole family having to sit together, next to each other on wooden toilets outside like that! And you... You haven't got any attachments yet, have you?'

There was a pause.

'Nothing serious, no.'

'You went to Nigeria once with someone, didn't you? You wrote to me about it at the time – I've still got the sketches you sent me. What happened to that boy? What was his name?'

I glance up at one of the apostles towering above us. There's something reassuring about the statue's permanence.

'I haven't seen him for years. His brother sends me occasional messages... Alec, his name was.'

'What a coincidence! There is an Englishman called Alec all over the Danish papers at the moment – you must have heard of him! I think he's over here...'

'Really? It's a common name.' I pick up my bag and stretch. 'Shall we move on?'

'He has been excavating a Viking boat with a team of Danish archaeologists. We saw a very good television programme about it only last week. Do you know, in the first programme he came on dressed as a Viking – it was very funny. Everyone thinks he is so sød.'

Sweet. Yes, I can see people might think that. But I can't sit around here all day contemplating Alec's sweetness or otherwise. Let's go upstairs and see if there are other pieces I remember.

*

Next day it's Sunday and still cold. Kirsten's not free to go out sightseeing, so my choice as I wake up in this comfortable modern hotel bedroom overlooking Tivoli, seems to be mooching around town on my own – or joining Kirsten's family. The pleasure gardens of Tivoli are closed in the winter, which is a shame because I could happily have wandered round there alone all day with my own thoughts. As a child it was a magic place full of fireworks and clowns, outdoor concerts and theatres – were there boat trips on a lake? – and ice-creams. Daddy once ate three whole candyflosses in one go because we dared him to. But sadly it's winter and the gates are shut. The whole place is covered in snow.

Kirsten was most apologetic: normally she would have done something with me, but this particular day she simply couldn't get out of the Quaker Meeting she belonged to. The Quakers are a very small band in Denmark, Kirsten says, and this Sunday is their Quarterly Meeting, when Kirsten herself had invited a speaker from the Danish Refugee Council to talk to them after their usual morning meeting and lunch. It sounded interesting – might provide more material for my book – and so here I am on my way out to Venders Gade by tram. It's a broad leafy boulevard where our parents rented a flat one summer, if

I'm not mistaken. Kirsten's pleased to see me. I've never been to a Quaker meeting before, and she tells me what to expect. 'Think of it as a bit like climbing a mountain with some friends, Eleanor. When you get to the top, you all sit down and look out in different directions, but leaning against each other's back for support.'

There are already five or six people sitting in the room, and one or two of them nod at me as I take a seat near the window. As I close my eyes the sheer tangible peacefulness takes me by surprise. I can feel myself relaxing as it washes over me, mingled with the smell of fresh furniture polish and the scent worn by the woman next to me.

So far, so good, then.

Plenty of ideas for the new book; memories, as well as new things to investigate. This guy from the Refugee Council might give me some insights into a modern Denmark that is completely alien to me, like nothing I remember from the past.

It's vaguely unsettling to think that Alec is probably in this very city himself just now, according to my cousin. But Alec will be associating with Danish TV types no doubt, being lavishly entertained in some five-star hotel. He's hardly likely to walk into a Quaker Meeting on the sixth floor of a block in Venders Gade! For God's sake get a grip, woman.

*

Lunch is a friendly affair with the usual smørrebrød. Ah good, I do love Danish open sandwiches. Kirsten and her friends have taken some trouble over making them, and look - they've even included my favourite, sildesalat: beetroot red, with a good deal of herring. I'll have to do some sketches of the best sandwiches for my book, but I must make it clear to my readers that the word in Danish translates as butter-and-bread, rather than bread-and-butter, since Danes have their priorities in the right place.

Over lunch I get introduced to the visiting speaker, a pleasant young man, and he tells me that the Danish Refugee Council was set up in 1956 after Hungary. Then Czech refugees had come in 1968, Jews from Poland, Ugandan Asians, Chileans under Pinochet, Vietnamese, and now the newest arrivals were Iranian. He sets up his slide projector with the help of a young Eritrean woman he's brought with him, who says she works as an interpreter for the Refugee Council.

'Don't you find it cold here?' I ask the woman.

'Oh yes! I have never seen sea frozen over before.' Her face lights up in amazement.

'Nor have I! I come from the UK, but I live in Rome. So is there a lot of interpreting for you to do?' I pass the woman a plate of chocolate gateau.

'Yes there is much to do. I used to be a kindergarten teacher,' she tells me, seizing a large slice of cake. 'I live in a working-class area because I feel more accepted there, but I had to give up teaching because some of the children said they did not like to be looked after by a Black woman.' She smiles and shrugs her shoulders.

I put my hand on the woman's arm. 'No, really? That's appalling!'

As the afternoon talk begins, I'm taken by a photograph of an Iranian family looking through the window of a butcher's shop and wondering what the hell that cut of meat is. The little boy in the picture clutches a teddy bear that someone gave him for comfort.

'We have to teach the refugee kids not to pee in the street over here, and the women very quickly learn not to talk to Danish men in certain parts of the city,' the speaker tells us.

The next slide shows an Iranian father sitting at a table with a tape recorder he's just bought as a symbol of the new society he hopes to join, and the means by which he intends to learn the language. 'But sometimes it's an advantage that the refugee children can't understand what the Danish kids say about them,' the speaker added.

*

It's wonderful to see Bedstemor again this afternoon. She still lives in the same flat just across the road from Husum station – even the smell in the lobby is the same, that ancient mix of freshness and cleaning fluid. As we climb up the two flights of stairs, Bedstemor is already outside her flat on the landing, waiting with arms outstretched.

We give each other a great big hug.

I've come home – I'm a little girl again. Maybe all those other things don't matter any more: just for now. Bedstemor is even shorter than me, and a good deal rounder. There's a whiff of eau de cologne about her, the same she always wore.

Damn - I've remembered too late that I should have brought a present, a bunch of flowers at the very least. Even in snowy January, blomster - flowers - are the Danish custom when you visit anyone. But it doesn't matter: Kirsten is clutching a huge bunch, and it will apparently do for all of us.

One day I'm going to organise presents for myself and not leave other people to buy wooden carvings for me, of little African boys climbing up palm trees to fetch down coconuts.

We are ushered into the sitting-room, which is just as I remember - but somehow smaller. As Kirsten predicted, Bedstemor has indeed made a wonderful spread. She must have been at it all morning. She's roasted a whole leg of pork, and made my favourite red cabbage with blackcurrant juice. The smell of the sizzling pork as my wonderful grandmother sets it on the table is to die for.

And look - the pudding is another favourite of mine - a creamy strawberry fool which the Danes called rødgrød med fløde: one of their hardest tongue twisters for foreigners, and one Mum has never mastered.

*

Next day - and there's a slight thaw at last. Kirsten has plans.

'Do you mind coming to Rådhuspladsen with me so that I can take that photo of Hans Andersen's statue the tourist board want? Won't take long, I promise! All we need is some kids.'

So here I am, back in this vast square, which is bustling with people despite the weather. We glance round and some English voices catch Kirsten's attention - a little girl of about four or five is chasing her younger brother round one of the benches and shouting at him. They are wearing bright coats which would show up well against the dark grey statue, Kirsten thinks, the boy in an orange anorak and the girl in blue, and they've got multicoloured scarves and green bobble hats.

'They'll do - just the right age, but I'll have to get permission,' she says, approaching the little girl. 'Hallo there. I wonder if you and your brother would like to help me?'

The child stops and looks up politely at Kirsten.

'I need a photograph of you two climbing on that statue there – it's to go in a tourist brochure so lots of people all over the world will see it and come to Copenhagen. Would you like to do that for me?'

'Yes, all right,' the girl says. 'Come here, David.'

'But first I have to ask your Mummy's permission. Is your Mummy here?' Kirsten glances round.

'No, Mummy's not very well. She'll be better soon,' the girl tells us solemnly. 'She's gone to hospital so they can look after her properly.' This must be what someone has told her to say.

'Oh dear, I'm sorry. So who is –'

'Daddy's over there with those people. Daddy!' she shouts. 'This lady wants you!'

A tall man turns and hurries across, stooping slightly, his feet turned out.

Oh God.

Step back quickly, nearly trip over. Pull my woolly hat down over my ears. Stay in the background.

Kirsten is stepping forward, smiling, holding out her hand. She offers the man the English version of her business card.

He reads it out loud. 'Larsen-Bruun Associates – surely no relation of the travel writer...'

'Daddy, this lady says we can climb up over that statue, and she's going to take our photograph! Can we, Daddy? Can we!' the little girl says, grabbing her brother's hand in case he escapes and spoils the fun.

'Well yes, I don't see why not,' he says, smiling down at his children.

'Oh thank you so much.' Kirsten turns to introduce me. 'And here she is – we are indeed related – I'm very proud to say that this is my cousin...'

He stares.

'Hallo, Alec. How's the marmalade doing?' As usual, the first ridiculous thing that comes into my head.

'Eleanor.'

His eyebrows are just the same – more bushy if anything, but still the odd gable shape. His hair's still thick, black and unruly, but his clothes are startlingly different: they are fashionable, even trendy. Must be all this appearing on Danish television. But he hasn't ditched the NHS glasses.

Kirsten is hurrying the children over to the statue. She helps them climb up and suggests that they should start by clambering into Hans Andersen's lap. She takes several shots as they scramble happily on the statue, shouting gleefully and waving to each other and to their father, who is not looking at them at all.

'How are you?' he says in the end.

'Cold!'

'Yes it's freezing, isn't it? But the forecast for next weekend looks a little better, in fact they are predicting temperatures...' He pauses. 'Oh God, why am I rambling on about the weather of all things?'

'Does your father still smoke a pipe that smells of vanilla?'

'I don't know – yes, come to think of it, he does. It does. Smell of vanilla, I mean. Fancy you remembering that!'

I remember everything.

'He still has nightmares, too,' Alec adds.

'Poor Norman.' I'm fond of his father, but I can't quite bring myself to ask about his mother.

'And I'm hoping to go to Monte Cassino and see the place for myself, maybe one day persuade him to come with me. Are you still...still living in Rome, Eleanor?'

'Yes but I'm not there very often,' I say quickly. 'I have to do a fair bit of travelling.'

'Oh yes, your wonderful books! We've got all of them... Tamsin loves the pictures, and David does too. What a pity they are all at home – you could have signed them for us!'

We both realise that is a ridiculous remark, and we fall silent.

Poor thing, he doesn't know what to say, any more than I do.

'You're looking well,' he begins at last, while at the same time I start asking him what his Uncle Ian's family is doing these days.

'They're fine. Matt's a journalist now, working in London.'

'Oh, yes?'

'And Owen's leaving school soon. He's going in for teacher training, I think Val said.'

I'm startled. 'Little Owen! I can't believe he's old enough...'

'It's nearly twelve years, Eleanor.'

'Yes, I suppose it is.'

I look down at my woolly mittens, and turn round as the children come down from the statue and run over, shouting.

'Daddy, you didn't look at us! We climbed right up to the top and I sat on the man's hat but I didn't let David come that far because he's too little... Why didn't you look at us, Daddy?'

'Thank you so much,' Kirsten is saying now, putting her camera away in its case. 'That was a great success – I've got some fantastic shots. Would you like me to send you some copies?'

'That would be great! My wife can't be with us just now, but I'm sure she'd love to see what the children have been doing. Here, I'll give you my address.'

He hands her his card, and Kirsten claps her hand against her forehead. 'Oh yes of course! I knew you looked familiar: we saw you on television the other day – it was so interesting.'

Alec grins at her. 'We've had a good time in Denmark.'

He turns to his daughter. 'Tamsin, this is the lady who wrote all those lovely books we've got – you know, with the drawings in them.'

The child's face lights up. 'Did you? Will you write another one?'

'Well yes, that's why I'm here in Copenhagen. Who knows, I might draw a picture of a big statue of Hans Andersen with a girl and a boy climbing on it!'

Tamsin thinks for a moment. 'Did you draw that ginormous bridge, that the Romans made to take water across to their town?'

'I did, yes. Did you like that one, Tamsin?'

'It's called an aqueduct, isn't it?' her father reminds her. 'The Pont du Gard. That was ages ago, when you were just born. Remember, I showed you the date in the book.'

Kirsten looks at Tamsin. 'I was so scared when you went right up to the top, onto the man's hat. My heart was in my mouth...' She clutches her throat, but she's smiling all the same.

'I've got a hat just like that, haven't I, Daddy? When I was a witch before Christmas...' Tamsin remembers.

'Oh yes, so you were,' he says. 'I took the children to a Halloween party.'

'You were a witch, Tamsin? How exciting!' says my cousin. 'So do you know any spells?'

Tamsin considers. 'Course I do. C-A-T spells cat, and T-A-B-L-E spells table.'

'Goodness, that's clever!' Kirsten is impressed. 'Our children don't start school as early as you, over here.'

Alec ruffles his daughter's hair. 'Not bad, old thing.' He glances at his watch. 'Oh dear, I'm afraid we must be going – we're late, we've got to meet some colleagues of mine.' He grabs David's hand. 'Don't forget to send me those photos,' he tells Kirsten as he turns away.

He's going to disappear now, and I probably won't ever see him again.

All of a sudden I take a step forwards. 'They are wonderful children, Alec. You must be very proud of them.'

I'm holding out my hand – which may be a mistake, but what the hell?

He looks at me for a moment, then he bends down and gives me a quick peck on the cheek. 'Good to see you, Eleanor.'

'And you...' I manage to say to the departing family.

David runs away, and Alec begins to chase after him. Tamsin turns round and gives me an angelic smile.

Chapter Six

1986

Eleanor

'Like bees round a honey pot – as I may have remarked before.' Gabriella is wiping her youngest child's nose on a yellow spotted handkerchief. I wish she wouldn't keep saying that.

'Just once or twice,' I remark. 'It's getting tedious.'

'I think you'll find that's what sisters are for. There, off you go –' She pats the kid on his bottom and sends him back into the garden with a biscuit. 'So this new guy of yours, what's his name?'

'He's not mine, and he's not really new either: he's been working for my publisher for years.'

Gabriella raises her eyebrows. 'Well?'

'Yes, OK, his name's Patrick.'

'How do you spell that?'

'Oh for heaven's sake! What do you mean, how do you spell that? How many ways do you know of spelling Patrick? Ah, now don't go putting him down on any family guest lists, Gabby – for God's sake! This is private. Light. Nothing serious, all right?'

'So what's he doing in Rome, then? If he works in London.'

'I told you, he's with my publisher. He's come over to discuss book launches in the spring with a few people, and we just thought we'd meet up again.'

'And how old is he, may I ask?'

'He's twenty-seven. You are so nosy!'

'You cradle snatcher! So are you having a book launch for your latest book?'

'Yes I am. You can come if you like; I'll get Patrick to send you an invitation. It's in March, in time for the Easter trade. I'm a bit scared – I've never had a proper book launch before! We're having it in London, at the Royal Danish Embassy no less.'

'Santo cielo! I might just do that... Your trip to Denmark went well, then?'

I lean forward and help myself to a slice of prosciutto from the dish my sister is preparing for supper. 'I wish you could have come, Gabby! It was wonderful seeing all those old places we used to go to when we were children. I went round with our cousin Kirsten - you remember her, don't you?'

'Vaguely. She was younger than me. I like the drawings you showed me - I do remember Rådhuspladsen, obviously. I like that one of the statue with the children climbing on it. Who were those children?'

I pause slightly too long. 'Oh they were just some kids Kirsten approached one morning.'

'You put their names on the pictures, though - I got the feeling you knew them? Tamsin, was it?'

'Well if you must know, they were the children of...of Alec Jenkins. The man I used to know in Cardiff.'

'Him! Whatever was he doing there? I didn't realise you were in touch with him again.'

'Oh no I'm not - Kirsten just ran into his children. It was a complete coincidence - he just happened to be filming in Copenhagen at the time. Gabby, don't look at me like that...'

'So you talked to him, did you? You didn't say anything at the time, when you came back.'

'Didn't I? I thought I had. It wasn't particularly significant...'

'No, I'm quite sure you didn't mention it. I would have remembered. So what did you talk about?'

'Nothing. The weather, I think. It was very brief, only while the kids were climbing on the statue.'

'So I suppose when you parted, you just shook hands, did you?' Gabriella laughs. 'He's probably very English.'

'Something like that. What time's supper, Gabby? I said I'd meet Patrick later.'

*

I'm in Patrick's compact - small - flat in London, and it's stuffy here, for the weather is unusually mild for March. I flung a soaking wet raincoat over the bedroom radiator half an hour ago, and it's beginning to smell. I stretch out; I might go to sleep in a minute. But Patrick sits up in bed suddenly. He has a restless energy about him, I've always thought. 'Everything's ready for the launch,' he tells me now. I do believe he's been ticking things off on a list in his head all this time. Do we have to talk about the launch?

I close my eyes. I've been tired all day, because I had to get up before six in Rome to catch my flight. Love-making always makes me sleepy, and it might have been nice to rest a while, just to savour the moment; but that's not Patrick's way.

'Have you thought what you're going to say, Hun?' he goes on, flicking his carroty hair out of his eyes. He looks extraordinarily young when he does that.

'Say? No idea.' Finding something to wear has been my biggest worry, let alone what to say. Gabriella took me firmly in hand, and we ended up buying a pinkish purple dress which cost rather more than I normally spend on clothing in six months.

'Tomorrow - at the launch! I shall be introducing the show - when they've all tucked happily into their sarnies and Carlsberg - and then hand over to you...'

'We're not really having beer, are we?' I crinkle my nose. 'I can't stand the stuff.'

Patrick grins. 'Ah, that woke you up, didn't it? No, house white, mainly. I just ordered a bit of Carlsberg to keep the Danes happy.'

'House white will be fine. With a choice of house red?'

'Yes of course, leave all that to me, Hun,' he growls impatiently. 'It's my job, remember? Then I'll introduce you, and you will have to speak. Briefly. When you sign the books, don't talk too long to each person - just ask their name, quickly, put it in the book and sign below it. And when you do your speech, keep it short for God's sake - less is more, remember.'

He waits for me to show I've taken this advice on board, then he leaps out of bed and begins to scrabble about in the pile of takeaway menus that he keeps by the phone. It's getting late and there isn't time, he judges, to go out and eat anywhere. We both need to be fresh for tomorrow.

*

54

The Royal Danish Embassy is an impressive modern building in Sloane Square, designed by Arne Jacobsen only a few years ago. Large rectangular windows covering most of the outside, with flags bravely fluttering in front: the Dannebrog so familiar from my childhood, and these days the embassy flies the flag of the European Union too. Would be nice to have time to sketch the place, but oh no! Patrick obviously isn't going to allow any hanging around outside. He ushers me into one of the larger reception rooms. Where have all these people come from? I thought there'd just be ten or twenty if that... Patrick seems to have invited everyone whose name I gave him, and obviously a few dozen more. I don't even recognise them.

There's a fresh smell from the banks of flowers stacked around the sides of the room, and a loud hum of conversation. As I follow Patrick into the room, I'm blinking in the bright light.

'Great to see you, my Sunshine!' Thank goodness, there's a familiar voice behind me. I turn round, and someone puts their arms around me and gives me a great big bear hug. I feel immensely cheered.

'Charlie! I didn't know you were coming,' I gasp when I can breathe.

'I got an invite through the post,' he tells me. 'Wouldn't miss it for the world. Hey, Eleanor m'dear, there are some seriously famous people here. People even I recognise, though I do live out in the colonies.'

'I didn't think you'd be in London, Charlie! What brings you here?'

'Oh, just family business – nothing important.'

Not sure that I want to know about the Jenkins family.

'Well it's my Dad, to be honest. He had a heart attack a fortnight ago...'

'Oh no! That's awful...'

'He'll be OK. He's still in hospital; had to have one of these new heart bypass ops. Mum's been marvellous of course, organising their friends to visit him in a rota, telling them what to bring him, keeping away the people she didn't want to visit him... Poor old love, she's shattered now.'

'I'm so sorry, Charlie.' Not sure how to put this next bit. 'Will you give Norman my...regards? If he remembers who I am.'

Charlie laughs. 'Not much chance of him forgetting you, Eleanor! For a start, he bought your books, in fact he gave me strict instructions to pick up a copy for him of this Danish book you're launching today – a signed copy of course!'

What on earth does Norman want with...?

'Hey, have you seen the food they've put out?' Charlie goes on. 'Sensational, or what?'

'I don't know if I'm allowed... I think Patrick wants me at the front.'

Charlie takes my arm and begins to guide me through the throng. 'Then you'd better stock up while you've got the chance, kiddo. Come on!' He leads me to the tables which stretch the whole length of the back wall. Wow! You couldn't call it a few plates of sandwiches, although Patrick would. This is an array of small works of art: I spot the fish, meat, salami, cheese, all laboriously decorated with various vegetables, some of them no doubt flavoured with dill or lemony mayonnaise, many of my favourite smørrebrød. Charlie hands me a plate. 'Here, grab what you can before they come to get you... What do you recommend? Have a glass of wine, Ellie – you need to relax.'

I take a glass of white wine from the table, drink half of it and help myself to one or two pieces – herring on rye bread, always a good start, and some pork liver pâté topped with diagonal slices of tomato and ribbons of cucumber salad made with vinegar, and some strips of fried onion. Then the sildesalat catches my eye.

'What's that bright red messy stuff, Ellie? Would I like it?' Charlie watches as I take a large helping onto my plate.

'Charlie, it is heaven! It's beetroot mixed with herring. Heavenly herring! My father used to make this. He minced the herring himself.'

'Well it goes with your dress, at any rate!' he notices. 'You're looking absolutely dazzling, by the way...'

I need another gulp of wine! I smile at him.

At the far end of the table I can see they've got an attractive array of puddings. I bet they've got rødgrød med fløde but I'm not going to get anywhere near it, am I?

Here comes Patrick... 'What the hell are you doing down here, Hun? You should be at the front.' He glares at Charlie.

He grabs my arm before I can pick up any cutlery, and propels me across the room. I balance my glass of wine precariously on my plate, glancing helplessly over my shoulder at Charlie.

He shrugs. 'Catch up with you later, my Sunshine!'

'I thought I'd just see what food there was...' I say to Patrick.

'Food can wait, Hun – there's a reporter here from the BBC, wants a word with you before we start.' Patrick steers me grimly towards the corner where a woman is waiting with a microphone. On the way I drain my glass and pop it onto a convenient tray that a waiter is carrying round; he offers me another glass of wine and I take it gratefully.

*

Well that went well; there were a couple of other reporters waiting to talk to me, and now I've spoken to them all I feel fine. I know just what to say in my address to the assembled company. My sister is hovering near the front, and she grins at me. Oh God tell me she hasn't – she's actually brought with her the large all-purpose canvas bag she normally uses for the kids' bits and pieces. Sometimes Gabby thinks she's Mary Poppins.

I grin back at my sister. This is OK – I can hack this, watch me! And so I get going...I pause and clear my throat about half way through my speech and I take another sip of wine. This is going well! The audience is engaged, laughing with me...

But suddenly Patrick stands up. What the hell? 'That is fascinating, Ms Larsen-Bruun – I'm sure we are all waiting eagerly for your next book. Thank you so much...' And would you believe it, he's starting to clap as he looks round at the company. They all take up the applause from him.

What?

Well I can take a hint; he thinks it's time to sit down! Graceful would be a good look here – but unfortunately I stumble finding my chair. I finish my glass.

'And now Ms Larsen-Bruun is going to sign copies of her book over by the window,' Patrick goes on, pointing to another table. 'So if you'd all like to pick up your copies over there, and form an orderly queue, please.'

I manage to grab my plate and carry it with me as I follow Patrick across the room. Another waiter is hovering with more wine. I put my plate carefully on the table as I sit down. The pork liver pâté is looking a little tired by now.

Wonder if I'll have time to eat any of this?

The first in the queue is Gabriella - how on earth has she managed that? Patrick stands by my side to make sure I keep the queue moving.

'How's it going, Gabby?' I whisper to my sister.

'Fine! You're doing very well. How many glasses of wine have you had?'

'I've no idea. What are you talking about, Gab?'

After I've signed about ten books, I take a tentative bite at the pork liver pâté. Some of the rye bread crumbles and falls on the table, and Patrick brushes it away impatiently.

'Me next!' It's Charlie, bless him, grinning down at me.

'Oh, is this one for your Dad?' With a flourish, I write 'To Norman with best wishes for a speedy recovery - love from Eleanor.'

He looks at it in surprise. 'Well thanks, Eleanor. That's great - he'll like that.' Then catching Patrick's threatening eye, Charlie picks up the book and moves away.

At last I get to the end of the queue. Patrick has just slipped over to the other side of the room, muttering something about some journalist he's been expecting. The room is beginning to clear now, and unfortunately the staff seem to be clearing away the food, too. They are picking up abandoned plates lying about. I grab my own plate and manage to take a large bite out of my sildesalat. Oh good, it's kept its sharp enticing taste in spite of the delay.

Over near the door I can see Charlie talking to a man with thick black hair. They are both looking across at me.

The guy detaches himself and walks slowly across towards me. I've got a feeling I know what's going to happen.

He's a tall man who walks with a slight stoop, and I see - I recognise - that his feet turn out. 'I'm sorry Eleanor, I hope you don't mind me coming - Charlie mentioned that he'd had an invitation, and

I thought as I was going to be in London anyway I might wangle my way in.'

'Alec.'

He looks at me.

'That dress, it suits you,' he says after a pause. 'What would you call it – puce, or something?'

Well thanks a bundle. I'm jolly well not going to miss out on the rest of my sildesalat. People do call me pig-headed sometimes, I must admit. 'Sorry, do you mind if I finish this? I don't want to lose it.' Shame I didn't grab a paper serviette when they were on offer – I can feel the gooey mixture smudging my face.

'Of course not – go ahead. I picked up a copy of your book for my children – they were so glad to meet you in Copenhagen last year. Your cousin sent us her photographs...'

It's nice to see him. Very nice.

Suddenly there's a loud shout. Patrick. I might have guessed. 'Eleanor, the woman from The Observer's just arrived.' He marches up to the table and grabs my elbow. 'She wants to write a piece about you. You're not still eating, are you? Hurry up, Hun, she's only got ten minutes before she has to be somewhere else.'

I'm not having this, and I jerk my arm away. 'Hang on a minute, I'm just - ' The rest of the sildesalat slips off the plate and lands fair and square on the front of my expensive new dress. Well Charlie did say it matched the colour, didn't he? About ten hours ago.

'Eleanor, watch out! Whatever are you doing?' It's Gabriella now, rushing round to my side of the table, clutching a – no, surely not? – the woman is actually carrying a terry-towelling nappy that she must have had secreted about her person, in her Mary Poppins bag no doubt. My sister starts to mop up the beetroot that is dripping down my bosom. 'Mum always said we couldn't take you anywhere,' she mutters.

'Holy Moses! I don't believe it...' Patrick gazes at the scene. Poor man, he looks as though he wishes it were part of an unpleasant but brief nightmare from which he will presently awake.

'I'm so sorry, it was my fault, I interrupted her...' Alec cries.

'Nice one, my Sunshine!' Charlie roars with laughter.

Chapter Seven

Alec

Magnificent.

She was drunk of course. Partly on the house white, but also on the adrenalin. I think she'd only just realised that she was capable of handling an occasion like this. People were listening to her, really wanting to hear what she had to say. I don't think that had happened to her before.

Not helped of course by that ridiculous prick, what was his name? Patrick. Kept calling her Hun, for Christ sake.

She looked pretty good - even when that purple gooey stuff slurped onto her chest. Her hair's shorter these days, rather elegant I suppose you'd call it, though I used to like it long. I saw an interview with her on television and I particularly noticed that.

I hope she didn't resent me tagging onto Charlie like that. I don't think she minded. Anyway, I had to get the Copenhagen book for the kids, didn't I? Tamsin loved it, especially the picture of her and David climbing all over that statue of Hans Andersen. I wonder if I could write and tell her?

*

Well I did write to her, of course. I suggested that we might meet in a café in London, next time we were both there. I didn't think she'd come, but she did. Briefly. She swept in, wearing a smart raincoat in a translucent greenish blue colour, and folding up an umbrella in matching jade.

My heart gave a ridiculous jump.

She spotted me across the room and came over to my table, pulling up a chair. 'Sorry to be late – I got held up at the publisher's. Thought it was only going to be a quick meeting but there were things to get clear...' she said breathlessly. She put her bag down on the chair next to her and smiled uncertainly. 'Have you been waiting long?'

'No, no – not at all. Just got here myself.' Which was a lie, of course. 'Well, not long ago. What are you having? I ordered coffee – is that OK? And a few muffins. If you want anything else, I can...'

She shook her head.

'No, coffee will be fine. I haven't got very long, I'm afraid.'

'No. No, that's OK. You said you would be in a hurry.'

She took off her gloves.

'Well,' I said after a pause. 'It's...it's nice to see you, Eleanor.'

'Yes. Yes it is, isn't it? I'm glad your children liked the book.'

'Oh yes, Tamsin specially.'

She looked across at me. 'Tell me about Tamsin. She's what, getting on for seven now? What's she like?'

I relaxed. Easy to talk about Tamsin; I was hoping she wouldn't ask me about my wife. 'Oh, she's just an ordinary six-year-old, I suppose. That is, we think she's pretty special, to be honest. She's very bright, and interested in everything that's going on. My father was telling her about India last weekend, showing her places in the atlas, and she was asking him the most amazing questions... He said there wasn't any oil, and she asked him whether in that case India squeaks!'

'How is your father, Alec? I was so sorry to hear about his heart attack. Is he OK now?'

'Oh yes he seems to be making an amazing recovery. But he's taking early retirement – well he's already sixty-four, and they've decided to sell the house in Lisvane and move out to the country.'

She was interested in that; asked me all about Cregrina, the little village they were moving to. My parents had bought this old stone cottage in the middle of Wales. Two hundred years old, in a beautiful narrow little valley full of sheep. Milly and I thought it would be good to have somewhere in the countryside to take our children. At least, that's what I thought. Milly wasn't that bothered.

Then Eleanor asked me about my old home in Lisvane. She remembered an amazing amount of detail about it – I suppose it was all the sketching she did when she visited.

She took a sip of coffee. 'Alec, is Milly all right now? She was in hospital that time we ran into each other in Copenhagen.'

Ah yes. She was bound to ask.

'Yes. Yes, she was, wasn't she?' I hesitated. 'I don't think I can say she's better, exactly. She gets these terrible depressions, you see.'

'Oh Alec, that's dreadful! There's nothing worse... Well, not much that's worse.'

'No. No one seems to know what to do about it. Every now and then she goes into hospital for a few weeks – like going on a cruise, she says!' I laughed. 'Because she finds herself in a strange place with her own personal sort of cabin space, forced to be with a lot of strangers, and meals keep appearing at regular times without any money changing hands. She says it's like being on a weird voyage on an ocean liner, going somewhere strange that she knows nothing about...'

'She's got a vivid imagination.'

'Yes, I suppose so.'

'What do the children feel about her being away so much?'

'David takes it in his stride, I think, but Tamsin gets terribly upset. She's very close to her mother. But I've had to have a housekeeper to look after them because I'm away so often. Mrs B., we call her. She's terribly motherly, nearly as old as my parents, and she even wants to mother me!'

She gave me a shrewd look. 'What?' I asked.

'People always want to mother you, Alec – it's just you never realise.'

That's how she sees me, then – a pathetic character who demands to be looked after.

There wasn't anything to say to that.

'And you're doing quite a few new programmes these days,' she went on. 'What are you into at the moment?'

I leant forwards. 'I'm looking at some political subjects – I may be involved in a series about India, but not for a bit. That's why my father was talking to Tamsin about India. But the next big thing – this is something I've only just got settled – I'm going down to Zimbabwe to look at a place called Great Zimbabwe... It's taken me months to get permission from the government to film there.'

'Oh yes, I think you mentioned it once. When we were in Nigeria, probably.'

'Did I?' I looked at her sadly. 'You remember a lot, don't you? Well there's a fortress and some amazing stone buildings there, built between the eleventh and the fifteen centuries. It's in ruins now of course, but it was once the centre of a vast empire...'

'That's fascinating.'

'Well I think so. Milly isn't too happy about my going so far away, but it needn't be for that long.'

'It must be hard for Milly.'

I nodded. 'I know, but what can I do?' I sighed. 'You know, visually it is a stunning place. You ought to think about sketching down there. Would you be interested?'

I was taking a risk, suggesting that.

'Oh, no! I mean, I can't just now – I've got a new project in Norway. It's just at the planning stage. My publisher wants me –'

'That guy I saw running your book launch, you mean? The one who called you 'Hun.' What was his name?'

'Oh, Patrick. Yes he's keen on Scandinavia.'

'He seemed pretty keen on you, never mind Scandinavia, I thought. Have a muffin, won't you? Not that your Patrick is any of my –'

I put my hand out to pick up a muffin and at the same moment Eleanor put out hers to take the other one, so that our hands brushed accidentally against each other. It felt like a double whisky.

'Sorry!' I said automatically.

She looked up. 'Listen, Alec, it's probably not a very good idea for us to meet.'

'Why not? We used to be friends.'

She put her cup down and carefully moved the saucer to one side without looking at me.

'We used to be a great deal more than friends, Alec. That's why... Surely you can see?'

I stared at her without speaking.

'I'm sorry – look, I knew it was a mistake coming here.' She stood up. 'I'm going to be late for my next meeting – I'm sorry, I'll have to dash. You have my muffin. Sorry.'

'For God's sake don't keep saying you're sorry!'

'Sorry... Oh this is ridiculous!' She picked up her bag and stood up.

'Eleanor, please don't go!'

She shook her head, turning away.

'Can I write to you – now and then?' I pleaded.

'No, don't! I mean, yes of course you can. Only I may not be able to write back...' She slung her coat over her shoulder and stepped out towards the door without looking back.

She was probably right. It was a mistake: I shouldn't have asked her to meet me. I picked up the bill and walked slowly across to the counter to pay.

Chapter Eight

1987-89

Gabriella admired the postcard of the ruins of Great Zimbabwe propped up carelessly on the kitchen windowsill among piles of saucepans.

'That's interesting – where is it?' she asked.

Gabriella was helping Eleanor to move at last into a bigger flat in Rome, close to the centre. They were surrounded by packing cases and the odd cardboard box. Eleanor seemed to have accumulated a great deal of stuff; her trouble, as Gabriella so often told her, was that she found it impossible to throw anything away.

Gabriella turned the postcard over. 'Good heavens – it's from him again!' She twisted her head round to look at her sister. 'I thought you weren't seeing him?'

'No of course I'm not! Look for heaven's sake, it's only a postcard. You know, the sort of thing Mum sends a couple of dozen of, when she's away on holiday.'

Gabriella read the card, which informed the world and anyone who cared to read it that Alec was enjoying putting together a series of programmes about the excavations there, which was to be broadcast in the autumn.

'You're not going to answer it?'

'Look, Gabby, let me tell you something about postcards.' She put down the bundle of waste-paper baskets she was sorting. 'They do not, repeat not, require an answer. They are not an intimate form of communication in any shape or form.'

'No? So why does he write "Good to see you last year," then? You saw him in London, didn't you?'

'Well yes, very briefly. We just happened to run into each other in a café, that's all.'

'What a coincidence! There do seem to be a lot of coincidences here.'

'All we did was have a cup of coffee. He told me he was going to make a programme about Great Zimbabwe.'

'Did he now. I hope he didn't expect you to drop everything and go off sketching there!'

Eleanor picked up a box of china and began to unload the plates. One of them was chipped, she noticed; she really would have to get some new ones. 'You're not answering. He did, didn't he?'

'What?'

'Want you to go and sketch this place in Zimbabwe. Did you want to go there with him? Did you?'

Of course I wanted to go with him – what's not to want?

'I couldn't go, anyway. I've been busy with my new Norwegian book, you know that. Patrick wanted me to go to Bergen straight after Christmas.'

'So it's still on with Patrick, then? In spite of the sildesalat!

*

From Alec Jenkins <anj@tomtom.net>
To Eleanor Larsen-Bruun <Eleanor@larsen-bruun.co.uk>
Subject: New horizons!
November 29th 1988   14:53:31 GMT

Hi Eleanor
How are you? We got your new book on Norway – it's got some great sketches in it! What's the food like – is it as good as Danish? I know how ATTACHED you are to Danish food! (Sorry, didn't mean that to be a dig; at least you've never cooked a chicken with the giblets still inside...) Been wondering what you are up to these days.

I've been planning what to do next, after Zimbabwe – hope you got the card I sent you from there. The series went down well, and they've sold it to a lot of other countries. I'm thinking of branching out into more political stories. There's going to be a series next year about the history of India, and I've been asked if I'd like to do the programme on partition after independence, which sounds exciting. I may even be able to call in on my aunt Valerie's family in Kolkata – you remember Valerie, don't you? We stayed with her and my uncle Ian in Nigeria that time. Val's father came from an ancient Kolkata family in the old part of the city, and she assures me that any relative of hers would be welcome.

Tamsin sends her love. So would David if he ever stayed still enough for anyone to ask him!

Yours, Alec

*

Patrick rang up from London early one evening in the spring of 1989, just after Eleanor got in from a day out with Gabriella and the children. She was tired and feeling slightly cross from an argument she'd been having with her sister, and was hoping for a quiet evening.

'Hi Eleanor – how are you? OK?' He sounded more breathless than usual, and in any case she knew from experience that he didn't expect much of an answer to this question.

'Fine – why, what's up?' She kicked her shoes off and flopped onto the sofa with the phone.

'You'll never guess what's happened, Hun!'

She sighed. 'What?'

'You've heard of the S.N.Choudhury prize? You must have!'

'Er...vaguely, I think.' She searched at the back of her mind. 'Something to do with travel writing?'

'It's only the most prestigious prize in the whole of eastern Asia.' Patrick paused, clearly expecting a reaction of some sort.

'Yes?' she said in the end. 'What of it?'

'They've gone and short-listed you for this year's award, that's what.'

'Oh!' Eleanor sat up. 'What on earth have they done that for?'

'Apparently they think you have been exploring interesting political questions in your more recent books. They liked the one on Iceland this year.'

She paused, taking this in. 'But they've probably short-listed a whole lot of clever people, Patrick! I'm not very likely to get it, am I?'

'I should have thought you've got a fair chance. They've had a string of solid serious writers in past years – word is they are looking for someone a bit different this time. Look, we can talk about it when you come to London. Are we still on for the Easter weekend? I thought we could take in a couple of shows, maybe dive down to Brighton... Eleanor?'

'Yes, OK. I'll get a flight on Good Friday if I can – I'll be busy 'til then.'

*

Gabriella paused while folding up the laundry and turned to look at her sister. 'Eleanor, that's amazing! Short-listed – wait 'til we tell Mum!'

'Oh don't get all excited about it, Gabby – I'm not going to get the thing! I'm sure I'm not. It's just nice, you know, to see that someone thinks I'm worth short-listing.'

'Don't be silly, of course you'll get it. My clever little sister, huh?' Eleanor frowned.

'And you think you'll know at Easter?'

'Patrick says the announcement will come on Good Friday.'

'Well mind you make sure to tell me the minute you hear.'

'Don't worry, you and Mum will be the first to know.'

'What does it mean? Will you have to go and get the prize?'

'It's awarded in Kolkata every August. There's an S.N.Choudhury Centre there, apparently...'

'Fabulous! Maybe I ought to come with you.'

*

Patrick met her at Heathrow when she arrived for Easter. He was characteristically late arriving, and she stood around for several minutes staring at the crowd, watching everyone else being lovingly greeted or disappearing towards the underground.

At last he turned up, looking flushed. He brushed her face with a swift kiss, then he put his hands on her arms and stood back to look at her.

'Well, Hun: you got it!'

'You don't mean...'

68

'We got a phone call this afternoon. You're officially the winner of the 1989 S.N.Choudhury Prize and you are expected in Kolkata for their international conference in August. You'll be giving the keynote address. You'll just be able to fit it in after you get back from Reykjavik. You've got those book shops promoting your Iceland book in July, haven't you?' She stared at him.

It wasn't until three hours later that she remembered her promise to Gabriella to let her know. They were eating in a hotel near Patrick's flat, and the steaks were on their way. Patrick had ordered a particularly good bottle of wine.

'Oh goodness, I really ought to tell my sister,' she said. 'Is there a phone in this place?'

He looked up in surprise. 'Yes, there was one in the entrance lobby. Can't it wait?'

She stood up. 'No, I promised... I won't be a minute.'

She grabbed her bag and walked briskly into the lobby. Ah there was the phone, in a secluded little alcove; luckily she had some sterling change in her purse. It would be good to tell Gabriella; she'd be so thrilled, and so would her ever-expanding family. Their unconditional support over the years had always given Eleanor a warm safe feeling.

Then there was the question of what on earth she would be expected to say in her keynote address; but Gabby wouldn't be much help there. Maybe someone else might be able to advise; she ran her eye idly down the list of phone numbers in her diary, then made up her mind.

The phone rang for a long time. There was probably no one in. Why should there be, this time on the evening of a public holiday?

This really is the worst idea you have had for...for an extremely long time.

Someone picked up the phone and a small voice said, 'Hallo?'

'Oh, hallo there.' Deep breath. 'I was wondering if Dr Jenkins is in?'

'Daddy's very busy tonight. Who is it?'

'Er...my name's Eleanor. Look, it doesn't matter if he's not available – I'll call back another time...'

But the owner of the small voice had left the receiver rattling on the table. 'Daddy! There's a lady on the phone for you.'

Then there was a very long pause, and various household noises wafted their way over the phone: someone was playing music in a nearby room – Mozart perhaps? A loo being flushed. Voices arguing in the distance. A dog was barking outside. Where was this, anyway? She had very little idea where exactly Alec lived.

Finally someone came to the phone. 'Alec Jenkins?'

'Alec. I'm sorry to bother you on a Friday night...' That's a stupid thing to say for a start: when would you not be sorry to bother him?

'Eleanor! How wonderful... Is everything all right?'

'Yes, yes, perfectly all right. It's just, something's happened and I wanted to tell you.'

'Yes?'

'I've been awarded this prize thing...'

Naturally he had heard of S.N.Choudhury – knew far more about the prize than she did. He knew who the original S.N.Choudhury was, the nineteenth century Bengali traveller who had explored the upper reaches of the Ganges.

'That's amazing!' he went on. 'I mean, no it's not really amazing at all, I'm just glad they've recognised your work at last. Congratulations!'

He asked her if she had decided what to say in her address. 'I could maybe give you some help there – I've been reading up a lot about India for the programme I'm doing in August.'

'Oh yes, you did mention that. I'd forgotten... When is it you are going?'

'Pretty much the same time as your conference, as it happens. Maybe we could meet up in Kolkata?'

She hesitated. You really shouldn't think of it. But then, you won't know anyone at all in Kolkata; it wouldn't do any harm to see a friendly face. Would it?

There was a crash in the distance, as though a whole dinner service of crockery was being chucked onto a stone floor. A child began to sob.

Alec muttered, 'Oh God, not again!'

'Look Alec, is this a bad time? I shouldn't have rung...'

'No, no, not bad at all! It's wonderful to hear your voice. Where are you, anyway? You sound as though you are in the next room. A breath of sanity. And your news is...great. I'm so pleased for you. Tammy, just a minute, can't you see I'm on the phone?'

'Daddy, Mummy's crying! You've got to come.'

Eleanor could hear Tamsin's voice, loud and insistent. 'Alec, we can talk another time – you must get back...' As she put the phone down, she heard him say he'd ring her.

Patrick looked up as she went back to the table. 'Well, what did your wonderful sister have to say? Don't tell me – she's going out to Kolkata with you, complete with her dozen children?'

'Oh!' Eleanor had completely forgotten Gabriella. 'No, actually she... She wasn't in.'

'Wasn't in? Then whatever have you been doing all this time? Your steak's getting cold. Who on earth...?'

'Her husband answered,' she lied. 'My brother-in-law, Giulio. He was very pleased. He'll tell her.'

'Well tuck in, then – the prices they charge in this place, we might as well enjoy it, Eleanor.'

She looked across at Patrick. Clever, single-minded, practical Patrick; not one to get entangled with people who threw dinner services onto the kitchen walls.

Suddenly Eleanor felt utterly exhausted.

*

Eleanor wrote her keynote address in Iceland that July.

She had gone there alone because a consortium of booksellers in Reykjavik had invited her to a grand book-signing ceremony to celebrate her collection of sketches of Iceland. Patrick was flying over later that week for the actual book-signing – Eleanor had the sense that he didn't like to let her out on her own in case she disgraced herself. He'd probably sent instructions in advance that they were not on any account to serve sildesalat with the refreshments; she wouldn't put it past him.

So here she was, alone with nearly a week to spare. It was chilly, and she was dressed in an anorak and jeans. She had hired a car for a few days, because she wanted to go again to some of the places where she had sketched when she was doing the book. This morning she was sitting on a bench looking across at a small pond, about the size of a child's paddling pool, which was surrounded by a raised edge of mud.

It was roped off, so she couldn't get right up to it, but she could see the surface ruffling slightly, as though a gentle breeze were catching it.

All at once one single huge dark bubble formed on the surface, like a giant cauldron coming to the boil. The bubble held for a few seconds. Then... Whoosh! Boiling water spurted up a hundred feet into the air.

Amazing! Eleanor had seen it many times before but she was still fascinated by it. Strokkur, they called it. It was at a little place called Geysir, which they said had given its name with altered spelling to all the other geysers in the world.

Spray splashed down onto the path on the gathered crowd, causing shrieks of laughter and delight from the tourists. A man grabbed his child; a young girl jostled her boyfriend. There was a party of Danish tourists talking loudly, several of them at once, enjoying themselves. It was wonderful just to listen to the language again; she hadn't been back to Denmark since Bedstemor died the previous autumn. Eleanor reached into her bag for her notebook. She'd already had a few ideas for the keynote speech, and here, folded neatly into her notebook, was an email from Alec with some suggestions for her address.

Alec seemed to live in her head these days.

She hadn't actually spoken to him since that alarming phone call on Good Friday, when there was obviously something badly wrong going on in his home. He didn't refer to that day in his email; instead he suggested that she might want to look at the striking changes afoot in the world that year. Gorbachev was an interesting new kind of Soviet leader, someone they could do business with, in Thatcher's famous phrase, so would it be worth illustrating the changes they were all living through with some of her sketches? He knew she'd been to see the Berlin Wall, for example; how many years was that destined to last? No one could tell.

Strokkur erupted again and a different set of tourists was splashed. Eleanor gathered up her things and headed for the restaurant, a bright modern affair with flags of several dozen countries flying outside it, and a cheerful mix of tourists inside, most of them on package day trips. She found a place for herself with an elderly Italian couple who told her that they had come here to escape the summer heat of their home.

After lunch she got into the hire car and headed back towards the coast. Interesting, Alec's email; maybe she could say something about Gorbachev. The evening before, she had wandered down to the sea from her hotel. It was a fine evening, if chilly, and it would not get dark at all, so she had struck out away from the harbour, and suddenly come across the municipal guesthouse, a mile or so along the coast. This afternoon she thought it would be good to take another look.

It was an unassuming white building overlooking the sea and the green hills on the peninsula across the bay. It was here in this guesthouse that Mikhail Gorbachev had first met Ronald Reagan in the autumn of 1986, not even three years ago. They had astonished everyone by agreeing in principle to remove intermediate-range nuclear weapons from Europe. Their own people back in Moscow and Washington had been horrified afterwards of course, but they had done it.

Eleanor parked the car and walked over to the guesthouse. She settled down on a wall by the sea and took out her sketchpad. Perhaps this peaceful place up here in Iceland, away from both Europe and America, had kick-started a process that would affect all of them in ways no one yet knew.

Chapter Nine

India, 1989

Eleanor

'This is ridiculous – how long is it going to take?' Apparently the woman in front of me in the queue is addressing me.

Here I am, on my own in Heathrow. Sweltering August weather, not the best time to be travelling, but I didn't have a choice - I just got back from Iceland a fortnight ago, and this is the only flight to Kolkata I could find. So I'm queuing up at the Biman desk, and we are in for a long wait. There's a tall broad-shouldered woman in front of me, also on her own. Distinct accent; can't quite place it. Everybody around us is in small or large groups, over a hundred passengers, sprawled on the metal barriers. Nothing seems to be moving at all.

'Yes, it is tiresome, isn't it?' I say, trying to sound friendly. 'I think they've gone off on their tea break!'

But my British sense of humour isn't appreciated, and the woman – who introduces herself as Susanna van der Merwe, from Darjeeling – proceeds to explain how very much more efficient an airport like Cape Town would be.

Normally I value my own space and stillness, but this time it might be just as well to have this stranger to talk to, for we've got to the middle of August, the very time Alec said he might be flying out to Kolkata to begin his programme. I've got no idea which airline he might travel on, but I'm beginning to feel that I don't want to be isolated here, a passenger on my own. Some company – even if this woman turns out to be garrulous and tiresome – might be useful camouflage.

So I smile, rest my weight on my suitcase, and ask the woman where she's going. It seems she's head of the geography department at St Teilo's school in Darjeeling.

'Ever been there?' the woman asks. 'You should – it's a beautiful place up in the foothills of the Himalayas; well worth a visit if you have time. What is it that takes you to Kolkata?'

I really don't want to go into the S.N.Choudhury prize– bad enough having to go and accept the wretched thing, without explaining it to strangers. To change the subject, I ask about Susanna's family background in Stellenbosch and the Transvaal, and Susanna is happy to tell me, at some length.

'My family didn't really approve of my London lifestyle,' she says some twenty minutes later. 'I've had to make my own way in the world. The odd relationship or three – but men are such bastards, aren't they? Except for the ones that up and die on you. Do you find that?'

There's no answer to that.

'So have you got a reliable mate to share the struggle?' Susanna peers down at me.

'Me? Oh, well...'

A reliable mate? No that isn't something I seem to be in possession of just now. Not as such. Patrick and I are more interested in our own careers than in each other. But why the hell should I want one? I'm a paid-up feminist, with a successful career that I love. Why should I need someone who is going to stick around for the rest of my life – that's hopelessly romantic. I'm a self-respecting person in my own right, I tell you.

'I'm sorry, I didn't mean to be nosy,' Susanna says when I don't reply. 'Oh look, is something happening at last?'

Passengers several rows ahead of us are picking up their luggage and inching forwards.

Toward the back of the queue, now stretching a long way behind us, there's a group with large and strangely shaped pieces of luggage – could there be the odd camera in there? I turn away quickly.

*

We must be somewhere over the Black Sea by now, at a height of roughly six miles. The cabin is mostly dark. I stir fitfully – maybe I ought to head for the toilets at the back? I haven't slept – I rarely do when I fly. Some hours ago there was a meal which I prefer to forget, though the smell lingers in the air. My eyes are aching and my mouth is dry. There's probably a tap at the back near the loos.

I'm tightly wedged between a large Indian businessman slumped in enviable noisy slumber to my left and a small child curled up next to his mother on my right. On balance the pair on the right look more negotiable, so muttering 'Excuse me – sorry – could I just...?' a few times I finally achieve the aisle.

I stand up straight and stretch.

It seems Alec has had the same thought.

'Ah – so you are on this flight, Eleanor! I wondered if you might be. Your conference is this week, isn't it?' He looks tousled, and his hair is sticking up more than usual.

'Yes, it's Thursday. I... It's nice to see you, Alec.' I look up at him.

'Yes. It is, isn't it?'

Oh God this is a dreadful mistake.

Alec goes on, 'I see the Guardian gave you pretty good coverage – all about this thing, the S.N. Choudhury prize, and your work. Nice photograph.'

'Oh, you saw that, did you?' The photograph was terrible of course; photos of me always are. There's a sudden lurch downwards and the 'fasten seat belts' lights come on. Alec puts out a hand to steady himself on the nearest seat. 'I hope we don't have too much turbulence. My sister's here, by the way – have you seen her?'

'Roz? No, I didn't realise. I wouldn't recognise her anyway – I haven't seen her since she was about twelve! What's she doing here?'

'Oh she's going out to be with Matt – they are an item these days. Our cousin, you remember? He asked her at the last minute to come and meet him in Kolkata, and I was able to get her a seat because one of our cameramen suddenly dropped out.'

It might be nice to meet up with Roz again.

'You've written your keynote address, I suppose. Were any of the things... Was it any help, the email I sent you with some ideas?'

'Oh yes of course!' I say. 'Thank you so much. I'm going to talk about the big changes in the world just now, in relation to little things going on in our lives.'

He nods. 'That sounds good.'

There's a pause, so for something to say I ask him if he's brought his children with him this time. Silly question of course.

'Oh no – I won't have time to entertain children: this is only a flying visit. They're fine, they are at my parents' new cottage in mid-Wales: I told you about that, didn't I? My mother is smothering them with attention as usual.'

What about Milly? I ought to ask him if things are any better – is she still throwing the crockery? But I don't know how to bring it up.

'So how are your parents adapting to the country life? Is your father all right now?'

'Dad's fine, and Mum's as busy as ever. Running the Women's Institute for the whole of Powys as far as we can make out. Sorting them out, telling them how things are done. Yes, Dad's made a great recovery, thank you. He's campaigning for a better transport system, thinks flying uses up too much of the earth's resources, but in my job I can hardly avoid it, can I? Anyway, where are you staying in Kolkata, Eleanor?'

*

It's broad daylight by the time we land at Dhaka. As I step through the galley onto the gangway, there's a humid banana-tinged smell outside and I'm smacked in the face by the bright fist of the Bangladeshi sun.

Transit passengers are being whisked away to a special lounge where there are issues with the air-conditioning, it seems, and we are all given tokens for cold drinks from a bar in the corner. Alec's film crew are making straight for it.

A young woman with long blonde hair detaches herself and comes over with a broad smile – this must surely be Roz. 'Hi, Eleanor – Alec said you were here!'

'Roz, how are you?'

'I'm good, thanks.'

We sit down on an elderly leather sofa to wait for the crowd round the bar to fade, and I take a tepid water bottle out of my bag. 'I don't fancy one of their drinks – it's bound to be fizzy.' I offer the water, but Roz shakes her head. 'So your parents have moved out into the country, I hear.'

'Yes, it's so cool, isn't it? I never thought Mum would give up all the things she ran in Cardiff. But she's just as busy. She's looking after my niece and nephew at the moment...'

'Yes, Alec said. I suppose his wife isn't...'

'Milly doesn't cope very well with the children,' Roz says, keeping an eye on the drinks queue. 'Look, why don't we find out how long we're going to be stuck here?'

Susanna van der Merwe is already engaging the official at the desk. There seems to be some sort of delay.

'What do you mean, delay? Kolkata is only half an hour's flight from here, just across the delta,' Susanna tells the man. He probably knows this already.

'I regret most sincerely, Madam,' he says softly, with a polite sideways click of his head. 'Incoming aircraft is delayed. We expect it in two and a half hours. Four hours utmost.

In another hour there's an announcement: an excursion is being laid on – we are invited on a tour of Dhaka in a small bus. Susanna declares that it would be better than sitting in the transit lounge, and Alec agrees. The film crew has fallen asleep over in the corner, but he and Roz join the party. 'Are you coming, Eleanor?' he asks.

'Sure.' I hoist my handbag over my shoulder.

The bus is old and badly sprung, with windows wide open, giving a sense of immediacy – we feel part of the bustling pot-holed street that the bus is hurtling along.

'You been to this part of the world before?' Susanna asks, turning to Roz and me. We tell her we haven't.

The air is thick with dust and black diesel fumes – and smoke which Susanna tells us comes from the two-stroke engines of the amazing little three-wheeler taxis. By the roadside there are open stagnant drains full of rubbish. There are people everywhere, and stalls selling everything you could possibly want.

'This is fascinating,' Alec says, peering out of the bus. 'I wasn't expecting to be here before Kolkata! We'll be back here filming in a few days...' He's got dark rings under his eyes, and he looks as if he could do with a good sleep.

Not the time to start getting all maternal on him.

'Good place for photocopying,' Susanna points out. 'As well as very sweet hot tea!'

There's a chaos of lorries, buses more battered than this one, and rickshaws all battling for space.

'You'll find Kolkata is very much like this. More crowded if anything,' Susanna tells us. 'What you should really do is not stay in Kolkata at all but come up to Darjeeling! It's such a beautiful place, up there in the Himalayas. Come and visit me.'

'I don't know what Matt wants us to do,' Roz said. 'But it's an idea. Alec, you must come with us!

'No time I'm afraid – we're filming flat out,' he says.

We turn a corner and look – there seems to be a political demonstration of some sort. A column of marchers, banners flying. No one else in the street seems to have noticed.

Our bus turns into a wide road to see the grand new parliament building which – the guide informs us – has been donated by the United States government.

Back at the airport the same official meets us at the desk, looking even more harassed than before. He's very sorry but there is still no flight available for Kolkata. Estimated arrival is several hours away, and the airline is pleased to accommodate all transit passengers at Hotel Zakaria, which is conveniently situated at the airport.

'A whole night!' Susanna is outraged. 'What are these guys playing at?'

'Not a lot we can do about it,' Alec points out. 'Matt will be told about it – he'll know to meet you tomorrow, Roz. And Eleanor, when is your keynote speech?'

'Tomorrow! Oh God, I'm not going to make it, am I?'

Susanna declares that she's jolly well going to enjoy the hotel and the sumptuous meal it offers, since it's free and the very least we deserve. Afterwards most of the exhausted passengers head straight for their rooms.

I'm going to take advantage of the pleasantly cool evening air to walk round the hotel gardens. There's a delightful scent of trees and plants that I wish I could identify. Alec falls into step beside me.

'I suppose you are used to public speaking by now,' he says with a grin. 'You seem to do a lot of it.'

'Nothing like as much as you, Alec! I'm not exactly a television personality...'

He laughs. 'I never expected to be!'

'To be honest, I still get horribly nervous.' I can't say that to anyone but Alec. 'Especially something like this – coming to a country I've never been to before. I mean, I've no idea whether what I've prepared will be at all what they expect, what they want from me.'

'Oh, you'll be great. You've got an easy, comfortable way of talking to people, Eleanor. They'll adore you!'

There's a small silence between us, as we walk around a branch that has fallen onto the path.

And you used to adore me yourself – but all that is deep in the past, in a different life, gone for ever. We cannot dwell in the past.

'So how... How are things with you, Alec?'

'Oh Eleanor.' He looks at me with an expression of utter despair. 'Milly's very unhappy. She's back in hospital at the moment – one of her cruises, she says!'

'She's got some spirit.'

'But I feel so angry with her – can you understand that? I just want to shake her, sometimes... I can't say that to anyone, of course.'

But he says it to me.

'That's only natural,' I try to say.

We have reached the gate at the end of the garden. Hey, wouldn't it be wonderful if we could escape through it, out into the world, and on... Ridiculous thought; of course we can't, and we don't, we turn up a different path back to the hotel.

'I'm sorry I couldn't talk to you properly,' he says. 'That night you rang up about your prize. It was a difficult evening...'

'Oh no – I was sorry myself that I'd bothered you.'

'Milly gets these sudden rages and it terrifies the children. Tamsin, specially. David just lets it all float by him, but Tammy is badly scared.'

'Poor kid.'

'I'm glad they've gone up to stay with my parents – my mother's so practical and sensible, you know. She'll spoil them of course, and do lots of exciting things with them, but she will make them feel secure at the same time. Everything will be safe and predictable for them.'

We've reached the hotel now, and he turns to say, 'Well I suppose we'd better get some rest before the jet lag kicks in, hadn't we? Goodnight, Eleanor.'

'Goodnight, Alec. God bless...'

I turn at once and begin to walk up the grand central staircase to my room without a backward glance.

*

Matt Beynon is waiting for us at Dum Dum airport. A tall lean figure now, thinning blond hair, I'd never have recognised him from his childhood days in Nigeria. He hugs Roz as soon as she appears, and then turns to greet Alec.

'Afraid we've got a slight crisis, Matt,' Alec says. 'We ran into Eleanor Larsen-Bruun on the flight – you remember Eleanor, don't you? She came out to Nigeria with me. She's got to be at the S.N.Choudhury Centre in... What's the time difference? In exactly forty minutes from now.'

'Oh, they are here for you.' Matt is quick to catch on. 'There was an elegant lady in a cream and pale blue sari in the crowd waiting for this flight. She's waving a big banner saying "Ms Eleanor Larsen-Bruun for the S.N.Choudhury Centre." I'll see if I can grab her.'

In no time Matt has located the woman, who introduces herself as Santi Choudhury, the daughter of the present head of the Centre. Santi is deeply relieved to see me at last, and points me to a yellow taxi which she has already booked. 'I am so glad to meet you. I think we will be in time,' she says with a smile which no doubt hides her anxiety.

'Don't forget – Darjeeling!' Susanna shouts. 'I'll try,' I shout back, breathless, as I climb into the taxi.

To my amazement, Alec climbs in after me. 'See you at the hotel,' he calls out to his producer. 'Just going to make sure this works out...'

Oh well. If that's what he wants.

The taxi swerves out of the queue and does a dizzy series of jerks and reverses to get round the jam of traffic. The young driver has clearly had the urgency explained to him. My stomach gets left behind somewhere as we sweep out of the airport and into the packed dual carriageway.

'It is not too far,' Santi assures us. 'We are lucky that we are located this side of Kolkata. We should be in time.'

Alec catches my eye. 'Might as well relax now, Eleanor. You'll be OK.' He takes my hand.

Wasn't expecting that!

It feels just the same: firm, solid – as though he means it. He hasn't held my hand since 1973. I ought to be terrified of giving this talk, but what the hell? I'm going to wow them at the S.N.Choudhury Centre. I know I am.

The journey is indeed, as Susanna suggested, reminiscent of our trip through Dhaka. There's the same chaotic mixture of rickshaws and cars, bicycles and pedestrians, all avoiding each other without the slightest sign of how they manage it.

Before long, here we are: the S.N.Choudhury Centre. It's a grand Edwardian edifice set in extensive grounds. The taxi draws up at the front, and we see an anxious group of well-dressed people waiting outside.

'You look absolutely stunning, by the way,' Alec whispers as we get out of the taxi. 'As you always do.'

Santi is introducing her father, old Mr Choudhury, who is extremely relieved to find that I am indeed their esteemed guest speaker. He shakes my hand solemnly and explains that he has the privilege to be the great-grandson of the famous explorer. 'But my daughter does all the work these days!'

'We are not late at all,' Santi says briskly, taking me by the elbow. 'If you and your husband would just come with me, you can refresh yourself for ten minutes and then I will introduce you to the conference. Please come this way.'

'He's not my husband, actually...' I cast a helpless glance at Alec, who's picked up my luggage. But he doesn't seem to mind; he grins and gives me an enormous wink.

*

It's a vast air-conditioned auditorium in several tiers. The lights are dim except for the stage, where I'm sitting with Santi Choudhury in front of a low table made of intricately inlaid wood. Santi pours out a glass of water for me, and then rises to the lectern to introduce me. Behind us at the back of the stage is a screen on which Santi is ready to project my drawings.

As the applause dies away I take a deep breath, stand up and walk over to the lectern. As I glance down, I can see Alec next to Mr Choudhury in the front row.

Time to begin.

'I have just been back to Iceland, to Reykjavik. A faraway place, about as different from Kolkata as you might find. It didn't get dark at all, for the whole time I was there, because it is so far north – imagine!'

Santi presses a button and projects the first sketch I've chosen – old Strokkur, spurting up its jet of water a hundred feet into the air.

'It was a very chilly holiday, for me – I live as you know in Rome, and I grew up in the UK. Yes, Iceland was certainly chilly. But something happened there.'

I pause.

'There was a new beginning, or perhaps just the beginning of a new beginning, which I believe will have an effect not just here in Kolkata but all over the world.'

The next slide is a sketch of the municipal guesthouse. There's an appreciative murmur from the audience, as they see the pleasant unpretentious white building overlooking the bay.

'Have a look at this. I found the place one evening when I went for a walk along the coast, not far from my hotel. It is a municipal guest house. This is the place where not so long ago, in the autumn of 1986, Mikhail Gorbachev first met Ronald Reagan.'

I take a sip of water from the table.

'Now we don't know yet how significant that beginning was, but we can get a sense that something is changing. In Europe the Poles have struggled for nearly ten years since the start of Solidarity, which was finally legalised four months ago. The Hungarians struggled for nearly ten months, and now the borders are open so that thousands of East Germans can pour into Hungary for their summer holidays this year.'

I nod to Santi, who clicks the button to show a sketch I made in the spring of the Brandenburg Gate, in the middle of the Berlin Wall.

'I don't know where all this is leading, any more than you do. Maybe this wall here – this great icon of the Cold War, the Berlin Wall - will last for another twenty-eight years, who knows? But I do get the sense, as perhaps you do too, that something is changing dramatically this year, and I see my job as simply to go round asking questions and sketching the individuals and places that interest me. I'd like to show you a few more of those people and places...'

I'm getting into my stride now, and Alec is leaning forward, smiling.

Eventually I come to the end. The thunderous applause takes me by surprise; I feel as though I've talked for ever. Alec's got a broad grin on his face as he claps – does he think I've done all right?

Santi chairs a brief question and answer session – too brief for the audience, it seems, but finally she wraps it up, explaining that I've only just arrived from the UK this very afternoon and will need to rest.

Old Mr Choudhury then walks stiffly up onto the stage, negotiating the steps with difficulty, and presents me with an envelope containing a cheque, the famous S.N.Choudhury Prize.

'Don't spend it all at once!' Alec whispers as he slips into Santi's taxi later. She's offered him a lift to his hotel, which turns out to be not far from where she and her father live. I'm staying with the Choudhurys of course.

'So you are making a television programme here, Dr Jenkins? I have read about it, naturally,' Santi said. 'It is about partition, is that right?'

'Yes it is. We're hoping to make a start first thing tomorrow morning, after our flight was so delayed. I'm doing a piece to camera down at Howrah station, to set the scene. Like to come along, Eleanor?'

'I don't know – I thought I might visit Matt and Roz tomorrow...'

'That's all right – they'll be there at the station too. Matt is going to write something for his paper. About ten o'clock, OK?' We've got to Alec's hotel. He jumps out and disappears into the entrance with a wave over his shoulder.

It was nice of him to come to my talk, though. For some ridiculous reason it gives me a warm feeling inside.

*

Howrah station is packed. There are travellers everywhere, family parties in colourful clothes, businessmen; long queues for tickets. Vendors selling all sorts of foodstuffs for innumerable journeys, and inexhaustible amounts of tea in charming tiny orange clay cups. There are hundreds of porters, steadily going about their business in their solid maroon turbans. There's a glorious smell, a mixture of spicy food cooking, human bodies in close proximity in rather too warm an environment, and of course the dirty bustling smell of the trains themselves: Howrah's twenty-one platforms handle over three hundred trains a day, I've learnt from Santi Choudhury.

It's a huge station with a roof high above, one of the two main Kolkata terminuses. I crane my head up to read the arrival and departure notices: the Ahmedabad Express, the Coromandel Express for Madras, the Amritsar Mail, the Rajdhani Express headed for Delhi and Bhubaneswar – names to conjure with. Later if there's time I'd love to make a few sketches of both the inside of the station and of the grand red brick exterior. I slept well in the Choudhurys' spacious house, and now that the dreaded talk is over I can relax.

There's Matt and Roz over by the main entrance - Roz turns round and waves.

'Hi, Eleanor - you made it. Alec said your talk was fantastic last night!'

'Oh, did he? Well they seemed to like it... Is Alec here?'

'He's sorting out things with the crew - come on, Eleanor, we're going over to find them,' Matt said. 'I think they are filming soon.'

Alec is in the middle of one of the platforms, surrounded on either side by swirling crowds of passengers. Looks as though he's about to start his piece to camera.

'I'm standing this morning in one of Kolkata's two vast train terminuses – Howrah station. It looks peaceful enough today – hundreds of people going about their normal daily travel – but let's go back forty-two years and we see quite a different scene. The station was packed with refugees. Many of them lived on these very platforms here for weeks on end before they could be resettled. Where had they come from?'

Someone calls 'Cut!' Alec walks over to the producer to discuss what archive footage is available.

'Fascinating, isn't it?' Matt says. 'My great-uncle Som was here in 1947. He's a doctor.'

Roz turns to me. 'Yes, I met Uncle Som at the house last night.'

Matt goes on, 'He's going to be filmed talking to Alec about how he spent months here looking after the refugees from East Pakistan – how cool is that? In the end he caught cholera himself and had to stop – he was lucky to survive.'

Some forty minutes later the producer declares a break of ten minutes, and Matt goes to buy more tea for us.

'How do you reckon Alec is, Rozzie?' he says, pocketing the change. 'He looks tired, to me. I haven't seen him for some time - he seems much older these days.'

Roz frowns. 'To be honest, Matt, I'm mega worried about my big brother.'

'Yeah?'

'Mum is too. He's so stressed out, because of Milly. Mum's terribly worried, she thinks he's heading for some sort of breakdown.'

'You're kidding! Does she really?'

I keep silent.

*

In the afternoon Matt takes me to visit his grandfather's home, where he and Roz are staying. It's an ancient building, dating back, Matt thinks, nearly three hundred years to the foundation of Kolkata itself, and his family has lived here ever since. A large rambling edifice in the centre of the city, built round four sides of a large open courtyard. This week it's decked everywhere in bright bunting, green, saffron and white, for the forthcoming Independence Day celebrations. The house is not far from the mighty Hooghly; Matt takes me up onto the roof garden, and we can see the wide sprawling river when Matt points across the flat rooftops of the neighbouring buildings.

'I'd love to sketch the view from up here, Matt, if there's time,' I tell him. 'It's amazing!'

'Plenty of time. Look - there, in the distance - you can just see the Howrah bridge that we came across in the taxi just now. The biggest cantilever bridge in the world. Four million pedestrians a day, if you can believe that...'

'Yes, you said. I wanted to stop there and then to sketch it - all those herds of cattle jostling with the people and the cars and rickshaws!'

Matt laughs. 'It's certainly different. You don't get much cattle on Sydney Harbour bridge, I've noticed!'

We approached the family home through a wide covered passageway from the street, which led straight into the central courtyard.

There was a crowd of children playing cricket there as we arrived, and Matt told us that he and Owen used to play cricket here too, when they came here with their parents many times. 'And Mum says my grandfather played here too.'

'Did he?' Roz said. 'That's so cool.'

'Yeah. Makes the hairs on the back of your neck stand on end.'

*

The two old men sit back in deep comfortable armchairs – Uncle Som, who was once a doctor at Howrah station when the refugees came flooding in from the newly created East Pakistan, and next to him his old friend and cousin-brother Krishna, who was himself a refugee from the east. Someone from Alec's film crew has fitted miniature microphones onto their long white loose-fitting Indian shirts. Across the room the crew set up their lights.

Alec sits in another armchair facing the two men.

I'm allowed to watch all this from just inside the doorway, perched on stools with Roz and Matt. I've never seen Alec at work before. He's concentrating hard, a sheaf of notes in his hands, and he speaks respectfully to the old men, greeting them first with a namaste, a deep bow over palms flat against each other.

He begins by asking Uncle Som whether he was taken by surprise when so many hundreds of thousands of refugees had arrived in Kolkata.

'Oh yes of course, everyone was,' Som says at once. 'It should never have been like that. The British were forced into leaving too quickly. Mountbatten was expected to hand over in 1948 but he brought it forward to 1947, before we were ready. We did not even know where some of the new boundaries were going to be drawn. We were supposed to be one country, but Jinnah insisted on a separate Muslim state.'

Alec encourages Uncle Som to talk about his experiences at Howrah station in the months after independence. He worked twelve- or fourteen-hour days there, continuously, until he became ill himself. Medicines were scarce and many people died.

'And you, Krishna,' Alec says. 'You arrived here yourself during that time, didn't you, sir?'

Krishna shifts in his seat and stares past Alec at some point in the distance. He doesn't speak.

'My cousin-brother lost several of his family members,' Uncle Som says at last. 'It pains him to think about them.'

'I'm sorry, please take your time, sir,' Alec tells the old gentleman.

Krishna takes a deep breath. 'We knew that the mobs were coming to attack us. There were rumours everywhere that the women were going to be raped and murdered. The attackers were people we had lived with for many, many decades, you understand. We had all lived in peace together until that time.'

Alec nods silently, encouraging Krishna to continue.

'I was very young. I thought that to protect my sisters I must kill them myself. I went so far as to purchase a small revolver and some ammunition,' the old man said.

Roz lets out a gasp from the back of the room.

'But when I returned to our family home my youngest sister was playing with our cat in the living room.' There's a long pause. 'I found that I was unable to shoot her.'

*

The film crew have long departed, and I'm sitting out on the terrace overlooking the courtyard with the others. We've had a splendid dinner with Matt's family. It's pleasantly cool now, and we all feel like relaxing, although the mood this evening is still sombre after Alec's interviews this afternoon.

'What I can't understand,' Alec is saying, 'is how people can behave like that to each other, to people they've known all their lives.'

'It wasn't just one side,' Matt puts in. 'When you go and film in Pakistan and Bangladesh, Alec, you will get stories just like these you heard today from my Uncle Krishna. Both sides took leave of their senses and went out and murdered the others. How can that happen?'

None of us can answer that. I glance across at Alec, his eyes tired from the effort of the day. He's handled the filming so well - he seems to be able to concentrate entirely on the job in hand, laying aside everything else. Does he think about his home life when he is working? Probably not; he puts all that into a separate box. How does he manage that?

In the end I break the silence by asking Matt about his family. 'And I hear your brother Owen is going in for teaching?'

'Yes that's right, he's just got his first job. And he's got an amazing marmalade girlfriend, that no one has met yet!'

'Marmalade?' says Alec.

'Yeah, that's just Owen all over. He calls her hair marmalade. And she's wonderful, apparently. Something high-powered in computing. I doubt if it will last – she sounds much too clever for him!'

'Oh, Matt, that is so not fair of you!' Roz chides him.

Alec smiles across at me and raises his eyebrow.

Matt stretches out his long legs and takes some more wine. 'Roz and I are planning to go up to Darjeeling at the end of the week. We'd like to visit that South African woman you all met on the plane – Susanna. Why don't you come with us, Alec?'

'Tempting,' Alec tells him. 'But I can't possibly come. We've got such a busy filming schedule. We are supposed to be flying to Pakistan next week, if the producer can get the various permissions we need.'

'Shame,' Roz says. 'Are you up for it, Eleanor? It was you that found Susanna for us – wouldn't you like to see Darjeeling with us?'

'I'm not sure. I promised to put in an appearance back at the conference, but that finishes on Tuesday. When are you going?'

*

The train journey is long. For the first eight or nine hours we are travelling across dead flat land, mostly farmed. Often the train goes on immense bridges across vast waterways. We are going north up the length of West Bengal.

Matt has brought our lunch in a metal tiffin carrier which his kindly relations have provided. 'Clever little thing, this.' He demonstrates. 'Look, it's got all these different compartments interlinking, so you carry it all by the one handle. Have some cashew nuts, Roz?' He undoes the top compartment. 'Have you noticed that whenever you look out of the window, you never ever see an empty landscape? There's always at least one human being somewhere in view – usually several.'

Matt's right – every scrap of space is used. Farmers plough with oxen and plant rice seedlings. Some workers are making bricks from river mud and repairing roads. Cattle are driven, and there are yet more overloaded rickshaws and buses with people clinging to the tops.

'Do you still make sketches of everywhere you go?' Alec asks.

Oh yes he's here too. Why, what did you expect?

I ran into Alec's producer at the hotel bar the other night; he told me over a double Scotch that he'd had a deeply frustrating day, trying and failing to get all the permits, visas and various permissions from high commissions that he needed to proceed with filming either in Pakistan or Bangladesh. Finally he'd had to go to Alec and confess that there would be a delay of at least a week. No, it couldn't all have been sorted out in London before they came out – he'd had his defences ready, because he thought Alec was bound to be furious with him. Alec Jenkins was a busy man, as everyone knows, and might well have clashing plans elsewhere.

But to the producer's utter astonishment, Alec had simply given him what he could only describe as a silly grin, and said right, in that case they would all have to take a week's holiday.

So here we all are.

Alec's quite right – I would normally want to sketch the scene out of the train window, but I don't feel like bothering today. By the middle of the afternoon the long plain is beginning to come to an end at last. Alec is standing by a window. 'Come and look, Eleanor – there's a tiny smudge on the horizon. That must be where we are heading. Can you see?'

I squeeze past him and lean right out of the window. 'Oh yes!'

There really is a faint line on the horizon.

Quickly he puts his arm round my waist. 'Careful, love! You'll fall out...'

He really mustn't touch me. I can't cope.

*

The train finishes its journey at New Jalpaiguri, where we have to stay at a rest house before setting off for Darjeeling tomorrow. It soon gets dark, and we sit out on the veranda after dinner.

'We should be sipping G and Ts, I guess,' Matt says. 'Sundowners.'

Roz grimaces. 'I'll make do with tepid coke, thanks. I'm not feeling that brilliant,' she confesses. 'Would you guys mind if I turned in early?'

Matt stands up. 'Good idea - I think I will too. Oh, by the way, some bad news.' He turns to Alec. 'They told me at the station that we can't go by train for the next bit. There was a landslide, and the line's closed. We'll have to take a taxi.'

'Does that matter?' Alec asks.

'It's a shame because this last bit is famous. Narrow gauge and very steep - like this...' He demonstrates with his arm. 'They claim it's the highest railway line in Asia. Ghoom station - on the bit we're missing - is seven thousand four hundred feet.'

'Wow!' says Roz.

As the other two leave the veranda, Alec offers me another can of coke, but I resort to my bottle of tepid water instead.

'I've never really liked fizzy drinks.'

'So you don't. I remember.' He puts down his glass. 'I remember most things about you. Eleanor...'

'Yes?'

'How have you been? I mean, really been.' He leans forwards and looks at me. 'Oh I know all the obvious stuff - you're a famous author: if I ever doubted that, my doubts would have disappeared the moment I saw the reception you got at the S.N.Choudhury Centre! We've got your wonderful books at home - but you know that. I suppose what I'm saying is, have you done what you wanted to do? These last sixteen years. Have you?'

That's an impossible question - I can't begin to answer him.

This book on my childhood roots in Denmark has set me on a new course - I don't any longer just want to draw things, I've started asking serious questions about what's going on, the challenges we are living through. To my surprise, people seem to like the new mixture.

This puts everything into perspective. Now that my work is becoming so important to others, has it actually become less important to me? Is it safe to admit that what makes me happier than any twenty thousand print run of a book of sketches is simply sitting here in a cheap hotel in New Jalpaiguri – with Alec?

I ignore his question. 'But what about you? Are you doing what you want to? I used to think that you were going to spend your life digging up potsherds and discovering ancient civilisations, but you've come a long way from all that. And there's your family...'

He looks at me. 'Eleanor... You do know, don't you, that I've always loved you.'

Deep breath. There's a powerful scent of strange tropical flowers drifting across the veranda, and a small gecko is scurrying along the ledge.

'Alec. It's no good now, is it? It's too late.'

'It's never too late.'

'You've got... You've got your children, haven't you? They need you.'

He takes my hand. 'Do you still fall asleep straight afterwards, Eleanor?' He smiles and raises one of his gable eyebrows.

Maybe it doesn't count, being here with him in New Jalpaiguri? Like when you're on a diet: anything you eat standing up, or you take from someone else's plate – it's a well-known fact that those calories don't count. Is this an unexpected extra bit of life, that doesn't count?

*

If I hadn't been told that we are missing the narrow gauge railway, I would have found this taxi ride up to Darjeeling quite incredible in its own right. On either side of the road there's dense dark vegetation. The road climbs fifteen hundred metres in only thirty-five kilometres, Matt is quick to tell us.

'Arggggggh! Look down there, Matt!' Roz screams as we lurched round one particularly steep corner.

'You're fine, don't make such a fuss!' Matt puts his arm tightly round Roz. 'The driver does this journey every day, no sweat.'

Alec rests his hand lightly on my shoulder. 'You OK?'

I don't trust myself to speak. I just want the dark forest that we are climbing through to go on for ever and ever. I rather doubt that it's possible for human beings to be as – well as happy as this, and frankly I'm far too busy just being it to have time for anything else.

It's all a huge mistake of course. I know that. I gave up on the gauche young archaeology student who took me to Nigeria all those years ago, and you can never go back. You really can't. Alec has gradually – amazingly – become a public figure in the intervening years. He's certainly not about to leave his sick wife, let alone his two vulnerable young children, in order to run off with an artist. No way. And nor should he – he would hardly be the Alec I love, if he did.

Watch it, Eleanor m'dear, I'm telling myself – you're letting go. It's dangerous to let go: you'll get hurt. But then what's the point of living, if you never risk getting hurt?

At last the forest gives way to vast tea plantations, and we glimpse rows of women in saris picking the leaves. Each woman has a basket hanging behind her, attached to her head with a cloth band.

The town of Darjeeling is shrouded in cloud as our taxi approaches, so there's no indication at all that we are surrounded by mountains. Matt points out that many of the public buildings are Victorian, since it was an old hill-station. The taxi deposits us near the centre, by the unused railway station, and porters appear – but unlike the ones at Howrah these are women, and not particularly young ones. They too carry the luggage on their heads, and set out at a cracking pace steeply uphill towards Tensing Norgay Road, to the government rest house where Matt's relations have booked us all.

It's hard to keep up, and I'm soon struggling for breath.

'Take it steady, Eleanor.' Alec turns back and offers me a hand. 'Don't forget, we are seven thousand feet up now – it takes a bit of getting used to. You'll be fine.' He smiles at me, and I take his hand. I will indeed be fine – for now at least.

It is pleasantly warm here; we've left the stifling heat of Kolkata far behind. The rest house turns out to be just across the road from a Buddhist monastery, where several orange-robed monks are going about their daily business. Peaceful people, clearly. I stand still and breathe in deeply; might even sketch some of them later.

There's running water and electric light at the rest house when we arrive, though Matt warns us not to take it for granted. I'm particularly impressed by the loo – more of a throne room, I think, as I sit high up in state in the centre of a vast and otherwise empty space.

'What about all these mountains that are supposed to be all round us, Matt?' Alec asks as we set out to find a restaurant to have an evening meal. 'When does the cloud lift?'

'Ah, just you wait! Five o'clock tomorrow morning, you want to go out onto your veranda and look out – it's magic! Sheer magic,' Matt tells us.

Roz coughs pointedly. 'Excuse me – I hope you don't think that I am going to wake up at five o'clock in the morning when I'm on holiday, Matthew Tarit Beynon.'

Matt laughs. 'You'll see, kid.'

*

Some ten minutes after everyone has said goodnight and retreated to their rooms, Alec knocks gently on my door.

'I was rather hoping that...well, that last night wasn't just a one-off?'

I'm sitting on the bed. 'No. No of course it wasn't, not while we're together up here, at any rate.'

'Good, I'm glad you think that. I don't think I could have managed the rest of this trip, otherwise. Matt going on about how fascinating everything is, and telling us the historical background, and all of us having to be interested...' He sits down next to me on the bed and begins to unbutton the front of my dress.

'Nonsense! You are interested, you know perfectly well you are. You're going to use the stuff he's telling you...'

He puts his arms round me and kisses my nose, which has caught the sun. 'Yes,' he admits. 'Maybe I am, in a different bit of my life – but I couldn't stand going round like a tourist all day with Matt if I couldn't come to your bedroom at the end of it all!'

'What about the view Matt wants us all to get up and look at, at five o'clock in the morning, then?' I remind him.

'Bugger five o'clock in the morning. Frankly.'

It's different tonight. Slower. More relaxed than at New Jalpaiguri. We're taking our time, exploring each other's bodies, discovering with delight how we've both changed in sixteen years.

94

He teases me, claims I've filled out. 'Tubby, you mean!' 'No, no! You're more beautiful than ever.'

*

Those peaceful Buddhist monks across the road who were going about their business serenely yesterday afternoon – remember them? They turn out to be surprisingly active at five o'clock in the morning. They sound as though they are scraping sticks over their dustbins. Enthusiastically.

This drags me out of a deep slumber. I stretch out my arm and bang it down. I seem to be shouting: 'What the hell's going on?'

'Watch it – that's my stomach you're attacking, darling!' Alec sits up and turns to look at me. 'Oh my goodness, you're still here!'

'Of course I'm still here – this is my room.'

He laughs. 'I know. It's just so amazing – I can't get over seeing you there, when I've just woken up. It's like a dream...'

Watch out. Don't get carried away. This isn't going to last. How could it?

The noise outside continues, and I sit up, leaning against him. 'What time is it? Is this when Matt wanted us to look out on the veranda?'

'I guess it must be. Maybe we ought to just...' Reluctantly he gets out of bed. 'It'll be cold – here, put this on.' He passes me a sweater. 'This won't take long, will it?'

Arm in arm, we go out onto the veranda.

What we see takes our breath away.

Yesterday there was nothing to see at all from this veranda, apart from the street below, the Buddhists across the road, a few other streets beyond, filled with a bustle of people and animals and stalls.

Now at dawn there's the most amazing view we have ever seen. Stretching far away into the distance are rows and rows of mountain peaks. Pale and ghostly, as if they don't exist in real life, they've just been put there by some gigantic scene-painter. Little curls of mist swirl about them, as if to say we'll be gone before you know it.

We are living in a fairyland – just for now. We are not part of Real Life. But it's only for a brief time.

I'm shivering now, and Alec hugs me more tightly. 'I guess it's not much use trying to go to sleep again. Eleanor?'

*

Matt's keen to take us to see a Tibetan Self-Help Centre some little way outside the town. By the time we go down after breakfast to look for a taxi by the station, the cloud has come down again.

'What's happened to those mountains, Matt? Did we imagine them?' I ask him.

'Oh good – you did see them, Eleanor. And you, Alec? Did you manage to drag yourself up at five o'clock? Your room is on the other side, though, so maybe...'

Roz laughs. 'Matt had to sit on me to get me to wake up!'

Matt takes her hand. 'It was worth it – admit it! Yes, the mountains are still there, Eleanor. You just have to remember that, when you can't see them. If we're lucky we ought to see Kanchenjunga from here – it's really close. It dominates the whole town, if you come in November. It's just bad luck we're here in August.'

Remember the mountains are still there, even when you can't see them.

Matt says he went to the Tibetan Centre a few years ago and he wants to see what progress it has made. He tells us at some length how impressed he was by the determination of the refugees to organise themselves and set up in business. We are shown into a big shed where we watch people spinning and weaving.

I like the delicate natural colours that they've chosen for the wool, very pale blues and purples. I want to say as much to the young Tibetan woman sitting at the spinning wheel, but she just smiles shyly at us foreign visitors – we have no common language.

Back in Darjeeling we walk up the road to a restaurant for some lunch. Roz links her arm in her brother's. 'How're you doing, Al? You're looking so much better today!'

'Am I? Must be the fresh air.' He grins at her.

Suddenly we turn a corner. Matt cries out, 'Look up there, everyone!'

The cloud has lifted for a moment and all at once we see Kanchenjunga above the town. Not even above it; the mountain looks so close it's almost part of the town. I think I can stretch out and touch its huge snowy slopes.

We all stop in our tracks.

'Oh Matt, that's wonderful!' I say.

'Wow!' That's Roz.

In the middle of the afternoon the streets are thronging with schoolchildren in neat old-fashioned uniforms in different colours – there must be dozens of schools in the town. Matt points out Tibetans, Ghurkhas, some hill people and a few Bengali children.

It's time to meet Susanna outside her school and she takes us over to her bungalow on the edge of the grounds.

'Well this is nice,' she says, pouring us glasses of homemade lemonade in the garden. 'At least there's something to be said for being held up thirty-one hours during a simple flight out from London! I wouldn't have got to know you guys, otherwise.'

We agree with her on this.

'While you are here you must go and see sunrise over Mount Everest,' Susanna tells us now.

Roz glances at Matt. 'Sunrise? Why do I have a nasty sinking feeling that this is going to involve more getting up in the middle of the night?'

'Oh yes, the car comes for you at four o'clock and takes you up to Tiger Hill. It's not very far,' Susanna says briskly.

'Four o'clock!' Roz echoes.

'Don't be such a wimp, Rosamund Jenkins!' Matt teases.

Before we leave, Susanna takes us on a tour of the school. 'So how are you, Eleanor? How are you adjusting to India?' she says, walking on as the other three stop to look at the cricket field. 'You look – different. What's happened?'

I don't answer.

'Oh I'm sorry – there I go again, jumping in with my size ten boots! It's none of my business of course. And now I've made you blush...'

'No, no. It's OK. I'm just... feeling the heat, that's all.'

'Eleanor, it's not hot here,' Susanna says dryly. 'Listen, Dhaka is hot. Kolkata is hot. Darjeeling is pleasantly cool.'

It's our last night here, just before our dawn trip to Tiger Hill. We've seen quite a bit of Susanna over the last few days, and tonight we are going out to celebrate her birthday.

She has an important announcement to make: she has decided to return to South Africa, now that things seem to be changing there.

Matt agrees that it is a good time to go back. 'My friend Seretse – you remember him, Alec? He was my best mate at school in Nigeria! He's a doctor in the States now, but like Susanna he's decided to go back to South Africa as soon as he can find a post.'

'Oh I remember your friend Seretse,' Alec exclaimed. 'He was such a kind boy – he offered to share his coke with me when I'd just been sick on the steps of the Health Centre!'

Matt grins. 'Yes, and that was also our first sight of you, Eleanor. Never forgotten!'

Susanna goes on, 'Well good for your friend, if he's going back home. We're going to need our doctors. So that's the next place you can all come and visit me – South Africa!' She beams at all of us.

Just as we leave the restaurant the lights go out.

'They still have load-shedding, I see,' Matt says. 'OK, Roz? Here, take my hand.'

Susanna has come with a hefty torch to light the way through the streets. 'Happens all the time,' she tells us.

Back at the rest house Matt finds some candles for everyone, for there's load-shedding here too. The water has also been cut off temporarily, which makes my trip to the loo – the throne room – slightly problematic. I balance a small guttering stub of a candle on its saucer on the edge of the porcelain shelf and count the remaining sheets of toilet paper.

Do you know, you've had better days than this! Let's see, no water, no light, distinctly dodgy in the tum, nine more pieces of loo roll. Or is it eight? But on the other hand, you are here. Just for now, you are here. You have never before been so completely in the right place.

'You OK?' Alec asks back in the room.

'I'll live! Yes I'm fine.'

'Everyone gets upset stomachs here – Matt says they are mostly caused by the malaria tablets people take,' Alec says. 'He may well be right.'

'I suppose you've travelled a fair bit, Alec?'

'Yes, I guess I have.'

'Does Milly ever... I mean, when she's not so ill, does she ever go with you?'

Careful! There are some things it really is better not to ask. But God I want to know!

He sits down on the bed.

'Not any more. She used to, years ago. It was fun, when the kids were small.'

'It must be terribly hard for Tamsin, this trouble of Milly's.' I sit down next to him.

'Yes, she hates any hassle. She always wants to get away. I suppose I was like that myself as a kid – Charlie was always getting inside my head and making a noise!'

'Oh, Val told me that about you, when we were in Nigeria.'

'Did she really? And you've remembered all this time...' He looks at me. 'Tammy's just like that with Milly.' He grins.

I put my arms round him. 'We don't have to talk about it now. We're leaving tomorrow, and then... We probably won't run into each other for a while.'

'No, I'm afraid we won't. But we mustn't regret this – must we?' He's not sure, is he?

'Regret?' Regret doesn't come into it. No way.

'Eleanor, this isn't the sort of thing I normally do. You do know that, don't you? I mean jump into bed with any passing woman when I'm thousands of miles away from home. You didn't think...?'

'I know that, Alec.'

'And you... You've hardly mentioned this Patrick of yours. He's a publisher, isn't he? I saw him that time at the Danish embassy.'

'That's different. Patrick and I have...oh dear, this is going to sound like a dreadful cliché, but we have an open relationship.'

'Yes?'

'He's got...lots of clients. And others. We don't want to live in each other's pockets, we never have.'

'I see.'

'Alec, let's just forget about everything else down there beyond these mountains! Just for tonight...' The mood changes suddenly as I kiss his neck and ease him down onto the bed.

*

Tiger Hill is cold. Very cold. A party of tourists from Kolkata stands shivering in tasteful but far too thin shawls, muttering their complaints. We have all been driven to a terrace at the top of the hill, in the gloom just before dawn. There's a fair amount of cloud and several people in the group are grumbling about it.

Suddenly the cry goes up: 'There, look!'

All I can see is cloud, a little lighter now – pale grey streaks.

Alec puts his arm round me and points. 'Look, Eleanor – it's going to clear!' For three seconds the cloud drifts away and I can see a tiny pink splodge in the distance. There's a half-hearted cheer from the rest of the group, and somehow we all persuade ourselves that we have indeed seen Mount Everest.

At once the party bustles over to the cars and relative warmth.

Back in Darjeeling Matt and Roz go off to look for a taxi, while Alec and I wait alone at the station with the luggage. All of a sudden, there's mighty Kanchenjunga again, huge and dominating the sky above the town, as if to say, well why on earth did you bother with all that ridiculous Tiger-Hill-at-Dawn business when here I am on your very doorstep? We gasp, and Alec takes my hand. 'Will you remember this, Eleanor?'

'Of course I will!'

'No, I mean the way old Kanchenjunga keeps appearing out of the blue – out of the grey – and reminds us that she's still there.'

'Ah, yes. So she does.'

'Like those willowy mountains,' Alec goes on. 'The ones we saw that first morning, remember? Stretching hundreds of miles into the distance. You can't see them during the day, when it's cloudy, but they are always there all the same.'

I feel a sudden chill, although the day is not cold.

'I understand what you are saying, Alec.'

'Look, Eleanor – I love you, you know I do. I always have. I always will.'

I say nothing.

'But just now, I have to go back to... It's not possible for you and me to...'

'I know, Alec,' I say quickly. 'You don't have to spell it out.' I've got a sudden feeling that I might start crying, and I want very badly to avoid that.

'But listen, Eleanor – this is important: we mustn't lose touch ever again. Not now. Please...will you promise? Will you? I need to know that we are friends.' He pushes back his wild unruly hair. 'Well?'

I look up at him. 'Yes, Alec – I think we always will be.'

Here come Matt and Roz with a taxi, and we begin to load all the luggage into it, ready for our descent down to the plain of Bengal and the long train journey back to Kolkata.

Chapter Ten

Alec

From Alec Jenkins <anj@tomtom.net>
To Eleanor Larsen-Bruun <Eleanor@larsen-bruun.co.uk>
Subject: Where are you?
October 4th 1989 14:53:31 GMT

My dearest Eleanor
Just surfaced after a hectic month sorting out Indian filming.
Have been thinking about you all the time – how are you?
And where are you, come to that?
I still can't quite believe Darjeeling! It seems as far away now
as those wisps of mountains that we saw early in the
morning, that were gone by breakfast. But they do exist, all
the same...

Love, Alec

From Alec Jenkins <anj@tomtom.net>
To Eleanor Larsen-Bruun <Eleanor@larsen-bruun.co.uk>
Subject Please write!
January 16th 1990 23:14:15 GMT

Eleanor – please answer my emails. No one else can access
my account, I promise you. A.

From Alec Jenkins <anj@tomtom.net>
To Eleanor Larsen-Bruun <Eleanor@larsen-bruun.co.uk>
Subject trip to USSR
April 23rd 1990 12.06:45 GMT
My dearest Eleanor

Funny running into you in that BBC studio last month. You looked so competent, handling the interview – I managed to watch a bit of it, before I got whisked away for my thing. I tried to look for you afterwards, but they said you'd gone... Milly seems a little better this year – almost as if she has turned a corner. Tamsin is still holding her breath, waiting for things to get worse again, but Milly herself is optimistic I think. So much so that she didn't object when my mother asked me to go with an exchange party to the Soviet Union with her this Easter, leaving Milly with the children. Of course my mother never travels normally – she only got roped into this because an organiser dropped out at the last minute. It's another thing she used to run when my parents were in Cardiff – I may have mentioned it. Cardiff is twinned with Luhansk, which is in Ukraine, so we exchange parties of visitors. My mother had only ever run the Cardiff bit of it before, entertaining the Russians who come over, sorting out their accommodation and so on, but this time she felt she had to go. Normally she calls on Charlie to get her out of problems like this, but he's back in Australia and a bit tied up at the moment. It's a new thing for her, to have to ask me instead! Quite an eye-opener for my mother – and I had to admire the way she coped with the foreignness of it all. At several schools in Luhansk the kids all flocked round Mum, keen to practise their English on her, and she lapped up the attention. The people of Ukraine are so hospitable. We were put up with a family in an incredibly hot apartment, where no one can turn off the heating because it is all controlled centrally by the authorities! We stopped in Kyiv on our way to Moscow, and we both found the golden onion towers on the churches stunningly beautiful.

Oh I must tell you this – they've just introduced a new chain of restaurants selling a continuous stream of succulent chicken joints – the people we were staying with in Luhansk took us there. It was delicious, far better than they are used to. The place was packed. Chicken always makes me think of you – but you know that.

When are you next coming over to the UK?   A.

From Eleanor Larsen-Bruun <Eleanor@larsen-bruun.co.uk>
To Alec Jenkins <anj@tomtom.net>
Subject: Prague
Date August 26th 1991

Alec,

Sorry I haven't been able to email you for a while – things have been busy. I got your email last year about going to the Soviet Union: how amazing that your mother went! I always thought she was determined to avoid Foreign Parts. How did your father manage?

Patrick and I have been in Prague for a short holiday; it's a lovely old place – have you been? I've been sketching the Charles Bridge over the Vltava, which is one of the most beautiful bridges I have seen anywhere. Of course this is the second summer of freedom here, and the atmosphere is amazing. People selling things in the open air. Entertainment. Music everywhere. Patrick especially loved the pancakes that you buy in the streets – you queue up in front of a big black open hob and they cook them while you wait.

Isn't it extraordinary the way things have turned out? We had no idea – we couldn't possibly have guessed. Patrick wants me to move in with him in London, but I haven't decided.

Eleanor

From Alec Jenkins <anj@tomtom.net>
To Eleanor Larsen-Bruun <Eleanor@larsen-bruun.co.uk>
Subject: What's happening?

Date December 19th 1991 23.42:34

Look Eleanor can we stop exchanging scintillating emails with each other about the exciting places we've been to and just MEET for once? We need to talk.

What are you doing about Patrick – are you moving to London?

Alec

From Alec Jenkins <anj@tomtom.net>
To Eleanor Larsen-Bruun <Eleanor@larsen-bruun.co.uk>
Subject: Where are you?
Date January 24th 1992 16.20:45
Did you get my email before Christmas? Charlie said he'd seen you in London – are you still with Patrick? Please talk to me! A.

From Eleanor Larsen-Bruun <Eleanor@larsen-bruun.co.uk>
To Alec Jenkins <anj@tomtom.net>
Subject: South Africa
Date 23rd February 1992 12.36:47
Sorry Alec – have been frantically busy. Yes, I did see Charlie when I was over in London; he says I should go to Australia some time. I just might. He had a friend with him from New Zealand, an interesting guy who builds his own boats and sails them round the coast. I might look him up some time.

Meanwhile I'm off to South Africa next week to see Susanna. She is back there, lecturing in Stellenbosch. She has joined the ANC, which is a big step for someone from an old Afrikaner family. She might even stand for parliament!

Oh yeah, and about Patrick: we've decided to go on with our separate lives in London and Rome – I couldn't bear the thought of leaving Rome for good. My sister would never forgive me!

Eleanor

Well that's something, I suppose. At the end of a spasmodic series of emails, we seem to have established early in 1992 that at least Eleanor wasn't moving to London to live with the odious Patrick. For now at least. Thank God for her sister, Gabriella, wanting her to stay in Rome! But how long was that going to last?

I still hadn't managed to see her since Darjeeling.

I hit a new low that February when I found myself at a conference in a dingy campus somewhere on the south coast of England – can't even remember where, now.

It had been an exhausting day, and as I came out of the conference room that evening I suddenly wanted more than anything else to run into Eleanor and take her off to some quiet restaurant away from everyone else, for a meal and just – well just to talk to her. For a start.

But Eleanor was a thousand miles away, wasn't she?

'Oh there you are, Alec! I was wondering where you had got to...'

Who's this looking for me now? Ah, Professor Falucci. Dark vision of elegance, she had dominated the conference that afternoon. I'd spoken to her briefly over lunch – she'd come up to me over the coffee. I really wanted to ask her some time about that dig she was involved in, a Benedictine monastery near Monte Cassino. Of course that's where Dad was during the war, and one day I hoped to make the connection - but not now. I was dead tired.

She had changed her clothes for some reason and appeared in a long faintly shimmering dress in a kind of bluish purple. 'I thought they would never finish today!' She smiled up at me warmly. 'That old man in the front row – he goes on and on, when he starts talking...' I knew what she meant, and I grinned ruefully. 'Yes, he is rather known for his views.'

'We must get away, before they all catch us and insist on continuing the debate. What are you doing tonight, Alec? Would you like to take me to dinner?'

What?

'Oh. Well yes, I suppose we could find somewhere...'She took my arm conspiratorially. 'Quick, we must go. Do you know somewhere quiet?'

'I hadn't in fact noticed much in the way of local eating places. I think there were a couple of Indian takeaways, a Pizza Hut and a McDonalds probably, and I'd seen a bright Italian restaurant – but presumably it would not be tactful to take her there, since she actually was Italian.

In the end I found a Chinese restaurant some fifteen minutes' walk away. So quiet it was deserted. Oriental music playing discreetly in the background; you know the sort. 'We are very similar to each other, Alec – do you realise that?' she said as the waiter brought our meal.

'We are?'

'We are two lonely souls surrounded by so many busy chattering people,' she went on. 'You have your poor sad wife at home... It must be such a strain for you.'

'Yeah, well, life does have its moments.'

'And as for me, I have nobody.' She put her hands down flat on the table and looked across at me, flashing her eyelashes helplessly.

'Oh but surely...'

'Oh yes there have been plenty of chances for me, but I am married to my work. I cannot compromise.'

Her work. I rooted around in my brain for what I ought to know of her work; well there was that Benedictine monastery of course, but what else?

She had become a professor at an early age – but hadn't there been some rumour about that? She had got the job in the face of sharp competition from three other good candidates; I heard it whispered that Cecilia had seduced one or maybe even two of the members of the appointment committee. Odd. But probably quite untrue – just the sort of ugly gossip that would attach itself to people like her – young, devastatingly clever, and quite...er...pleasing on the eye. Unfair – and she probably didn't even know about it, I thought now as I passed the prawn crackers.

'You must come and visit my dig when I have set it up, Alec – you would find it so interesting!'

'Yes I'd like to, when there's time. I've read about it, of course. I enjoyed your thing this morning.'

Cecilia had given a passionate presentation that morning about her plans to excavate the monastery, which was some miles south of Rome. 'You should make a programme about it! Do you know the area?'

'Yes, funnily enough I believe it's not very far from where my father fought during the war...'

Suddenly I felt an overwhelming desire to yawn. I tried to cover it up with my hand, but she laughed.

'You are tired, I can see. We have all been so busy today! Perhaps we should go back to the hotel. Are you staying in the same place as the rest of us? I have a beautiful big room on the first floor...'

I turned and beckoned to the waiter, making a sign for the bill.

'I'm sorry – do you mind if we don't have a dessert?' I said. 'I really need to get back to work – I've got some documents to check before tomorrow. I'll have to make a move, I'm afraid.'

'Oh, tonight? Can it not wait?'

'No, I'm sorry. I need to catch two of the London people tomorrow morning, and I have to check something first.' This wasn't entirely true, but it was the first thing that came into my head. 'I'm sorry – it's been, er, it's been a lovely evening.'

Chapter Eleven

1993, Alec

'Why the hell don't you ever take the children away with you?' Milly's eyes were blazing, and I wondered if she had remembered her medication that morning.

'What do you mean? I take them away all the time!'

'Only up to your sainted mother's cottage! Why don't you ever give them a proper holiday?' She brushed her pale hair away from her eyes.

'Perhaps it's because I have a job. It takes up my time, that's what jobs do...' Blimey - maybe I ought to listen to myself sometimes?

'Oh yes, the famous media personality, the darling of press and public alike. We can't have the great Alec Jenkins inconvenienced by having to take his own children away anywhere...' There's nothing to say when Milly is in this mood. I turned towards the door.

'Where are you going?'

'Out.'

'Oh don't be so teenage! It's Tamsin who is supposed to be a teenager, not you!'

I sighed. 'I did say I was going out this afternoon. I promised to meet up with my cousin Owen. He's down from London, visiting his parents this weekend. I told you, OK?'

Val and Ian were settled in Cardiff by then, retired from Nigeria. My Uncle Ian - I can hardly believe I'm telling you this – Ian had actually taken up golf, but Val had thrown herself into the local ward of the Labour Party and was intensely busy organising all the canvassing and leafleting and stuff. In fact she had just been elected to the council in a surprise bye-election. Surprise as in the amazement of our whole family, not to mention the shock to everyone else from the sudden fatal heart attack of the previous holder of the seat.

'Oh do what you damn well like!' My wife took a deep breath now and stood looking out into the back garden, her hands on her hips.

I closed the front door with exasperating gentleness and set off on foot to the pub where I'd arranged to meet Owen.

My cousin it seemed was hardly in a better mood.

'What's up, Owen? How's school?'

'Oh, not too bad, I guess. I'd rather get a job here in Cardiff – Mum cuts out the job ads in the Western Mail every week! But given that we have to live in London for Donna's work, it could be worse. You know she's a systems analyst, don't you? She's seriously clever.'

Ah yes – I remembered the marmalade girlfriend, who was not only still around after four years but living with Owen in a broom cupboard in east London. I had not met her.

'Why are you so down, then, Owen?'

Owen took a swig at his beer and settled back. 'Oh, Donna's got to go to Helsinki this August. Her company is providing the software for some firm that makes kitchen units, and it needs servicing.'

'Oh, yes? Sounds interesting.'

'Not really. It means she'll be away for a good bit of August, and then she won't have time for a proper holiday afterwards.'

'Couldn't you go to Helsinki with her? It's a fantastic place.'

'Not if you're all on your own, waiting for someone who is too busy with kitchen units to talk to you.'

'Ah, I see.' I glanced out of the window. 'You're pretty keen on your Donna, aren't you?'

Owen looked at me mournfully. 'I asked her to marry me the other day.'

'Really?' I sat up. 'What did she say?'

'Not a lot. I picked a bad moment, I guess; she was packing for Brussels. She just told me to move my arse so she could get at the chest of drawers because she was in a hurry.'

I grinned. 'Maybe try again later?'

'Yes, probably. You know I envy you, Alec.'

What an extraordinary thing to say!

'Whatever for?'

'You've been married so long. Settled down. And your children are great. I don't suppose Donna and I will ever have children...'

There was nothing to say to that, but then an idea struck me.

'I tell you what, Owen: if Donna really has got to go to Finland, and you want to go with her – why don't I come too, and bring Tammy and David? We could have a holiday while Donna is working – what do you think?'

110

Owen's face lit up. 'You're not serious?'

I nodded. 'Sure. They'd love it. What dates are we talking, here?' I fished in my pocket for my diary.

*

It was a long shot, I knew. I hadn't been able to see Eleanor since Darjeeling – four whole years! I was still emailing her now and then, with news of work and the family, and just occasionally I got an answer. When she did respond, she had a knack of saying just the right thing – brief, supportive comments that showed understanding and kindness. But I hadn't actually seen her.

I decided to tell her that I was taking the children to Helsinki with Owen, and suggest that she might like to be there at the same time, perhaps sketching – she had said something last year about Patrick's firm wanting more on northern Europe after the success years ago of her Danish and Norwegian books. Would Helsinki fit the bill?

Eleanor replied that she thought probably not, as she and Patrick were planning a few days together in Italy.

*

My first impression of Owen's girlfriend Donna was of a determined young woman with a small, delicate face, full of freckles, and a wonderful way of screwing up her nose when she was concentrating, as she was at the airport. You had to admit that 'marmalade' was a fair description of her long flowing hair.

But not the sort of marmalade that you'd put on your roasting chicken, as no doubt Eleanor would observe – if only she wasn't a thousand miles or more away.

Owen was delighted to see us, and he'd brought some books for the children, and picked up some leaflets. 'We don't have to stay in Helsinki all the time that Donna is working,' he told us. 'We could all go to Lapland!'

'Aren't you thinking of Father Christmas trips in December?' I said, heaving my hand luggage up into the overhead locker.

'Dad!' Tamsin protested. She knew at thirteen just how embarrassing fathers can be.

'No, no,' Owen said. 'You can go to Lapland all the year round. Loads of things to do there. No darkness, you see. Well, not this time of year. Up beyond the Arctic Circle.'

I groaned.

'We could even play pooh-sticks,' Owen went on. 'You get all kitted out in protective stuff and a life-jacket, and they throw you into the Pajakkakoski river and then you float down it, over the rapids and everything...'

He's taking this seriously, is Cousin Owen.

'Mega!' said David, and Tamsin brightened up at this idea.

'And they give you hot chocolate afterwards, and then you go in for another turn!' Owen told them. 'I've got a leaflet.'

'Somehow I thought you would, Owen,' I said with a sigh.

When we landed at Helsinki, we were met by Donna's client Juhani, who had brought his wife Saara along to entertain the rest of us while Donna was busy at work. Saara said that after we'd had a day or two in Helsinki we were all welcome to come out to her family's summerhouse and swim in the lake. 'The summerhouse is on an island – we can only get there by rowing boat,' Saara added.

'Wicked!' said David.

'Yeah, OK,' said Tamsin.

This prospect seemed to satisfy the children, and the following morning they were prepared to put up with a short tour of downtown Helsinki. There were a couple of contrasting cathedrals Saara wanted to show us, the Lutheran and the Russian.

'Then in a little while we'll go down to the harbour and get some ice creams and drinks,' Saara promised. 'We can look at the big ships there.'

Inside the dimly lit Russian cathedral, I said to Owen, 'As a matter of fact there is a slight possibility that Eleanor Larsen-Bruun might be coming over to Helsinki this summer.'

'Oh, really? Is she doing another book?'

'Yes I believe her publisher wants a follow-up to that one she did on Copenhagen and then the one on Norway – covering more

Scandinavian countries. She wants to draw some of the sights of Helsinki.'

'My brother told me he and Roz met up with her in India a few years ago – but I haven't seen her since that time you brought her to stay with us in Nigeria. I thought she was great, when I was a little boy! When is she coming to Helsinki?'

I glanced at my watch. 'I don't know if she will make it at all. She and her...er, her boyfriend, seem to have had other plans. But I told her the times when we would be here, just in case. I said we'd be down at the harbour at eleven o'clock this morning.'

Owen laughed. 'Oh you did, did you? Then we better had be!'

We found Eleanor in one of the many outdoor cafés which lined the harbour. She was sketching a large ferry which would be leaving shortly for Riga, the passengers already clambering up the gangway laden with rucksacks.

I caught sight of her suddenly as we strolled along to the harbour. My heart started thumping ridiculously fast.

Eleanor looked up. 'You're ten minutes late,' she said, putting her pencil down on the table.

'Sorry! Got held up in a cathedral...' No, I wasn't daft enough to try to kiss her in front of this lot - why, what did you think?

She stood up. 'Good heavens, you must be Owen – how nice to see you again. You've grown since I last saw you!' She shook Owen's hand, laughing, and everyone fussed around introducing people and gathering up extra chairs from surrounding tables to join Eleanor. Ice creams were ordered for the children, and coffees with cream for everyone else.

'Can I be one of the children too?' asked Owen. 'I'd like a double chocolate flake in a Helsinki Glory!'

Saara mentioned that they did good pastries here, and Eleanor said they reminded her of Copenhagen.

It was a relief to get the children out of Helsinki the next day. Donna and Juhani stayed on to work, while Saara piled everyone else into a large car she'd borrowed to go to the summerhouse.   'It's very kind of you to let me come too,' Eleanor said, sitting in the front next to Saara. She had been effortlessly included in the trip.

We'd hardly spoken to each other alone. Polite inquiries as to each other's health and the progress of our respective work; oh and she said I was looking tired. Lines around my eyes, she noticed. Well, no one else was going to tell me that!

She on the other hand was looking great. Younger than ever. Flourishing.

Finally Saara said we were leaving the road and setting off along a narrow track to take us to the shore of the lake. She untied her family's rowing boat and she and Owen rowed everyone across to the island.

The summerhouse was a wooden building on the opposite shore, just next to a natural harbour. The living area was the whole of the downstairs, and there was a ladder leading up to the open space which went round the edge under the roof, where there were several beds and some bunks. It was a family home, and there was not going to be a great deal of privacy. None, in fact.

'Can I sleep on the top bunk?' said David.

'Whatever,' said his sister.

As soon as we had dumped the luggage, I got changed and dived into the lake. 'Come on kids – it's warm!'

'Dad, you're lying,' Tamsin told me, dipping her toe cautiously into the water by the landing stage. She was right of course.

David jumped on her from behind and pushed her in, following after her. He'd swum far out beyond the boat before poor Tammy emerged, spluttering 'Dad, tell him!'

Eleanor observed all this from the bank, an inscrutable look on her face. She was seeing a different side of my life, I guess.

Later Saara got out the barbecue for supper, and afterwards we lay by the shore, pleasantly tired and full.

'How long are you staying in Finland?' Saara asked us. 'There are lots of other things you can do.'

'I heard there are trips by train across to St Petersburg,' I said. 'It's called the Sibelius. Only takes six hours, and you stay a couple of nights in a hotel there.'

Eleanor sat up. 'Really? I'd love to see St Petersburg,' she said.

'Oh, no! You must not take the children there.' Saara was adamant. 'They would be bored, I think. And in any case, Russian society is very unsettled now, with the collapse of Communism. It would be dangerous to take the children.'

'Pity,' I said.

David jumped up. 'Dad, can we go to Lapland? I want to play human pooh-sticks like Owen said!'

I sighed and turned to Eleanor. 'My cousin picked up a leaflet about Lapland.'

'Oh, Juhani would love to go to Lapland again – it is such a long time since we went. We will come with you if you like,' Saara offered. 'When they have finished their work. What about Donna, would she like that?'

Owen smiled. 'I think I might persuade her. She's always in a good mood when she's finished a project.'

'And you, Eleanor?' I asked. 'Do you fancy Lapland?'

'Well...' she said reluctantly.

Owen sat up suddenly. 'We don't all have to go to Lapland. Tell you what, Alec – why don't Donna and I take the children up to Lapland with Saara and Juhani? If you are really more interested in the train trip to St Petersburg, why don't you go on that? I'll take care of the kids for you.'

I looked doubtfully at Tamsin. 'How about it, Tammy? Would you like to go to Lapland with Owen?'

She shrugged. 'So long as I don't have to pretend to go and see Santa Claus and his little elves getting all the presents ready for Christmas.'

'Result!' David punched the air in delight. 'When can we go?'

*

'God, surely not! Hold still a minute...' Eleanor leaned across the railway carriage and put her hand on my head. 'It is, it's a grey hair!'

The Sibelius rattled through the Finnish countryside towards the border.

I laughed. 'Just the one? That's what comes of being the father of a teenager, I tell you.'

And other things.

'I know,' she went on. 'But they are lovely children, Alec. You're very lucky.'

'I wonder what they are up to now? Owen will have them under control, I hope.'

'Bound to. He is a teacher, after all,' Eleanor said. 'He's a competent lad, underneath the vague front he puts up for the world. And Donna's got her head screwed on.'

'Owen seems very smitten with her, don't you think? I wonder where that's going...'

Some hours later at St Petersburg a taxi deposited us in front of a large blank building near the city centre.

'That's a hotel?' I questioned. 'Looks more like the Lubyanka to me.'

'It'll do,' she said, taking my hand. 'I love you, Alec Jenkins.'

I looked at her.

'Yes I know. I still can't quite believe it.'

We went in and found the reception desk. The corridors were uniform and dark, and it was impossible to tell how anyone ever found their way to their own room – but it would be anonymous, we agreed.

Eleanor thought this was another of those places that don't count, like Darjeeling. Even more so – no one could possibly recognise us in Russia.

'At least it's comfortable,' she said, bouncing on the bed. 'Well fairly comfortable – avoid that bit there if you can...'

'I've missed you so much, my darling,' I said, sitting down next to her.

'Are you sure no one is going to mind...' she said. 'Us being here? Aren't you supposed to be taking your children on holiday?'

I kissed her neck. 'I love that little brown dangly spot just there – you've always had that! No, they'll be deliriously happy with my cousin Owen up in Lapland.'

'But what will Milly say when she finds out?'

'There's no reason why she should, is there? She won't be interested in what they've been doing. Tamsin will think she's got to make a big effort to tell her things, but Milly will just be bored – she told Tamsin last year that it was actually quite tedious when Tamsin came

116

home with some great long story about something that had happened in school.'

'No, really! Wasn't the poor girl hurt?'

I shrugged. 'I don't know. I took her and David out for a pizza just afterwards, so I imagine the memory faded.' I began to take off my shoes.

Breakfast next morning was confusing. There was a vast gloomy area downstairs with empty tables laid out neatly – several adjoining rooms, looking more or less similar.

'Where are we meant to go?' Eleanor wondered.

'Anywhere, I should think. Those tables over there, look – they've got orange juice on the trolleys: shall we try that?'

The orange juice was a mistake. No sooner had Eleanor picked up a couple of glasses and made for a table than an irate waiter appeared and demanded to see our documents. Some instinct made Eleanor drain one of the glasses of orange juice at once, while I fished in my pocket for any papers I could find.

The waiter's English was not perfect – hey, why should it be? – but he made it crystal clear that we were not on the package that offered orange juice. Niet was the one word we recognised. He indicated another set of tables altogether, which was apparently where riff-raff like us belonged.

'Stop laughing, Alec! You'll set me off,' Eleanor begged me as we sat down. 'What are we going to do today? The Hermitage? The Winter Palace?'

I put my hand lightly on hers across the table. 'I don't care what we do. We're here, and we're alone, and we have one more whole night in this wonderful hotel...that's enough, isn't it?'

She looked at me without speaking.

'Why did you decide to come, darling?' I asked her. 'When I told you I was going to Finland with Owen, you said you were too busy – you said you and Patrick were spending some time in Italy. What happened to that?'

'I...I suppose I just wanted to see you. It's been a long time...since Darjeeling.'

'Too long,' I said.

Rejecting the possibility of simply staying all day in our hotel bedroom – for Eleanor had spotted the army of cleaners hovering at the end of the corridor – we decided to begin with a guided tour of the city, which apparently the hotel offered.

'Are you sure we're not on the wrong package?' I giggled. 'We are probably only entitled to a tour of the cement works.'

'Shut up, you!' Eleanor dug me in the ribs – which was hard to do since I had my arm tight round her waist. 'I'm listening to the nice young man.'

The nice young man was called Sasha, a tall dark-haired and unbelievably thin man who had a sister dancing with the Kirov Ballet, which he recommended. He had assembled a party of around a dozen tourists and was telling us about the legend that St Petersburg was so beautiful that it must have been built in heaven and lowered down here in one piece. Various members of the party murmured appreciatively, and an American woman whispered loudly to her husband that that idea was just so cute.

The first part of the tour was to be a boat trip on the canal, as good a way as any to see the famous buildings. As we walked down to the canal we passed a demonstration of Communists in the street, banners waving.

'Do you have many demonstrations?' Eleanor asked the tour guide.

Sasha considered the question. 'Yes, I would say that people are much more unsettled nowadays. Some people are much poorer than they were under Communism. Our birth rate in St Petersburg is falling. But in the old days we were not allowed to have demonstrations...'

As the boat glided silently under bridges and through the centre of old St Petersburg the sun came out and we saw the lovely pastel-coloured buildings at their best. Eleanor sat back and enjoyed them, her hand lightly in mine. She didn't seem to feel in the least like getting out a sketchpad. The American couple were now at the other end of the boat, but I was getting the uncomfortable feeling that the woman was staring at me while at the same time pretending not to.

At the end of the boat trip Sasha stood on the bank and asked everyone to leave in an orderly procession. As they approached the gangplank, the American woman plucked up courage and came up to us. 'Do you mind my asking you – my husband simply insists that I do...' Her husband looked embarrassed, as though he insisted on no such thing.

I looked up. 'Er... Yes?'

'You look so much like a guy we saw on our television last fall! A programme about the early voyages of the Pilgrim Fathers. It is you, isn't it?'

So much for no one recognising me in Russia!

'Well actually...yes, I did do something about that last year.' I let go of Eleanor's hand.

'Oh now, Elmer, didn't I just tell you it was him! How amazing that we should run into you here in St Petersburg of all places!'

'Yes indeed. Actually we were just going on to see...er...'

'The ballet,' Eleanor said quickly. 'Sasha said if we were quick we might just get tickets for the Kirov Ballet. But we do need to hurry!'

'Don't look round,' I growled as we walked smartly away from the canal.

'It's OK, she's so overcome at seeing you that she doesn't dare follow us,' Eleanor said dryly.

When we had safely turned the corner, I asked her, 'Do you really fancy the ballet, darling? Or was that just a brilliant invention?'

'Sounds a good idea to me.'

We were lucky – the Pushkin Theatre had a couple of returns for that evening's performance of Sleeping Beauty. It was a wonderful evening. This is what normal people do, they go to the theatre with their partner and sit enchanted by the music and the dancing. Hand in hand in the dark.

'I love ballet,' Eleanor said as we came out of the theatre. 'I don't go nearly enough.'

'I took Tamsin to the Bolshoi last year when it toured Britain; she thought it was wonderful,' I told her.

'You do a lot with Tamsin, don't you?'

'I try to when I'm around. Milly thinks I neglect them. I wish there was some way we could contact the children now, find out if they are OK – but there's no chance of that with the telephones here, and we don't really know exactly where in Lapland Owen has gone.'

Slight confusion over finding the right room in the hotel – the corridors really were all identical – but eventually we found room 1497 and went in. I took off my jacket and flopped down on the bed. 'It's getting warmer – I don't suppose I could get away with shorts tomorrow, could I?'

Eleanor laughed. 'I haven't seen anyone else in shorts! But I suppose it might stop you being recognised.' She got out her favourite green cotton summer skirt with the voluminous pockets in the front, and put it on a chair for the next day – our last in St Petersburg. She looked at me. 'You minded that woman recognising you, didn't you?'

'Yes, to be frank I did. Some of the paparazzi are beginning to take an interest in...well, in me and Milly. I don't want to give them any ammunition if I can help it.'

'No I see that,' she said quietly.

I sat up and put my arms around her. 'Oh darling, I'm sorry! I didn't mean...'

'It's all right. I know we can't meet very often. It's not easy for me either.'

I kissed her. 'I may be in Italy quite a bit next year, or at least the year after.'

'Really?'

'Have I told you about my Italian colleague, Cecilia?'

'No I don't think you have.'

'She's set up a dig a bit south of Rome, a Benedictine monastery.'

'Oh?'

'Cecilia is so enthusiastic! Typical Italian, so passionate that she gets things done. Well you know all about Italians, of course. She wants me to come and do a programme about it, when it's up and running. And then I could write a book next year about Benedictine monasteries in Italy. It was Cecilia's idea, as a matter of fact.'

'Right.'

'I met her at a conference some time ago, and she was at a bit of a loose end...'

'How old is she?' Eleanor asked casually.

'Oh, I don't know. Never thought about it. About our age, I guess. The interesting thing is that it's quite near Monte Cassino. You know, where my father fought. I'd love to involve Dad in some way.'

Next morning we packed up early and decided to walk along St Petersburg's most famous road, Nevsky Prospect, leaving our luggage at the hotel, since the return train was not until the afternoon. So that was it, then. We were going back – we'd had our last night together for God knows how many months – years, probably. 'Do you see much of my brother?' I asked, taking her hand as we reached Nevsky Prospect.

'No – we just run into each other now and then, that's all. Nothing planned.' She smiled up at me.

'Last year you said something about going out to Australia to visit him.'

'Did I? I don't remember that. Just a chance remark maybe... I forget.'

'You said he'd introduced you to a man from New Zealand. Who was that?'

'Oh, I don't know... Let's not worry about that now, Alec. Look at those kids over there! Where have they come from?'

We'd come to an open area where the pavement got much wider. A few metres away there was indeed a large crowd of children, mostly very young, surging suddenly towards us. They were a ragged bunch: several in bare feet on the dirty pavement, with strange clothes. Torn, squalid clothes.

One girl, a little taller than the others, thrust herself forward and we saw that she was carrying a baby in her arms.

'Look – baby!' the girl cried in English.

Eleanor recoiled – she has never liked large crowds of children – but we were surrounded. The baby we were being asked to admire had a runny nose and old layers of grime on its face; it was on the point of bawling. 'Yes OK, very nice,' Eleanor said, clearly wishing they would all go away.

I fished in my pocket and found some loose change to offer them. They seemed grateful, and eventually moved off, presumably to find some other tourists to persecute. We wondered vaguely where the parents were, but we weren't that troubled.

Then Eleanor stopped abruptly.

'Alec – my purse isn't here.' She had her hand in the left-hand pocket of her skirt.

'What? Are you sure? You didn't leave it in the hotel, did you? Packed it, maybe.'

'No, no I didn't,' she said impatiently. 'I remember picking it up. I thought we might want to buy something this morning before we leave. God how stupid of me!'

'Oh darling – don't worry!' I put my arms round her, there in the street, and kissed the top of her head. Never mind my being recognised by tourists - Eleanor was upset and I had to comfort her. 'We'll go back to the hotel and ask about reporting it.'

The man behind reception at the Lubyanka had not recently won any awards for courtesy and helpfulness when dealing with the general public. After fifteen minutes it emerged that the only thing we could do was report to the police, who would then require us to stay in St Petersburg for twenty-four hours.

'But that's ridiculous! We have a train at three fifty-five,' I told him. 'We can't possibly miss it.' I glanced at Eleanor, and for a moment she must have thought I was going to suggest that we should go along with this, and spend an extra night together here in this vast anonymous hotel.

She looked up at me.

'We can't...' I said quietly. 'I promised Owen I'd be back with the children tonight. They'll be worried. I'm so sorry, Eleanor.'

'No,' she said quickly. 'Of course we can't stay here. Let's just pick up our bags and leave now.'

*

Owen had not drowned either of the children in the Pajakkakoski river. Nor had he allowed them to contract pneumonia, or to break any of their limbs. Tamsin had acquired quite a suntan and seemed to have enjoyed herself.

'Dad it was ace!' David declared. 'I want to go again! Can we go next summer?'

Owen was beaming all over his face. 'There is some news, as a matter of fact.'

'Oh yes?' Eleanor asked. 'Good news, I assume?'

My daughter grabbed Donna's left arm and held it up. 'Dad, they're going to get married, and they are going to invite us! Look at this... Isn't it lush?'

Donna smiled. On her finger was rather a large emerald ring which went beautifully with her hair.

Chapter Twelve

USA, 1995

'Hit the floor, lady!'

Eleanor stared up at the only other passenger in the elevator, a broadly built, thick-set young white man who'd just got in on the eighteenth floor, two floors below Eleanor's room. He looked ill-intentioned.

'What?' she whispered.

He had his right hand in his jacket pocket and appeared to be fingering something fairly large.

In the next three seconds Eleanor regretted again her agent's choice of hotel in downtown Los Angeles: the Westin Bonaventure was a strange square building, glass windows covering the whole of the outside, with four towers on each corner where the elevators were. She was currently suspended somewhere on the north east corner, God knew how many thousand feet above the land, alone with this maniac.

'I said hit the floor! Lady,' he added with what she took to be a smirk.

She had of course been warned not to go out alone on the streets of LA, and indeed she had no intention of doing so, for to her surprise Charlie had emailed her a fortnight ago to say that he would be visiting LA himself this week, and he wondered if they could meet up for a drink some time. In fact he ought to be waiting for her at this very minute, in one of the bars downstairs.

'Oh...well, all right then...'

There was nothing for it. She knelt down on the floor of the elevator, which – odd how you notice such things in an emergency – was spotlessly clean but one single cigarette had been stubbed out in the corner, and someone had dropped a screwed up scrap of paper.

She glanced up at the man. Was this far enough down or did he want her flat out? She held her bag up above her head as a sign of compliance. After what happened at St Petersburg the year before last, giving up all her money was getting to be a habit.

'Oh no! I'm so sorry, Ma'am... I didn't mean... I only wondered, are you going all the way down? Do you want the floor? The sidewalk?'

He leant across her and pressed the button to take the elevator down to the ground floor. On second thoughts, he was actually quite a pleasant young man. He bent to help her up and dust her down.

*

Charlie went on laughing for most of the evening. 'Could happen to anyone, Eleanor my Sunshine,' he said, pouring out some more wine.

'Don't be so mean, Charlie,' she said. She looked him up and down: still slim, unlike his brother, but his hair was thinning at the front, which was perhaps expected at forty. He looked healthy, though. Sunburnt. Nearly twenty years running a company that hired out surfing equipment, or whatever it was, had put their mark on him.

'I think we might change the subject now,' she said archly. 'What brings you to LA? You still live in Melbourne, right?'

He nodded. 'Business, just boring business. Seeing a few old friends at the same time. It's good to see you, Eleanor. Where would you like to eat?'

There was plenty of choice of places to eat in the hotel complex itself - no need to venture out onto the dreaded sidewalks, as Charlie pointed out. 'Never know who you'll meet, out there.'

'Shut up.'

They chose Mexican.

'You heard my divorce came through?' he said, picking up the menu.

She nodded. 'Yes, er...someone mentioned it.'

'Kids staying with the ex, but I guess it was as amicable as they get. I needed a break from all that hassle. So you are here on your own, are you? What happened to that guy who was running your book launch - or is that ancient history?'

'Patrick. Oh he's still around, you know. On and off.'

'Yes?'

Eleanor made no further comment so Charlie went on, 'Well Patrick or no Patrick, what you really ought to do while you are over here is book a flight to the Grand Canyon. It's an amazing place.'

'No!' she said sharply.

'What?'

'Sorry, I just meant, I won't have time. I've got other plans.'

'Other plans? You're being very mysterious, kiddo. Come on, you can tell your Uncle Charlie!'

She shrugged her shoulders and studied the menu in silence.

Charlie glanced up as the waiter approached. 'Shall we start with the enchiladas?'

'Sounds OK to me,' Eleanor said.

'Yes, and a side order of guacamole,' Charlie went on. 'And some salsa verde. Thanks.'

'Sure,' the waiter said.

While the food was coming, Charlie told her about Owen's sumptuous wedding, which he had been able to attend because he happened to be in Britain at the time.

'Oh yes I ran into Owen and his girlfriend in Finland. How did it go?'

He grimaced. 'Well if you set aside little things like my mother taking over the entire proceedings... But Donna gave as good as she got. She's a spirited young woman. She's pregnant, by the way. Don't know what she sees in dear dozy old Owen, mind.'

'Oh come now, people always say that! She's devoted to him.'

'If you say so. Pity you weren't there, Ellie: we could have done with lightening up a bit on the Jenkins-Beynon side of the family.'

'Was... I suppose Matt and Roz were there?'

'Yes but they were hardly a riot of joy. Roz is pregnant too...'

'Oh, I didn't know.'

'No, she's only just got pregnant, so she kept rushing off to be sick every half an hour...'

'You exaggerate, Charlie. That's great news; I must email her.'

'And Matt kept rushing off after her to see if she was OK, which obviously she was, and my father kept asking my mother if it wasn't time to go home yet, which obviously it wasn't.'

'Sounds like a great family occasion, then.'

'That wasn't the worst of it: listen, Alec and Milly had the most spectacular row!'

Eleanor picked up her knife and began to fiddle with it as the waiter approached, laden with food.

Do I want to hear about this?

'She really can be a right little cow when she wants to be!' Charlie declared.

'I always thought she was rather timid. Frightened of life,' Eleanor said. 'Not that I've seen her since her eighteenth birthday party.'

He looked at her sharply. 'She's changed a lot since then. Since she's been married to my brother. Milly was flirting shamelessly with Donna's father, of all people – poor chap, he must be sixty or seventy if he's a day, dead embarrassed, and Tamsin goes up to Milly and tries to prise her away. The kid could see everyone was looking at her mother.'

'That was brave of her.'

'Yeah. Then Milly turns on poor Tamsin...'

The waiter put down their plates, which were twice the size of a British dinner plate and piled high with food. There was a delicious spicy smell.

'Thanks.' Eleanor looked at the waiter over her shoulder.

'Uh-huh.'

'And Milly starts shouting at her daughter, "Leave me alone you fucking stupid child" – I think she'd had a fair bit to drink by then – and everyone turns round to look, and there's this deathly hush throughout the room, and then Alec comes over and lays into her. "Leave Tammy out of this." He's dead calm, controlled, a block of ice. Everyone was listening: you could have heard a prawn drop onto a barbie.'

'How dreadful. How did it end?'

'Oh my incredible mother, of course. She clapped her hands and said now, now, darlings... Let's not spoil it for the happy couple. Does anyone else want any more of the delicious Black Forest gateau? Coffee is being served in the garden room.'

*

The Pacific Ocean stretched out endlessly ahead of them, nothing but the odd island between them and Japan, Charlie told her. The sea was calm, lapping enticingly on the shore. It was a warm day, and the sandy beach at Santa Monica was already full of parties of swimmers, although it was still early April.

Charlie stood with his hands on his hips, surveying the scene with pleasure. Apropos of nothing in particular, Eleanor thought she heard him say, 'Shall we go to Venice?'

'What? Did you say Venice?'

He turned to her. 'It's real beaut. We could...'

'Charlie, listen.'

'What?' An amused smile played on his lips.

'I know perfectly well that Venice is, well, beaut is not quite the word I would have chosen but I agree it is an amazing place. I was there last summer, sketching gondolas on the Grand Canal.'

'Ah.'

'Charlie, it's great to see you again after all this time, it really is.'

'Likewise.'

'And I'm sure we'll run into each other again some other year, some other continent...'

'Oz perhaps?'

'Yes, quite likely. But I'm not in a position... Look, I'm very fond of you, Charlie, and I know we go back a long way, but I don't actually want to have any sort of...'

To her amazement he doubled up laughing, gasping for breath. When finally he could speak, he took her hand lightly and pointed with his other arm. 'Venice is another place just along the coast from Santa Monica. It's a gentle stroll over there, look, along the beach. Bare feet on the sand? Worth seeing because there are some ace markets, and you said you wanted a swim – Venice would be a good beach. You have brought your bathers, haven't you?'

'Oh!'

'You always did look magnificent when you blush, my Sunshine. No drama; Big Bad Charlie isn't trying to have a naughty. Not today, anyway. Just a walk along the beach before the sun gets too hot?'

And the wretched man was quite right – Venice was an interesting place. Eleanor found a large green tee shirt hanging in one of the markets behind the beach. It was on sale for only eight dollars. She tried to buy it from a tall sunburnt blond guy in shorts and sandals. 'For you, four dollars,' he said, popping it into a bag for her. 'Have a nice day, now!'

Charlie and Eleanor swam in the sea, which was just warm enough to be comfortable, and then they lay flat out on the sand to soak up the sun.

'I suppose you're used to all this at home, Charlie?'

'Well yes, I guess it's what I make my living out of.'

'Of course, so it is. Will you stay there, now – after your, you know, your divorce?'

'Oh yes. Mum wishes I would come home but after all these years I don't know if I could face the British winter. What would be really good...' He sat up and turned to her. 'I've always had this dream that I could get my mother to come out to Oz for a holiday. She promises she'll think about it next year.'

'What, you mean she's never been? But you've lived there for nearly twenty years, Charlie!'

'Yes but they don't travel, my parents – don't you remember? My father was at Monte Cassino during the war – which was a million years ago. He won't even get a passport.'

'But your mother went to the Ukraine a few years back, didn't she? Before the Soviet Union broke up.'

He looked at her shrewdly. 'You heard about that, did you? I'd forgotten. Oh yes, she made Alec go with her on this Cardiff exchange lark she used to run.'

'Something like that – I forget. Roz must have mentioned it to me.'

'Really? It must be my sister who is keeping you so closely up-to-date on our family news, then.' He gave her a knowing look. 'Anyway Alec is working on getting Dad himself out of the country some time in the next few years.'

'Is he?'

'There's this glamorous Italian archaeologist called Cecilia – you might have read about her, in fact.'

'I don't believe I have, no,' Eleanor said. Which was not strictly true, but reading about Alec in the tabloids was not a habit she wanted to admit to, not to Charlie of all people.

'Well Gorgeous Cecilia is digging up some monastery not all that far from Monte Cassino, and Alec is trying to persuade the TV people to let him make a documentary about her dig, in the hope that he can do one on war time Monte Cassino at the same time. He wants to get

Dad out there to talk about it on camera. Milly isn't too keen on the idea, of course.'

'Why ever not?'

Charlie laughed. 'Because she can recognise a woman with her claws in Alec at five hundred paces!'

Eleanor said nothing, and Charlie went on, 'Would you believe, the daft man actually invited this woman to a meal at home, and expected his family to fall about in admiration and wait on her hand and foot. Tamsin told me about it.'

'Did she?'

'She summed up the whole evening in one word: yuk.'

*

The young woman in the automobile hire office at Grand Canyon airport looked up from her desk and gave her professional smile as another passenger from the incoming flight walked in. A shortish man, lean and sun-tanned, pretty fit-looking. Probably Australian, to judge from his hat.

'Hi,' the customer said, mopping his brow and putting his documents down on the counter. 'I've booked a car. Name of Jenkins.'

'Sure. I'll check for you, sir.' She ran her finger down the list. 'Oh-oh. That is so strange.'

'What is? Look, I hope this won't take long...'

'We do have an automobile listed here, booked in the name of Jenkins – but Mr Jenkins picked up his auto yesterday morning. A green one – I have a note here: he specifically requested a green auto because it's his friend's favourite colour. Isn't that neat?'

'What? I never said anything about green...'

'He is staying at the Moqui Lodge,' she went on.

'No, no – that's me: I'm booked in at the Moqui Lodge. I ordered a car for today. I've just come in on the Las Vegas flight. Look, I've got all the documentation here.'

She picked up the man's booking forms and examined them. Then she turned back to her own lists.

'Now that is so weird. There are two cars here, both in the name of Jenkins: what are the chances of that happening in two days? We

have yours right outside, waiting for you, if you could just sign here, sir?'
She handed him the keys. 'Maybe you'll meet the other Mr Jenkins at
the Moqui Lodge.'

He closed his eyes with a sigh. 'Maybe I will.'

*

Eleanor sat on the ground on one side of the path, beside a slight bend.
She was trying out a sketch, but the scene unfolded beneath her was so
familiar from thousands of world-famous pictures, that it was impossible
to offer anything original. Yes the Grand Canyon was indeed beautiful,
or rather awe-inspiring – you had to grant that: a great series of chasms
down through the Colorado Plateau, up to a mile deep in places, carved
by the river itself, a process which had taken millennia. The colours
were amazing – the oranges, the pinks, the lilacs.

Eleanor had reached her limit. Everyone they met had been
anxious to warn them of the dangers – wear a hat, carry plenty of water,
never take longer to hike down into the Canyon than one third of your
available time, because it will take two thirds of your time to get up the
trail again. So here she was, convinced that she could walk for no longer
than twice the time they had already walked down that morning.

Reluctantly they'd left her sitting on a ledge here. There were
plenty of folk about, hiking up and down, even children; she assured
them that she would be fine, and she knew they were keen to go a little
further down for it was still morning. Both the brothers – she was
ashamed to reflect – were considerably fitter than she was herself.

Even Alec had more energy than she had, though he was looking
dog-tired this time. She hadn't seen him for over a year, and she'd
noticed a few more grey hairs when they were in their room last night.
He seemed to be under strain; he hadn't wanted to talk about Milly, but
when she asked about the children he lit up. David was learning the
violin and still badgering him to take them all back to Lapland. As for
Tamsin, she was thinking of giving up Guides after several years and
showing a new interest in archaeology; in fact she was wondering about
joining a student dig, which of course Alec hoped would be with his
colleague Cecilia.

Eleanor put her pencil down and looked around. There was a temporary lull in people passing by, and it was suddenly so silent that you could hear the wind whistling. She glanced down at a small patch of grass some twenty or thirty feet below her, far away to the right of the trail, and noticed there was a group of deer there, just standing quietly, nibbling at the grass. She hadn't realised that you could see wild animals here, when there were people everywhere.

Four or five hundred feet below the ledge where Eleanor sat, the others were coming to a halt.

'Maybe we should turn round,' Alec said, squatting down beside the path and offering Charlie the water bottle. 'Best not to leave Eleanor alone too long.'

Charlie was breathing heavily and was glad to sit down. He took a long swig at the water. 'You run into her a lot these days, do you?' he asked. 'I heard that Owen saw you both in Finland a bit back, and Roz said...'

'No, not really,' Alec said abruptly. 'We hardly ever meet. We're both so busy. And she lives in Rome.'

'So I gather. Of course you have to fit in that other Italian we've all been reading about, haven't you?'

'What?'

'Come off it, Al – it's been all over the red tops. You and Cecilia Falucci, is she called? Mum's been keeping it from Dad – it hasn't got into the Telegraph yet!'

'There's nothing at all in it. Just ridiculous rumours...'

Charlie looked at his brother. 'Eleanor must know, I would have thought. You treat Eleanor pretty shabbily, you've got to admit – and I mind about that.' He stood up and looked out across the canyon. The wind was getting up, and sand was blowing around their feet. Finally he spoke again. 'I have to say you seem to have got everyone in your life just exactly where you want them, big bro.'

Alec too got to his feet and glared at Charlie.

'When we were kids,' Charlie went on. 'I always thought I'd be the one to make a splash in the world. You were the boring one – the swot, the one who came top of the class...'

'You broke my birthday bicycle!' Alec's voice was suddenly raised, and his face was flushed.

A couple of children who were hiking past looked up in surprise at the unexpected commotion. Charlie took no notice of them.

'So what? Dad bought you another one, didn't he? You always did have people where you wanted them!' Charlie too had raised his voice. 'And now you've got the lot – fame, fortune and all that goes with it: for God's sake, I tell people that I'm your brother and they look at me with awe! And you've got a nice respectable marriage, AS WELL – it is only just beginning to dawn on me – as well as no less than two compliant long-distance mistresses...'

'That's a ridiculous word! No one has a mistress nowadays except French politicians.'

'Alec, face it. Don't bandy words with me. Face it: you're using Eleanor, big time. And she's much too good a person to be treated like that. Think about it.'

Alec stared at his brother in disbelief. 'You have no idea, have you? You are accusing me of using people! You, Charlie Jenkins...'

'Well?'

'You're the one who uses people, you always have. Look at when we were at school...'

'Holy dooley, Alec!'

'You were seeing Milly, but you had a string of other girl-friends at the same time...'

'So? What are you saying? We were seventeen, for Christ sake!'

Alec looked at him. 'She loved you, when you were seventeen. But you didn't care. She was just one of the crowd, for you. Another boring one, like me!'

'That's absurd. And anyway, I didn't marry her, did I? You were the one who married her, when you were still in love with someone else! How's that as a recipe for ruining someone's life? No wonder she suffers from depression, or whatever it is.' There was a silence between them, as clouds drifted over the sun.

'Look, Alec, I'm serious here: Eleanor is the one who matters. She actually wants you – God knows why. But don't just assume – don't be so bloody arrogant – don't expect her to wait patiently for you for ever.'

In the end, Alec spoke quietly, so that Charlie had to strain to hear. 'How dare you? How bloody dare you, Charlie!' he said. 'You don't know what you are talking about. You never have.'

*

'So are you going to tell me what's going on?' Eleanor closed the window of the bedroom and turned round to look at him.

'What do you mean?' Alec sat down wearily on the bed.

'The atmosphere this evening – it would have been warmer inside a freezer at the south pole. Oh I know you were annoyed yesterday when Charlie turned up here, but you thought that was funny this morning – something happened when you two were hiking down the trail. You were hardly speaking to each other when you came back up. I've never seen Charlie look so grim, and as for you, you were purple in the face. I was worried.'

He put his head in his hands.

'I'm sorry, Eleanor. I'm so sorry.'

'What on earth for?' She was beginning to be scared. 'What's the matter, darling?'

'I'm no use to you, Eleanor. To anyone. Maybe...maybe we should stop seeing each other?' He looked up at her sadly.

'What? You can't mean that.' She sat on the bed next to him. 'No, don't push me away. Listen, Alec – after all we've been through... This is not the time to give up. Trust me,' she said.

Chapter Thirteen

Wales, May 1997

Norman Jenkins followed the parking signs up a narrow lane and turned right towards a vast soggy field sloping uphill. A teenager took money off him at the gate and a series of other determined youngsters gestured to him to keep driving towards them, then to turn sharply up one of the ordered rows of cars and park exactly there, where he was told, next to the car before him. Norman obeyed.

By now it was pouring as though rain had just been invented, so before locking the car he decided to change into wellingtons. Glancing up, he saw that the green hills which rose gently round Hay on Wye were disappearing in mist: not a good sign.

Easy to see where he was supposed to go: there was a host of white tents two or three hundred yards away in the next field. It was like a medieval encampment in front of a battlefield. He set off along a track three inches deep in slippery mud, and stepped into a cowpat.

Norman had never bothered with this festival before, though it was only half an hour's drive from the cottage. Some literary caper; the Guardian Hay Festival, they called it. This year Alec had just published a book on Benedictine monastery life, and he was here to be interviewed about it by the journalist and feminist Joan Cowdrey. Alec had invited his father to come over for the day, since Barbara if you please was at that moment enjoying – if that was the word – the high life in Australia with Charlie.

Norman caught sight of Alec straight away, standing under the awning at the entrance talking to some friends. He broke off when he saw his father, and waved.

'Hi, Dad – glad you made it! Cup of tea first?'

'Just the ticket.'

They went in. It was a damp place, full of cheerful people scurrying about in wet clothes, clutching umbrellas and programmes, bags of books and sandwiches. Alec steered his father along the pathways between the various tents. Although the paths were roofed with plastic, the rain was often horizontal and the green matting that covered the walkways was soaked. Swaying up and down on the wet paths, Norman had the illusion that he was negotiating a ship in perilous seas.

They stopped at the Fairtrade tent and Alec found his father a seat near a screen which was relaying the current session from inside one of the neighbouring tents.

Alec glanced at it for a moment before joining the queue for drinks. 'They are reading poetry from the First World War – I thought that session sounded interesting. Look, that's Benedict Dacre.'

They don't know the half of it, Norman thought.

After they'd had drinks, Alec took his father off to find the tent where he was due to be interviewed. Several people stopped him for a chat on the way but eventually they reached the place. A long queue had already formed, snaking round some posts at the back, and Alec presented Norman with his ticket and said he would see him afterwards.

'I shall have to sign copies of my book in the book tent, but then we can go for some lunch,' Alec said as he left.

A quarter of an hour later, someone called out Norman's name – odd, surely no one at this festival would know him?

'It is Norman, isn't it?' A young woman from further back in the queue was waving at him. Curly hair, looked vaguely familiar. 'I'm Eleanor – I don't suppose you remember?'

'Good lord! Yes, yes of course I remember you, my dear. What are you doing here?'

'Oh, I just thought I'd catch Alec's performance. Are you on your own?' She glanced round nervously, as though she expected Alec's mother to emerge from underneath a copy of The Guardian.

'Oh yes, quite alone. The Duchess has gone to Australia for five weeks!'

'Oh I'm so glad! I mean,' she added hastily. 'I mean because Charlie said he so much wanted her to go out and visit him.'

'You've seen Charlie?'

'We...er...we ran into each other in the States a year or two ago, yes.'

The queue began to move, and he waited for her to catch him up. Inside was a large square tent, with rows of seats flat at the front, and sloping steeply up towards the back. They found a couple of seats towards the front.

'So you've moved up near here, I gather?' Eleanor said, taking off her wet anorak and folding it under her seat. The tent was rapidly filling up, and there was a strong smell of damp clothing.

'That's right, it must be nearly ten years now. We've got a little cottage... Tell you what, why don't you pop in now you're here?'

She hesitated. She wasn't going to be able to see Alec this time: he had emailed her a week ago, when she was in Canada, to say that he'd been called away to Italy immediately after his event at Hay. He was now working with Cecilia the Italian archaeologist, and she had summoned him urgently: some problem with the finances of her dig.

'Well that would be lovely, of course, but I've got to sort out my accommodation first. I only flew in from Canada this morning. They'll be booked up in Hay, so I'm driving over to Builth or somewhere this afternoon, before the jet lag kicks in!'

'Oh but we've got plenty of room – why don't you come and stay at the cottage, my dear? You couldn't find a quieter spot if you want to sleep off your jet lag.'

She peered at him to see if he really meant it.

'Why yes – that would certainly solve a major problem for me. Thank you, Norman. Yes, I'd love to.'

The audience quietened down as a young man in black led the two performers out from behind a curtain onto the stage, Cowdrey followed by Alec. They sat down on armchairs on either side of a low table and waited for the applause to die down. Outside the wind was howling, attacking the metal structure which held this huge tent together. The posts rattled loudly and the canvas flapped ominously. Alec laughed and made some joke about the Welsh monsoon season; then Cowdrey introduced him.

Eleanor hadn't yet seen Alec's book on Benedictine monastery life. She sat back and listened, as the audience gradually forgot the noise of the storm outside. Alec was describing the daily routine of the monks: prayer, farming and reclaiming wasteland, caring for the poor. They copied manuscripts and were busy with study and devotional exercises. After some twenty minutes Alec produced a few slides of excavations.

'There's a particularly interesting one that a colleague of mine is digging up,' he said, and he showed several shots of an archaeological site. Eleanor assumed that the elegant woman clutching a trowel and beaming into the camera must be the peerless Cecilia Falucci.

Cowdrey asked him what were the major hopes and fears of medieval monks, and he began to describe the Saracen raids up through Italy during the ninth century. Alec was a good story-teller, and Eleanor felt her flesh creep as he talked of the blind panic of the monks as hordes of Saracens were sighted pouring down the hillside towards the abbey, to plunder and destroy it.

Towards the end of the session, questions were invited from the audience, and several assistants roamed the tent with microphones. People were clearly engaged and interested. Some of the questions were from people Eleanor recognised – was that Simon Schama?

At the end, someone came onto the stage and presented Cowdrey and Alec each with a single white rose on a two-foot stem. Finally they walked off, Alec looking somewhat at a loss to know what he was supposed to do with his rose.

*

They took Norman to lunch at the Swan in Hay on Wye.

'You got my message, did you?' Alec said to Eleanor. 'I'm sorry I can't stay on for your sessions here – you are performing on Thursday and Friday, aren't you?'

They were shown to a pleasant table by the window, and Norman took off his damp coat.

'That's right,' Eleanor said. 'I'm chairing a discussion on Thursday, and then I'm doing a presentation on Friday about my new sketches. And your father has been so kind – he's invited me to stay at the cottage...'

'Has he now?' Alec was startled. 'Your latest sketches – that's the African ones, isn't it? You must tell me about them – you've been to see Susanna van der Merwe, haven't you?' He hung up all their coats on a rack.

'Yes I have – and she sends you her greetings, and wonders when you are going out to visit her yourself.'

'I'd love to – but I have to get this Italian programme sorted out first. Dad, you know I'm going to Monte Cassino, don't you?'

138

Norman grunted.

'The dig is not far from the famous Benedictine monastery at Monte Cassino - which is rebuilt now, of course, since it was destroyed in the war - you know?'

Norman looked at him steadily. 'So I gather.'

'I hope to interest a producer in making a documentary about the battle there in 1944 - the capture of the monastery.' He took a deep breath.

Eleanor looked at Norman; this was terribly important to Alec, she knew.

'I was wondering, Dad,' Alec went on. 'Would you consider coming out to Italy and, well, and taking part in the documentary? Since you were actually there at the time...'

'Oh no. Definitely not. Out of the question, Alec. Quite out of the question.'

Alec glanced at Eleanor, but she shrugged. 'Right then,' she said, pointedly changing the subject. 'Well I for one am having the lamb, and the pavlova for pudd, if anyone wants to know. There's something about jet lag that makes me starving hungry for a while, just before I keel over!'

The three of them finished their meal, talking about neutral things like the possibility that the mist might clear from the hills and what Barbara could possibly be up to in Australia - Eleanor had an agreeable vision of Alec's mother taking up wind-surfing in a wetsuit, tutored by Charlie, which would make a great cartoon, but she kept it to herself. Finally they got up to leave, and Alec said reluctantly that he would have to go almost at once if he was to catch his flight to Rome. Norman went to the gents while Alec paid the bill.

'Eleanor...' Alec said. 'My darling, I'm sorry it's been so short.'

'Can't be helped, if you've got to go,' she said tartly.

'Cecilia is in such a terrible muddle about the fees people have been paying her for working on her dig...'

'Yes, you said.'

'I just couldn't say no. She trusts me, I can't think why...' he went on with a wry smile. 'We must meet again - soon, Eleanor! Maybe you could come down and see the dig for yourself in the summer - it's quite spectacular. I'd love to show you.'

'Maybe. I don't know what my plans are yet.' She picked up her bag from behind her chair, putting the distance of the table between them. 'Good luck with your documentary!'

As Norman walked stiffly back towards them, Alec picked up the white rose he'd been presented with and thrust it at Eleanor. 'Here – you'd better have this, sweetheart,' he muttered. 'I'll never get it onto the plane!'

*

Eleanor drove her hired car into the little village which stretched along the bank of the river Edw and parked it outside Norman's cottage. A good thing she'd had Norman's car to follow, else she would never have found her way along all these narrow confusing lanes.

She got out and looked around. It was an enchanting place; there was a strong smell of blossom, and across the road a little stream bubbled its way down towards the Edw. The grey stone cottage was very old – about two hundred years, Norman said, but Barbara had made it very comfortable inside.

'Welcome, my dear,' Norman said, reaching for her suitcase. 'Here, let me take that. Come and sit down. You can have the end bedroom upstairs – nothing will disturb you there. All you can hear is the brook across the road! I'll make up the bed for you directly, but shall I make us some tea first?'

'Oh Norman, what a charming place!' She went into the sitting room, which looked out over the long garden. Alongside the cottage and garden was the river. 'It's so peaceful.'

'Sometimes I think it's a bit too peaceful for the Duchess, but she manages to keep busy. She's found things to run here, remarkably like the things she used to run in Cardiff. I'll just go and put the kettle on...'

While he was gone, Eleanor glanced round the room. Yes, recognisably Barbara's stamp here: neat, functional but attractive furniture, and everything so tidy. No piles of stuff lying around, as there always were in Eleanor's own home in Rome. No work in progress, no correspondence pending.

There was a pretty vase of flowers on the coffee table, flowers which Norman must have picked from the garden, and their smell added to the general sense of ease in the room. Over in the corner was a bright red plastic box full of toys, presumably for when Roz and Matt came to visit with their little boy. There was a copy of the Radio Times on the coffee table, and Eleanor was amused to see that someone had ringed a short piece about Alec's latest programme. Readers were invited to agree that Alec had become a lovable eccentric in his middle age, practically a national institution. He'd first attracted attention years ago when he dressed up as a Viking with a helmet and horns – would he now be dressing up as a British squaddie when he turned his attention to second world war battles, the writer wondered?

Several bookcases along the walls; always fascinating to see the books other people keep. There were a few books by Alec in pride of place by the fireplace – oh, and above the mantelpiece she recognised the wooden carving that Alec had brought his parents back from Nigeria, what, twenty-four years ago? More than half a lifetime! She touched it briefly, feeling the smooth edge of the wood. It hadn't changed in all that time. The boy was still climbing up the sloping palm tree to fetch down the coconuts. Yet the teenager who'd bought the carving in that market in the old town of Ile-Ife had himself altered immeasurably.

'Here we are.' Norman broke into her thoughts as he came in with a tray of tea things. 'I found one of the Duchess's fruitcakes, and I thought this would be a splendid occasion to sample it. Can you manage a slice?'

'I'd love one.'

'She does like to leave me food, you know – a bit like a dog, Monday, Tuesday, Wednesday and don't eat it all at once! And I don't, I'm very obedient.'

Eleanor laughed. 'Does she often go away?'

He shook his head. 'Only odd days – meetings in Llandod, that type of thing. Oh, once she went to the Soviet Union, would you believe? Not her cup of tea at all!'

'I heard. You don't travel, do you, Norman?'

'I had enough in the war. When I came home from that, I promised myself I'd never do it again.'

'I can understand that,' Eleanor said, biting into Barbara's delicious fruitcake.

After a small silence, he said, 'I had a brother, you know. In the war.'

She looked up in surprise. 'Did you? I never knew that!'

'Stanley. We were twins; he was forty minutes older than me, as a matter of fact.' The veins on his neck were standing out as he spoke.

'Really! I had no idea. Alec never said a thing!'

'He was... He was quite different from me. Clever. Everyone thought he was wonderful. He was going to be a scientist. But Stan was musical, too - he could turn his hand to any instrument, and he had a good singing voice. I've never been able to sing. Nor has Barbara, poor dear.' He gave a small laugh.

'Charlie's musical, isn't he?'

'Yes I suppose so. He was when he was a boy - but Charlie never kept his music up. Couldn't be bothered. Stan would have... I don't know, he'd have made something of his life.'

'He died, didn't he?' she said quietly.

'He was killed at Monte Cassino. We were in the same regiment. We'd always been together, d'you see - at school, at home...'

'How terrible. And awful for your parents, too, of course.'

'They never got over it. Our whole world was gone. My mother died the following year - a broken heart, my father always said. And he died himself only a few years later, cancer. My father only met Barbara once.'

'I didn't know any of that, Norman. No wonder you don't want to go back to Monte Cassino and talk on television about it!'

He shrugged. 'I hope Alec understands that.'

Eleanor sat up, a new thought striking her. 'So is Stanley buried in the Cassino War Cemetery?'

'I suppose he must be. I've never...'

'Because I've been there myself, Norman! You know I live in Rome? The cemetery is a morning's drive, south east of Rome. I went there with some friends a few years ago. We took the A2, the autostrada, down towards Naples and turned off at Cassino... It's very impressive, the cemetery. The monastery at the top of the hill dominates the place, of course.'

Norman was silent for a moment as he glanced out of the window. A blackbird was singing on one of Barbara's bushes outside.

'So that's where old Stan ended up?' he said eventually.

'His grave would be marked, I expect. It's a beautifully kept place. They have all the names catalogued.'

'Do they?' He stood up. 'Well I mustn't keep you – your jet lag will be catching up with you! I'll just go and dig out some bedding for you. Do feel free to sleep as long as you want – you won't be disturbed.'

*

Some ten thousand miles away on the other side of the world a day of crisp winter sunshine was beginning, and Charlie decided to take his mother out for a drive along the famous Great Ocean Road going west from Melbourne. They stopped on the way to look at the pillars of rock sticking out into the ocean, with towering white cliffs.

'Magnificent, isn't it?' Charlie said, framing his mother in a photograph with the sea and cliffs as a background. 'You know, Mum, there's nothing between here and the Antarctic.'

Barbara pulled her scarf more tightly round her neck. 'Do you remember that holiday we had on the Isle of Wight? You must have been about ten.'

'Er...yes, as it happens. Roz got lost on the beach and Alec had his nose in a book the whole time. Why?'

'This reminds me so much of the scenery there, don't you think so, Charlie? Those columns of white cliff!'

'Oh, I see,' Charlie conceded. 'But I reckon the Great Ocean Road might be, well, marginally bigger than the Isle of Wight? And anyway, Mum, it's much more interesting! Over a thousand ships were wrecked here, on their way out from Britain. People came out here to start again, getting so near the end of the journey, then wham! A sudden storm, and your whole new life has gone walkabout.'

'Pity they didn't stay where they were, then.' Barbara sat down on a bench. 'Where did you say we were going this afternoon, dear?'

'Torquay for lunch, and a gentle drive back to Melbourne. Tomorrow we've got a real treat, Mum! Down to Phillip Island to see the fairy penguins on their evening run. You'll love them.'

'I'd better telephone your father when we get back to Melbourne, Charlie.'

'Leave it 'til the evening, then. Give him a chance to get up in the morning, Mum!'

'What? Oh, I see. Yes, well you work it out for me, dear, and tell me when to ring. I do hope he's managing all right on his own...'

'Bound to be! No worries, Mum - he can look after himself. Alec said he was going to invite him over to the Hay Festival. He's doing an interview there about his latest book. That'll be a nice day out for Dad.'

'Oh he won't like that! He can never be doing with people standing up and spouting about books. I shouldn't think he'll go.'

They drove on to Torquay and settled down in a restaurant.

Charlie looked at his mother over the steak. She was - what? Getting on for seventy soon, she must be. She wasn't looking too bad. Slight folds around the neck, that he hadn't seen the last time. Her hair was a solid grey now, cut shorter than he remembered, but neat; none of this nonsense with artificial colouring, she'd told him - she was grey and she didn't care who knew it. She certainly hadn't slowed down at all; she and Dad still got out on plenty of bracing country walks, evidently. And to be fair, she had stood up to the marathon journey across the world remarkably well. Charlie had organised a stopover for her in Singapore, but she hadn't said much about that.

'So how's everyone back home, Mum?' Charlie asked her as they waited for the dessert.

She folded her hands on the table and leant forwards. 'To be honest, Charlie, I'm rather worried about...'

'I know, don't tell me: Roz?'

She shook her head impatiently.

'Matt and Roz? Their baby? What's he called, Kit?'

'Will you let me finish! Rosamund is perfectly fine. Busy, of course, but perfectly happy. No, it's Milly that I'm worried about.'

'Ah.' He looked up. 'How are things, there?'

'Worse than ever, as far as I can make out.'

'Really?'

'We had the children up to stay with us at Easter, and Tamsin said her mother was going round jumble sales buying up old crockery to throw at the walls!'

Charlie threw his head back and laughed. 'Nice one!'

'It's not funny, Charlie! I'm afraid she is a desperately unhappy woman.'

Charlie said nothing.

'And it is affecting the children badly,' Barbara went on. 'Especially poor Tamsin. And I don't know what Alec can do about it.'

'I think, Mum,' Charlie began carefully. 'I think that that marriage may have run its course.' He looked at her, unsure how she would take this.

'Poor Alec,' she said after a long pause. 'I'm afraid he must be very unhappy. They both are. Well, you know from your own experience, dear.' She smiled across the table at him. 'You had to cope with all that nasty divorce business on the other side of the world from us.'

He inclined his head. At the time of his divorce, Charlie had not been entirely sorry that half the world lay between himself and his mother.

'So...' Barbara went on. 'You think, do you, that Milly and Alec will have to separate?'

'It looks like it, Mum.'

'Well let's hope it doesn't attract any unpleasant publicity in the newspapers when it happens, then.'

'No indeed,' Charlie said.

'Any more than we've had already, that is...' she went on archly. 'There ought to be some way of stopping them writing such dreadful stuff! I tell you, Charlie, prison's too good for these scum.'

The waitress arrived with enormous ice-creams, and Barbara leant forward with glee, the subject safely changed.

After the meal they made their way gradually back to Melbourne, stopping once or twice on the way to admire the view.

Next day Barbara discovered that there was a lot of hanging around in the dark waiting for penguins. They had driven down to Phillip Island from Melbourne after lunch, and were standing on a wooden platform which stretched above the sand. Charlie explained that the fairy penguins came up from the sea every single day at the same time and waddled across the sand to the dunes where their patient offspring have waited in their nests all day for their tea.

'No fancy photography allowed, Mum!' he said with a grin.

'Don't be silly, dear.'

She shifted her weight and wondered how long they would have to stand here. 'So what do you think Alec will do, then, if he and Milly have to...' she said.

'I don't know, Mum.' He looked at her.

'I suppose... Does he ever see that girl he used to go out with when he was at the university? She's become quite famous now, I gather.'

Charlie was surprised at his mother's question. 'Eleanor Larsen-Bruun, you mean?'

'That's the one. Norman has got a book by her. Nice drawings.'

'Yes I know, I bought it for him when it came out. And yes, Alec does see her. Quite a bit, as a matter of fact.'

'Really? I didn't know that.' She smiled with satisfaction. 'That's nice. I'm so glad.'

'Are you?'

'Oh yes. It's just what Alec needs.'

There was a sudden cry at the front of the platform, as the first of the evening's penguins were spotted waddling up from the sea. Charlie took his mother's arm and edged her closer to the barrier so that she had a good view.

It was quite dark, and the penguins seemed to have no idea that other creatures were watching from far above. Each one waddled single-mindedly up the beach, intent upon finding their own particular infant and feeding it. How conscientious of them, Barbara thought; but then that after all is what matters in life: finding out what it is that one's offspring needs and doing one's best to provide it. If one can.

*

Eleanor slowly emerged into a woozy consciousness. She had no idea how long she had slept, but it felt just about enough. She stretched out – this little bed was very comfortable, in the small snug room with the sloping ceiling and slightly uneven floor. The window was open, and she could hear the brook babbling across the road. The sun was shining. The scent of blossom floated in, but from downstairs there was a stronger smell – bacon frying! Ah, she rather thought she could manage a decent breakfast, in due course.

She lay in bed some time, gathering her thoughts. No need to hurry. She didn't even need to go back to the Festival until Thursday. The last fortnight had been one mad dash in Canada and she needed a day or two doing absolutely nothing. Shame Alec had had to scurry off last night to pick up Cecilia's pieces - but there was no point dwelling on that.

Remember, Eleanor m'dear - we don't do regrets: that's how we get through.

Eventually she stirred and found her way to the bathroom. By the time she went downstairs, Norman had finished his breakfast, but he'd left out everything she could possibly want. The back door was open, and glancing down the garden she saw that he was busy cutting the lawn at the end, with a noisy old machine. After the previous day had been so wet, he was taking advantage of the sunshine to get the job done.

She cut some bread and stuck it in the toaster. Norman had left plenty of bacon ready to fry, and a box of eggs.

The phone rang.

Ah. Probably someone local. They'd ring off if she ran down the garden to call Norman - he'd never hear her if she shouted above the lawn mower. Anyway, suppose it was Alec ringing from Italy?

She picked up the phone. 'Hallo?'

'Hallo! Who is that? Is that Hundred House 997?' A cut-glass woman's voice, belonging to a somewhat put out cut-glass woman.

'Er... I'm not sure, hang on.' Eleanor hadn't got her glasses on and couldn't read the front of the telephone. 'Sorry, this is Norman Jenkins's home - he's just cutting the grass - shall I fetch him for you?'

'Who the dickens are you?'

'Oh, no one, I'm just staying here. Do you want Norman?'

'This is Barbara Jenkins speaking. I am telephoning from Melbourne, in Australia.' She said this very slowly and clearly, in case there was any doubt about the miracle of telegraph wires encircling the world.

'Oh, right! Sorry... Hallo, Barbara, it's Eleanor Larsen-Bruun. We met a long time ago, I don't suppose you remember... I was a friend of Alec's at university. Look, I'll just go and get Norman...'

'Why yes of course I remember you, er...Eleanor. How nice to talk to you again! I do hope Norman is making you comfortable?'

'Oh! Yes, very comfortable, thank you...'

'I made some lemonade before I came away. Oh, and I left a fruitcake in a big square tin in the cupboard on the right of the sink, with a silly rustic scene printed on the lid – if he hasn't found it yet, perhaps you could have a look? You might like to try some – do you like fruitcake?'

'Oh yes! Actually we had some yesterday at tea time – it was delicious, Barbara.'

'Ah good – I'm so glad: one is never quite sure how these things are going to turn out, you know. Are you able to stay long?'

*

Some hours later Eleanor lay relaxed on a deckchair in the garden with her eyes closed. She felt ridiculously lazy. Norman was just finishing some repair work on the riverbank, which had to be maintained to prevent flooding. He had an old straw hat on his head, and there was a smell of fresh earth where he had been strengthening the bank. When he was satisfied, he came to sit on the other deckchair and helped himself to some of Barbara's lemonade from the garden table.

'There, that should hold for a few months,' he said. 'Want some more lemonade, my dear?'

Eleanor opened her eyes and held out her glass. 'Yes please – it's very refreshing.' All the more so for Barbara wanting me to have it! What was that about?

Norman refilled her glass and she took a sip.

He looked at her for a moment, then began abruptly, 'That programme Alec wants to make about Monte Cassino – I don't suppose you know anything about it?'

She sat up. 'He's told me a bit, yes.'

'Just wondered, that's all: d'you think the boy realises what hell it was?'

She put down her glass on the table. 'Tell me, Norman.'

A dog barked in a distant field, somewhere beyond the river.

'You've been there yourself, d'you say?'

'Yes I have, as a matter of fact. I went there with some friends some years ago. It's a beautiful place, the new monastery – it was completely rebuilt after the war. It's very large, a fresh white building, covering the hill top.'

'It's a very steep hill,' Norman said. 'Very steep.'

'Oh yes I remember – we went in my friend's car, round all these hairpin bends. There were so many they were actually numbered. My friend's driving was so scary I threatened to get out of his car and walk when we got to Bend Sixteen – but I couldn't because it was far too hot to walk!'

'Certainly wasn't hot when I was there.'

'No?'

'It was bitterly cold in 1944. The worst Italian winter in living memory. Rain, sleet, snow. The lot. We were there for four months, out on the hillside. No tents or cover.'

'Really? That's incredible.'

Norman took out his pipe from his pocket, filled it and lit it slowly. All at once Eleanor remembered the old smell of vanilla.

'The Germans looked down on us on all sides, with their heavy machine guns,' he went on at last. 'Stanley was in a dug-out next to mine. He was furious when the Americans went in with their bombers a day early. They'd promised they'd bomb on February 16th, d'you see – dropped leaflets so the civilians could get out. There were only a handful of monks left, but dozens of refugees from the town, women and children.'

'So what happened?'

'They came in a day early, February 15th! Only because the weather changed, gave them a window. Stan simply couldn't understand it. I was more worried about being so damn cold and wet, myself, but Stan was furious.'

A squirrel ran across the grass and disappeared down the riverbank.

'I still dream about it.'

'Do you? I remember you used to when I first knew you but I hoped perhaps...'

'Oh yes, it died down for a while. A good many years, I suppose. But you know what brought it all back?'

'What?'

'A year after we moved into this cottage, the Duchess and I - the preparations for the Gulf War.'

'Really? But surely that wouldn't affect you up here?'

'Oh it certainly did. They flew their planes right overhead, along this narrow valley. Great huge things - so close, Barbara even thought she could put her hand up and touch 'em. Huge grey monsters.'

'Good heavens! I've never seen...'

'It was just like when the American bombers came down on the monastery. The whole ground shook. We looked up at them, we saw the bomb doors opening...'

He wasn't talking about this village any more. He'd gone back.

'So the monastery was captured in February?'

'Oh lord no, it took another three months fighting. It fell in May, in the end. The Polish soldiers played a big part in it. No, the bombing just reduced the whole thing to rubble, the perfect place for the Germans to defend. Blasted landscape looked like the Western Front.'

'Yes, I can imagine.'

I say I can imagine, but I can't, not really. No one could who wasn't there.

'Stanley said it was all quite pointless, d'you see?'

'Why was that?'

'He said it was a mirage, attacking the Gustav Line up here. A hundred thousand casualties on each side! All for a mirage, an obsession. It was the river valleys down below that mattered, Stan said. Once spring came, the Allies could cross the rivers and go north - cut off the German supply lines. The Allies entered Rome on June 4th.'

'Oh, wasn't that just before D Day?'

'Exactly - Nancy Astor got up in parliament and called us the D Day Dodgers!'

'What an extraordinary thing to say!'

The old man took his hat off and put it on the table.

'Norman, what happened to your brother?'

'He was killed right at the end. Early May. Trod on a landmine. Blown in two. I was a dozen yards behind him.'

'Oh Norman how dreadful!'

'I remember it as if it was one sleep away from the present,' he said, turning to look at Eleanor.

'Of course you do, Norman.'

'I felt as though something came suddenly, a big thing, it came and filled me right up and choked me. I couldn't stop shaking. I thought, NO! THIS IS NOT WHAT I WANT. There's been a terrible mistake here... I mean, I'm not a religious man, of course, but I felt that something - someone - had FAILED TO UNDERSTAND what was important. They'd got it wrong. It shouldn't have been Stanley, you see. Stanley of all people. It was a mistake...'

Eleanor took his hand.

'I never told my parents what really happened, you know. I lied and said it was a clean bullet.'

'Yes, I'm sure that was the right thing to say.'

The two of them were silent for several minutes, while the birds sang overhead and swooped down to the river.

'Norman, what you've told me is impressive - graphic - so detailed after fifty years. Don't you feel that you ought to share this with people? Alec can't do that - he wasn't there, he wasn't even born. Doesn't it need you?'

Chapter Fourteen

Italy, August 1997

Eleanor

'Look at these colours, Eleanor!' Alec's eyes are shining.

We're standing on a muddy bank overlooking the latest find at Cecilia's dig.

I've come down here for the day, and finally met this wonderful Cecilia that everyone's talking about. Yes, this may be a terrible mistake, but here I am.

We are looking at the floor of the crypt, Alec explains, newly uncovered after eleven centuries underground. The mosaic is a delicate pattern, a picture perhaps.

'Is it a biblical scene?' I ask.

'Yes, we think it's Jesus preaching to the crowds – perhaps the loaves and the fishes: look at that bit, over there.'

'It's so bright!' I say. 'I wasn't expecting that.'

'That's because we only uncovered it yesterday. This is what it must have looked like when it was first made. Just imagine! Cecilia's thrilled.'

I bet she is.

I take a step forwards to have a better look, then suddenly I skid.

He grabs my arm. 'Careful! This mud is slippery – don't get too near the edge.'

'Thanks!'

'You know you really ought to do some sketches of this, don't you think?'

Ah that would be difficult. I don't think I can stand the atmosphere here – I can't stay long enough for sketching.

'Oh, I don't know... I must get back to Rome this evening. There's things to see to, you know.'

'So soon? But we've hardly spoken to each other.'

He doesn't realise that he's completely surrounded down here at the dig. No one can get near him; Cecilia makes sure of that.

We turn round - there's the sound of loud voices drifting across the site. It must be Cecilia coming towards us, followed by an entourage of students. She's explaining the significance of the crypt.

'There!' Cecilia declares, coming to a halt on the bank. She glances briefly at me as though she thinks I would have left by now. Then with a flourish of her arm, she indicates that her students should gather round. She is wearing a long flowing skirt which she has not picked up in any Oxfam shop, and a cream blouse with a large bow. As Cecilia points out the salient features of the mosaic in the crypt, she flashes her eyes at Alec. 'Dr. Jenkins was with us when we uncovered this...'

After a while the students go back to their work, and Cecilia turns to Alec with a dazzling smile and asks him when his daughter will be arriving to join the dig.

'Oh God – it's soon, isn't it?' He brushes his head with his hand. 'I'm supposed to be meeting her. Milly rang at the weekend. What day did she say?' He fishes in his pocket for his diary and discovers that Tamsin is due at Fiumicino at three fifty-five today.

'I'll have to go...' he says.

'Oh no you cannot go! You promised you would give the students a talk after they finish their work this afternoon! They are so looking forward to it.' She pouts at him. Yes she actually pouts, like a cartoon character, a child being thwarted. It flashes across my mind that the elegant professor may be about to burst into tears. 'You must not let me down!' she declares.

Alec frowns, running his hand through his unruly hair. 'God, why am I so bloody disorganised?' He turns helplessly to me. 'Er...I don't suppose you could meet Tammy, could you? You did say you had to get back to Rome today...'

*

I'm late meeting Tamsin's plane, of course. With that traffic, I'm lucky it's only half an hour.

Poor kid, she's so proud of managing her first flight on her own, after all the fuss her grandmother made – I can imagine Barbara! It was dead easy, no hass. Until there was no sign of her Dad in the waiting crowd.

She hasn't got a mobile – unlike a few of her school friends with more compliant parents, she tells me; and she hasn't even got any currency for the phone. Her mother had been going to get it for her, but in the end she hadn't had time. Milly had had one of her bad days, and she said she had been too busy; too busy to get out of bed, Tamsin had reflected bitterly after school as she washed up the breakfast things and put away the cornflakes. So what to do?

Luckily that's when I turn up, dashing breathlessly through the arrivals door.

'It is...isn't it? You are Tamsin Jenkins, aren't you? I'm Eleanor – we met in Finland a few years ago, didn't we?'

'Oh yes – you're Dad's friend!' Relief at someone familiar, obviously here to pick her up. 'Did he ask you to meet me? He didn't tell me...' Some annoyance now, at the way grownups always decide things about you without telling you.

'Yes...' I'm still out of breath. 'I'm terribly sorry to be so late! I didn't realise you were coming until this afternoon, and then the traffic was terrible... Your father's got to give the students a talk this evening about his latest book – he'd promised, he couldn't get out of it. I can take you down to the inn where you'll be staying.'

'Oh, OK. Cool.'

In no time I whisk her out to the car park and we set out towards the autostrada, the windows wide open.

'It's been swelteringly hot these last few weeks,' I tell her. 'All the natives have fled – only people like you flocking in!'

Tamsin grins. 'I've been dying to come.'

'I bet. You're still at school, aren't you?'

I look at the young girl. She's grown considerably since that holiday in Finland four years ago. She isn't a child any more – she's turned into an attractive young woman. Her eyes are a piercing brown like her father's.

Tamsin groans. 'Yes, unfortunately. One more year, then I'm free!'

I smile. 'What are you going to do then?'

154

'I'm having a gap year. I can't wait. I've been emailing a friend of Dad's in South Africa – maybe you know her too?'

'Oh, Susanna van der Merwe? Yes, I've known her for years. We actually got to know each other in Darjeeling, of all places...'

'I know, Dad told me.'

'Did he?'

'He said it was a fantastic place, where you could see rows and rows of wispy white mountains stretching away for hundreds of miles.'

I concentrate on joining the southbound section of the autostrada.

'Yes, Tamsin, yes that's right,' I say in the end. 'I remember the wispy mountains too. You could only see them very early in the morning, but I've...I've always remembered them.'

'You've been to South Africa too, haven't you, Eleanor? We've got a book of your sketches from there.'

'Yes, I stayed with Susanna a bit back.'

'I love your books! We buy them all as soon as they come out. Do you remember when we met you in Copenhagen? When we were little? You drew pictures of Dave and me climbing that statue.'

'In Rådhuspladsen, yes. The Hans Andersen statue. My cousin Kirsten wanted to photograph you for a commission she was working on.'

'Oh yes, we've got the photos, obviously – Dad made her send them to us – but they aren't half as good as the drawings you made of us!'

I turn to her and smile. 'Well thank you, Tamsin.'

'Will you be around when I'm on the dig?'

'Me – no. I'm nothing to do with archaeology. I'm going back to Rome first thing in the morning. I've got to go to New Zealand in ten days or so, as a matter of fact.'

'Oh, cool! What are you doing there?'

'Some sketches for a book a friend of mine has written. Well he's a friend of your Uncle Charlie's as a matter of fact.'

'Yeah?'

'He's written a book about how he built his own yacht and sailed it round the coast. He wants me to draw his boat in Auckland harbour, and then we're going to sail down to the South Island and...'

As we come off the autostrada, it suddenly strikes me that we might make a small detour and go and look at the site of the dig.

'There won't be anyone there now - they'll all be back at the inn - but if you're not too tired we could have a quick look? It's a huge place, as big on the ground as some of the great French cathedrals. Won't be able to get in of course, but you can see a lot through the mesh of the outer fence, if you like?'

'Oh yes please!'

As we drive along the track leading to the entrance of the site, I'm startled to see a break in the blue chain-link fence above us. 'What's going on here? I've got a bad feeling...' I pull up opposite a small bridge over a stream. At the top of the slope is a still-locked gate in the fence, where I was earlier today, but next to it someone has pulled the fence down.

We get out of the car and walk up to look.

'There's something badly wrong here, Tamsin. This fence was perfectly OK this morning. We'd better tell someone. Cecilia needs to know.'

There's a jumble of fresh footprints around the break in the fence.

'Oh but now we're here,' Tamsin says. 'Shouldn't we go in first and find out if anyone is around?'

'Well I don't know...'

But before I can stop her, Tamsin leads the way through the fence onto the walkway. She sets off briskly around the edge of the site.

'There's someone down the far end - I can hear voices,' she calls over her shoulder.

'Tamsin, I'm not sure that we ought to be trespassing...' I hurry after her.

Tamsin's right, there are voices: as we get closer I can see a young woman balanced on the edge of a trench, shouting at a man who is waving a camera. They are above the crypt that has just been uncovered - precisely where I was this afternoon.

'You can't take pictures here - you promised! Professor Falucci will kill me if she finds out I've let you in!'

I suddenly realise that I recognise the girl - she's Tracey, one of the students on the dig.

'Shut up, you fucking bitch!' The cameraman is Italian. 'There is a story here, and it will be me who gets it!'

He takes several photos of the crypt below them. Poor Tracey stares at him in horror, then she lunges at him, trying to wrench the camera away.

'Careful, stupido – this camera is worth big bucks!' he shouts.

The two of them struggle and as they move towards the edge of the trench, she suddenly slips on the mud – overbalances – and crashes down with a thud as she hits the floor eight feet below.

'God! Is she OK?' Tamsin shouts.

I grab Tamsin's arm to stop her joining the unfortunate Tracey.

'Who the fuck are you?' Noticing us for the first time, the photographer turns and stares.

At the bottom of the trench the girl begins to scream. She's lying spread out awkwardly on the crypt floor, her right leg twisted under her.

'Where does it hurt?' I called down. 'Have you broken anything?'

'Fucking broke my camera!' the man mutters. 'She's all right, the bitch. Get up! Get out of there before the police come!'

'I don't think she can get up,' I tell the odious man. 'She's broken her leg, I'm pretty sure.'

Tracey screams again.

'I have, it hurts – it must be broken! Help!'

'It's all right, don't panic,' I say. 'We'll fetch someone straight away. Don't worry, I'll climb down...'

I find a foothold on the side of the trench and jump down. I can see what's happened.

'Thought so: that is definitely a broken leg. Don't try to move it – you'll make it worse.' I look up at the man. 'Now can you get help? You must have a phone – mine's in my car.'

With great reluctance he produces a mobile from his pocket. 'Who are we calling? Not the carabinieri – there's no need for that! The hospital maybe?'

'Here, give me that,' I stretch my hand up to him.

I'm staring hard at him, and unwillingly he hands his phone down.

I dial rapidly, a number I know by heart. 'Not sure if we'll get a signal down here. Ah yes – it's ringing. Oh hi, Alec – it's me. Listen love, we've got a crisis. Can you get an ambulance over to the site at once? Tracey Thompson has fallen down onto the crypt and broken her leg. Quick, Alec. Look, I'll stay here with her. I've got Tamsin, she's fine... I'll have to stop now; you're breaking up.'

Chapter Fifteen

Italy, September 1997

Alec

'I just don't know what to do, Alec my friend!'

Cecilia stood at the kitchen table, pausing as she chopped onions for what she'd called a light supper. Her hair was straying wildly – quite out of character – and her eye shadow was smudged, but she was wearing an elegant white silk blouse.

I'd just arrived that afternoon and I was hot, hungry and pretty exhausted. She'd phoned with another S.O.S. for help with her accounts, and luckily I had a few days to spare before I was next due to work on a broadcast. I got a last-minute cancellation flight.

'It's that wretched girl, Tracey Thompson. She broke her leg and flounced off home to Australia, or wherever she came from – and now she wants all her money back...'

'Yes, you said.'

'And it just isn't in the right account. There are so many separate accounts...'

The onion slicing had ceased – temporarily, I hoped. 'Look, there's no point worrying about it tonight, Cecilia. We'll go into your office first thing tomorrow and look at all the books. There'll be insurance cover, surely. And meanwhile there must be other accounts you can take Tracey's money from.' I tried to smile encouragingly at her.

'Oh you are such a rock to me, Alec! I have no one else to turn to.' She spread out her hands. 'You are a wonderful man!'

Hardly what Milly would have called me! And as for Eleanor... She seemed quite out of reach. She'd vanished back to Rome the very next day, after she and Tammy had discovered the break-in at the monastery site. Oh, she made sure Tracey Thompson was taken safely and quickly to hospital, but I never saw her again.

In the end I helped Cecilia cook the pasta, while she finished off the sauce. She opened a large bottle of Italian wine, and my exhaustion began to drain away by the time I reached the second glass. At last we sat down to eat, and she told me how the dig was developing, and how much difference my recent book on the Benedictines had made to interest in the site.

As we finished the meal I began to clear the table.

'Oh no – leave these: they can wait 'til the morning,' she said, putting a precarious pile of plates on the draining board. She turned and gave me a radiant smile. 'You have already made me feel so much better, Alec.'

'Well I don't really think you've got anything to worry about here...'

She sniffed suddenly. 'You see, I try so hard to put on – what do you English call it? A brave face?'

'Yes?'

'Everyone thinks I am absolutely in control. Only you know how weak I am...' She picked up her glass, which was still half full of wine. 'But tonight you have made me feel like a queen!'

'I have?'

'I am not going to let these problems conquer me!' She took a deep breath and quite suddenly began to sob. Loudly.

Oh dear. There was me thinking we were getting on well, and I'd even been wondering whether before long I could make my excuses and go back to my hotel.

I stared at her as tears rolled down her face.

'Good grief... It's not that bad, surely?' Maybe it was a mistake to hold out my hand and take her elbow just as she had another sip of wine. 'Chin up, old bean, my mother used to tell us as kids!'

'What?'

She jerked her elbow and the rest of the wine slurped down her blouse.

'Oh, sorry!' I stood back in horror.

'No, no, Alec, it does not matter. This old thing – I have had it for a long time.' Carefully she began to unbutton the blouse. 'I must put it to soak at once – then all the wine will come out, you will see. Oh, it is stuck – can you help me, Alec?'

I hesitated, then I began to peel the dripping garment off her shoulders. Underneath she was wearing a white lace bra. Some of the wine had unfortunately got through to it, making a red pattern across her breasts.

'Oh dear...' I said.

'This is one of my favourites! I will have to soak it too. Can you help me?' she pleaded again.

As I tried to put my hands behind her back, she suddenly stretched up and reached around my neck in order to kiss me firmly on the mouth.

*

Birds were singing their cheerful morning songs outside the window as though they hadn't a care in their bright Italian world. They probably hadn't. I sat up and leant on my elbow.

Cecilia was still asleep, stretched out in abandon, her luxurious dark hair spread out across her shoulder. It had been another blisteringly hot night and she had not felt the need for clothing.

What the hell had I done?

My head was aching furiously – I must have drunk far too much of that wine last night. I could murder some strong coffee. I wondered what sort of breakfast she went in for. Cautiously I slipped out of the bed and padded over to the door. Cecilia didn't stir.

In the kitchen I found her percolator and set it going. It was a neat, tidy kitchen. Everything in its place; like Cecilia herself, indeed. I'd always thought her a self-contained character, dedicated to her work, and utterly professional.

I hunted round for some cups and poured a couple of coffees. Milk? Yes, of course – Cecilia had milk in her fridge, even though she herself took her coffee black; she was ever mindful of the needs of any passing visitor. I found a tray and carried everything into the bedroom. Cecilia turned over and opened her eyes as I came in. 'Oh Alec, you've made some coffee. What a wonderful smell!' She sat up and patted the bed. 'Come and sit next to me...'

'I hope these are the right cups... They were all I could find.'

She burst out laughing. 'Oh you are so English, Alec! What does it matter what cups we use? After last night! It was magical, wasn't it? Fantastico! I had no idea...'

After her anxiety of the day before, Cecilia did not seem in too great a hurry to get back to the accounts in her office. After a while she found some eggs in the kitchen. 'No fresh rolls today, I am sorry, but I have a loaf – I can make you toast. What would you like?' By now she was wearing a pale blue silk dressing gown, wrapped loosely round her supple body.

'Oh yes, toast would be fine.'

She smiled. 'I think the English like toast. Oh and here is something you will need, I am quite sure...'

She turned to a wall-cupboard over the cooker and began scrabbling at the back of the top shelf. 'I am sure I have it here somewhere!'

'What...'

She seized something and brought it out with a cry of triumph. On the table she placed a jar of Marks and Spencer's Sicilian blood orange medium cut marmalade.

'There! Isn't that right? All English people eat marmalade.'

I stared at it.

'Why, what is the matter? You look as if you have seen – what is it you say? – seen a ghost!'

*

A couple of hours later we went over to her office and she opened the books of accounts.

'I don't think he is here today,' she said, glancing out of the window onto the courtyard.

The temperature dropped by twenty degrees.

'Who?' I demanded.

'Oh some photographer. He's been around lately, asking questions. I think he is the same man who was there with Tracey Thompson when she fell and broke her leg. I don't like him.'

I knew exactly who she meant. He had his fingerprints on several photos of me in the past, which he'd sold to the tabloids. Not good news. 'Maybe we should be careful for a bit,' I told her.

'Why should we?' she said suddenly.

'There is no point in hiding what we feel, Alec.' She looked at me across the table. She had been about to open the file of insurance documents, but now she deliberately placed it on a pile of books. She took a deep breath and brushed her hand lightly over her hair. 'It is time now, I think. It is time for you to leave your wife so that we can be together. Then it will just be accepted and no one will have anything more to write about.'

I stared at her.

*

From Alec Jenkins <anj@tomtom.net>
To Eleanor Larsen-Bruun <Eleanor@larsen-bruun.co.uk>
Subject: Oh my God!!!!!
October 19th 1997 14:53:31 GMT

My dearest Eleanor

I guess I owe you some sort of explanation, if I can manage one.

DON'T TAKE ANY NOTICE OF THE PHOTOGRAPH THAT'S DOING THE ROUNDS OF THE NEWSPAPERS. It isn't what it looks like, I promise you.

Look, Cecilia is an old friend. I told you about her.

That student you found down the crypt - when she broke her leg she had to withdraw from the dig, obviously, and she claimed her money back from Cecilia. Unfortunately it wasn't there in the right account. Turned out that Cecilia had spent it on entertainments for the students; she very kindly organised a welcome party for Tamsin.

Cecilia asked me to come down and look at the figures. The photographer was looking for a scandal and he thought he had found it when he caught us together as we were coming out of Cecilia's office last month.

Why did you disappear so suddenly? I was so grateful to you for bringing Tamsin down to the dig, but I never got the chance to thank you. Where are you now? Tamsin said you

were thinking about New Zealand. Surely not? Look, I need to talk to you.
All my love – Alec

From Alec Jenkins <anj@tomtom.net>
To Eleanor Larsen-Bruun <Eleanor@larsen-bruun.co.uk>
Subject Where the hell are you?
November 6th 1997 14:53:31 GMT

My dearest Eleanor
Haven't heard from you for weeks – did you get my last three emails? Where are you?
David isn't speaking to me at the moment. Milly is still desperately upset about that ridiculous publicity in September, and now David thinks it is all my fault: at least that is my guess. Since he won't actually communicate, I don't know. Tamsin is more understanding.
All my love – Alec

From Alec Jenkins <anj@tomtom.net>
To Eleanor Larsen-Bruun <Eleanor@larsen-bruun.co.uk>
Subject: Happy Christmas!
December 24th 1997 14:53:31 GMT
My darling Eleanor
Are you still in New Zealand?
Things are pretty icy over here.
Love, Alec

*

There was another burst of fireworks and this time the whole sky was lit up - gold and silver, with cascades of red and blue, over and over again, falling gently down on the Manhattan skyline. 'Magnifico!' Cecilia cried, snuggling into my scarf.

'Yes, they do a pretty good display here, don't they? I thought they would. You're not too cold, are you?'

New York was having an exceptionally mild winter, and there had not even been snow so far. Of course it was a last minute decision to come here for the New Year. There were people at CNN that I wanted to contact in the near future, and suddenly at home on Boxing Day I'd had enough – what the hell, why not fly over this week instead of waiting? So why did I invite Cecilia to come with me? I don't know, to be honest. Well obviously no one else was going to hop over to New York with me - not even Tammy. I could have gone alone, but that was even more bleak a prospect than staying at home. Maybe I just asked her because I was lonely? Burning my boats, of course; it wasn't going to endear me to Eleanor, if she ever found out.

We were standing on the shoreline of downtown Manhattan, a huge crowd surging cheerfully all round. Behind us was the forest of skyscrapers stretching back towards the centre, where our hotel was, and in front the sea, dotted with islands. In the distance we could just make out the Statue of Liberty, holding up her torch of hope.

'What a wonderful idea to come here! I was so surprised when you telephoned me...' she said, leaning up to kiss me.

I'd been pretty surprised myself, come to that. The air was filled with loud hoots from a mass of boats on the Hudson River.

'Would you like another coffee? There's less of a queue over at that stall...' I suggested, pointing across to the corner of the ferry terminal.

We threaded our way carefully through the throng to the coffee kiosk. A small child was eating a very large ice-cream, which dripped down his coat, and some good-humoured teenagers had begun to sing God Bless America, out of tune and not quite together. We reached the front of the queue.

'Welcome to 1998!' cried the woman behind the kiosk, handing us a couple of cartons of coffee. 'And have a nice... ah, have a nice year, now!' she added with an immense cackling laugh.

Chance would be a fine thing.

I had absolutely no idea what 1998 was going to bring. Tamsin was leaving – that much was certain: she should do well in her A Levels, and go off on her gap year, so long as she wasn't too upset by me and

Milly. No, Tammy would be OK – she was used to us by now – she'd seen enough crockery thrown when she was a small child. Took it in her stride. And David lived in a world of his own.

As for Milly herself, she seemed different this autumn. That last lot of photographs in the Mail, was it, or the Sun, in September – '...tensions between Jenkins, 43, and his wife Millicent, 42, have been running high since she discovered he was cheating on her with dark seductive work colleague Cecilia Falucci, 46...' – had drawn a line for Milly. She had withdrawn from me.

Of course I was worried it would tip her into another depression, but to my surprise it didn't. Far from it. She began to make plans. She wanted us to separate, she said, and sell the house as soon as David left school. She planned to move down to Dorset where her parents had retired, and meanwhile she had enrolled on a course in counselling: she had decided to use her own terrible experiences to help others.

So that was Milly settled, after a fashion. And the children would be gone in a year or two. But whatever had happened to Eleanor? I had no idea where she was; she never answered my emails these days. She must have seen the press photographs, unless she'd abandoned New Zealand and gone to live in Ulan Bator; so had she finally given up on me, after all these years?

'I was feeling so lonely this Christmas,' Cecilia said, opening her carton of coffee. 'All my friends were away, or busy with their families, and they did not want me to disturb them.'

My own Christmas had not exactly been a laugh a minute. 'Shall we walk back up to the hotel?' I said. 'I'm afraid my jet lag is beginning to catch up on me...'

Chapter Sixteen

From Susanna van der Merwe SvdM23@Maties.sun.ac.za
To Eleanor Larsen-Bruun <Eleanor@larsen-bruun.co.uk>
Subject: Catching up
January 3rd 1998 14:53:31 GMT

Hi Eleanor
Thanks for your Christmas email – sorry I haven't written for
so long: life has been hectic as usual this summer. New
friends...tell you more when we meet. You seem to be having
fun over there – have you recovered the use of your hand,
after that incident when he took you paragliding?
Alec Jenkins sent me a desperate email before Christmas
asking if I knew where you were. Am I supposed to tell him?
He says you haven't answered any of his messages for
months. What's going on? I thought you were quite involved
with him – or have I got that wrong? Maybe I'm out-of-date!
I read something about some other woman he was mixed up
with but I didn't pay much attention to it.
Some Italian academic?
Your African sketches are selling well down here; the
university bookshop has a big display of them, I noticed the
other day. People are particularly interested in your visit to
the Cape Flats and your interview with that Cape Coloured
soldier, Henry, was it? They like the detail about his little boy
trying to get into the football team.
I'm getting heavily caught up with the ANC now; we've got
an election next year and I've finally made up my mind to
stand. You know here in Stellenbosch we have three
establishments – the rugby, the wine and the university, and
if you annoy any of those three you really are persona non
grata – well, Eleanor old friend, it looks like I'm going to

annoy all three of them! Not to mention my family... A woman spat at me in the street last week.

Have to prepare a lecture for tomorrow! Take care – Su

From Eleanor Larsen-Bruun <Eleanor@larsen-bruun.co.uk>
To Susanna van der Merwe <SvdM23@Maties.sun.ac.za>
Subject RE Catching up
January 15th 1998 11:34:57
Hi Su

Good to hear from you. About telling Alec where I am: NO, PLEASE DON'T! After that business that got into the tabloids last year, I decided to give myself a break.

I'm having a great time in New Zealand – can't write any more as someone is queuing up to use the computer in the post office...I should be back in South Africa by the end of June – see you then... Eleanor

From Susanna van der Merwe <SvdM23@Maties.sun.ac.za>
To Eleanor Larsen-Bruun <Eleanor@larsen-bruun.co.uk>
Subject RE Catching up
Date March 5th 1998 23:16:47

Glad to hear you are coming back here soon; lots of my friends want to meet you, after buying your African sketches! And I want to hear what you've done in New Zealand.

Your friend Matt Beynon has settled in Cape Town for the time being – did you know? He's a foreign correspondent for some paper – so I am seeing quite a bit of him and Roz, and their little boy, Kit, who is lovely – he's about two or three. Matt's old friend that he was in school with in Nigeria, Seretse, has returned with his family to South Africa and has just taken up a job as a hospital doctor in Lesotho. He wants everyone to visit him there. He says he remembers you very well from your visit to Nigeria when he was a boy, and that I'm to include you in the general invitation to Lesotho for sure! Oh and another connection with you – Alec Jenkins's daughter Tamsin has asked me if she can start her gap year here with me at the end of the winter, as soon as she finishes her A Levels; she says she'll arrive in late August. Maybe I should send her to Maseru to visit Seretse? Matt could take her. She sounds an interesting young girl; she's had good offers from universities for next year – oh and she's just passed her driving test first time, which I admire: I must admit I took three goes, myself.

In haste – as usual! Su

From Seretse Hamakwayo <seretse@hamakwayo.net>
To Matthew Beynon <matt.beynon@freesurf.net>
Subject: Your trip here
Date September 15th 1998 16:24:53 GMT

Matt, OK, will meet you off Friday's flight. Yes fine to bring Roz's niece, Tamsin. Plenty of room – empty house. Lots for her to see.

Sorry my family is not here just now – Ebba has taken the kids to Norway to see their grandparents, but I will try and take some time off to take you out and about. We must go to the mountains. We can camp and take canoes. I've booked you into a place called Malealea where you can ride horseback through great scenery and live in little round huts. It's a wild country here, completely unenclosed and very high up. What are you like on a horse? I learnt in the States.

Don't take any notice of anything you might have heard about trouble here: it's OK. Bit of fighting in the city since the botched election last May – machine gun fire round the palace, rebels gathering there asking for support from the young king. My kids are at the International School just next to the palace and they sometimes hear the rebels singing, along with the odd burst of gunfire wafting through the classroom windows – but nothing's going to happen, I'm certain.

Cheers – Seretse

From Matthew Beynon <matt.Beynon@freesurf.net>
To Seretse Hamakwayo <seretse@hamakwayo.net>
Subject RE Your trip here
Date September 18th 1998 17:33:58 GMT

Sorry Seretse – last minute hitch: Kit has gone down with something, a high fever. Don't know what it is but Roz is panicking – well to be honest so am I. Think I ought to stay here. Do you mind if my plane ticket goes to Eleanor Larsen-Bruun? She is staying with Susanna in Stellenbosch and says she'd love to see Maseru.

Catch up with you soon I hope – Matt

Chapter Seventeen

Lesotho, September 1998

'The tanks rolled into Maseru at dawn on Tuesday 22nd.' That's how Matt Beynon might have started his piece if he could have been there, and Eleanor felt that the least she could do was make some notes for him. That was what tanks did, they came at dawn. 'The tanks arrived half an hour before lunch' just wouldn't have the same ring to it. And no, he probably wouldn't appreciate any little sketches of them. Not this time.

So dawn it was. Five o'clock. Six hundred crack South African troops, who should have been backed up by two hundred Botswanans, only Botswana was two days late. Operation Boleas, they called it. They were apparently there to restore democracy and the rule of law.

Eleanor leant out of her bedroom window in Seretse's house on the Caledon Road and stared at the column of tanks advancing steadily on Lesotho's capital.

'What's going on?' Tamsin came up behind her and squeezed past. 'God, it looks like an army!'

'Yes I think it probably is, Tamsin,' Eleanor said dryly. 'Come away from the window, love.'

The invasion was immediately reported in Britain on Radio Four's Today Programme. Barbara listened in horror at the cottage in Cregrina and rang Alec down in Cardiff at once.

'What on earth is South Africa up to?' she demanded. 'Why are they invading Lesotho, of all places? I jolly well thought you told me, Alec, that it was a peaceful little kingdom the size of Wales that never gets into the news?' She paused for breath. 'And you've let Tamsin go there for a holiday?'

'Yes, I gather that was the plan. Matt was supposed to be taking her up to Maseru to see an old school-friend of his, a doctor. Tamsin is there now, she only arrived a few days ago.'

'What do you mean, Matt was supposed to be taking her? Did he take her or didn't he?'

'Well no, I'm afraid he couldn't make it in the end. Little Kit got a temperature or something. Oh the kid's fine now, don't worry, Mum – but Matt had to cancel.'

'You're not telling me you let Tamsin go alone into a war zone?'

'We didn't exactly know it was going to be... No, listen, Mum, she's not alone. She's with Eleanor. You can trust Eleanor to look after her.'

Barbara hesitated. 'Oh I see. Eleanor is there?'

'Yes, apparently. Matt told me. I don't hear from her myself.' He paused. 'I gather she was staying with an old friend of ours in Stellenbosch.'

'Well that's... That's good. I'm glad to hear that. But what are you going to do about the situation, Alec? You can't do anything from Cardiff, can you?'

'No, you're right. I may see if I can get a flight out to Cape Town...'

*

Seretse could tell there was no hope of driving his car into work at the hospital. 'I'll have to try and get there on foot,' he told his guests. 'Through the back streets, if I can.'

'We'll come with you,' Tamsin said quickly, picking up her camera and popping it into her pocket.

Maseru was not a very big place – about the size of Guildford, Eleanor had read, and well over a hundred years old. The older parts of the town consisted of low square buildings made from reddish beige sandstone; the name Maseru did in fact mean the place of the red sandstone. Eleanor thought it was beautiful, and had already made some sketches of the old buildings the day before.

The streets that morning were obviously not as bustling as usual for the time of day, but there were a few Basotho about, dressed for the cold in their colourful traditional blankets pinned at the neck. There were no other foreigners about, Eleanor noticed nervously.

'Oh look, that guy's carrying a rifle,' Tamsin exclaimed in surprise as they turned a corner. 'Is it loaded?'

'I would imagine so,' Seretse told her, taking her by the elbow. 'Don't hang around, Tamsin.'

Eleanor glanced up at the parched hills which encircled the town, and caught sight of a burst of gunfire. 'God, what's that?' She gripped Tamsin's arm in fright. 'What's going on, Seretse?'

'I didn't think it would come to this,' Seretse muttered, ushering them down a side street. 'It's a protest against a rigged election last May.'

He had had to meet them at M'shoeshoe Airport the week before in a borrowed car, much to his annoyance, for his own car had been hijacked. Cars had been stolen at random and parked outside the palace in an attempt to bring down the government – he had only just got his vehicle back. It was, he told Eleanor, the largest car hijacking in one city, ever in the world.

The first thing Seretse did when they reached the hospital was check his supplies. It wasn't a large hospital: only four hundred and fifty beds at most. They had a limited supply of drugs, and some amount of food. Already people were being brought in with gunshot wounds, and Seretse said that quite a few of the regular staff were missing, having had trouble getting past the tanks.

'Why don't Eleanor and I go into the town and find out what's happening?' Tamsin suggested brightly.

'Well I don't know...' Eleanor was cautious.

'Tell you what,' Seretse told them. 'There's an old motor scooter in a shed round the back – you could borrow that. Easy to ride, if you're used to driving a car, Eleanor? Room enough for you both. Might get you out of danger quicker!'

'Cool!' said Tamsin.

He took them round to the back of the hospital. 'And while we're about it, I might as well give you a couple of white coats to wear. Give the impression that you're official.'

'Great! I've always wanted to wear a white coat,' said Tamsin.

It struck Eleanor that a journalist like Matt Beynon would probably wear a flak jacket rather than a white coat in these conditions, but she kept quiet.

Though old and rusty, the motor scooter was still in reasonable working order and Eleanor quickly grasped its salient features, like how to brake. They set off for Kingsway first, the main road through the centre of town, the heart of the economy, full of banks, tall offices and big supermarkets, as well as the tourist office.

Also in Kingsway was the Basotho Hat, a striking building topped by a thatched roof modelled on the traditional straw hat. They had visited it the day before. It was a cheerful two-storied edifice faintly reminiscent of a Swiss chalet, but conical in shape. It was the main marketing centre for the Lesotho Co-operative which sold village handicrafts, and Tamsin had bought tiny model Basotho straw hats for her mother and David. She'd hesitated over getting one for her father, then decided against, saying he probably wouldn't like it. Eleanor had raised her eyebrow questioningly but it was after all none of her business how Tamsin felt about her father. For all Eleanor knew, Alec might actually be living with That Woman by now. She did not ask Tamsin because - well to be honest, she was afraid of what the answer might be.

'I guess I'll find something else for Dad,' Tamsin had said in the end. 'He's been sad this year.'

Sad. A telling way of putting it, Eleanor thought, and she'd given Tamsin's arm a reassuring squeeze before turning to her own purchases. She had bought a straw basket to take back to Susanna, and promised herself a luxurious Basotho blanket before she left the country, to use as a throw over an armchair, or perhaps as a rug.

Today there were masses of people out on Kingsway, and looting from the shops was already well underway. Hardly surprising, Eleanor thought, with such high unemployment here. With people as poor as this, you'd expect looting, but what puzzled her was why the South African soldiers didn't just stop the looting. That first morning the tanks were parked to the side of the wide road, and the soldiers were standing around awkwardly looking on as a stream of local Basotho came out of the shops staggering under the weight of televisions, washing machines and piles of clothes. It was noisy.

'This won't last,' Eleanor murmured to Tamsin over her shoulder. 'Something will snap and then people will get hurt.'

What the hell am I doing down here with Alec's daughter? If it's that dangerous...

They parked the motor scooter by the side of the road. Tamsin reached for her camera to take a few shots, her eyes shining with excitement.

Suddenly Eleanor heard a familiar voice above the din.

'Eleanor! It is you, isn't it? What are you doing here?'

She looked up, and saw that one of the South African soldiers was leaning out of his parked tank and waving at her. She stared – it was, it really was Henry, the Cape Coloured man whose family she had visited in the Cape Flats when she was doing her African sketches. They'd been displaced a generation ago from the old District Six, which was how she had met them. She had drawn sketches of Henry's little boy kicking a football around on the dusty ground; she had written in her book about how the boy wanted to get into the team.

'Good heavens, Henry! Hallo there, how wonderful to see you! I might ask the same of you – what on earth brings the armed might of the Republic of South Africa into this poor little kingdom?'

Henry didn't sound too sure; he thought they'd been invited in to prevent a coup, but he wasn't clear who'd asked them. 'And the white coat suits you, Eleanor!'

She introduced Tamsin, who immediately took a photo of Henry and one of his tank.

'And how are your children?' Eleanor went on. 'Has your son got into the football team yet? My friends who've read the book all want to know...'

But Henry received an order at that point, and they had to stand back and wave to him as the tanks began to move off slowly.

Eleanor wondered if anyone was going to object to all these photos Tamsin was taking, and she wished there was a tactful way of stopping her. 'Tell you what,' she said. 'Let's go up to the Lesotho Sun and see what's happening there, shall we, Tamsin?' The Lesotho Sun was a tourist hotel up on a hill well outside the centre of town; Seretse had already taken them there to swim in the pool. 'All the foreign journalists will be there; we might find out what's happening.'

As they rode the scooter briskly up the hill, the day was beginning to get warm. It was still only September but after a chilly night they were glad they were only wearing tee shirts and light trousers.

After ten minutes Eleanor came to a halt because she'd suddenly noticed what looked like a row of tanks ahead of them on the road to the hotel. 'What are they up to?' Eleanor said over her shoulder. 'There's nothing political up this way, just the hotel and a housing estate for foreign workers. I can't think why...'

'Let's go and find out,' said Tamsin.

'Well OK, I suppose...'

They overtook several stationary tanks as they came round the bend to the Lesotho Sun. The tanks had just stopped in a row, awaiting further orders. Eleanor looked for Henry, but she didn't see him again. As they approached the entrance to the hotel they saw a group of white officers standing outside, consulting some journalists.

'No, no, this is not the palace,' the hotel doorman said. 'The palace is in the middle of town. It is a long way from here.'

'Try turning your map the right way up,' one of the journalists muttered under his breath.

With some hesitation the soldiers got back into their tanks and someone gave the order to turn round. As Eleanor got off the motor scooter, one of the officers came over and said, 'Excuse me, madam, can you tell me how many gates the palace has? It's only got one, no?'

'Oh no,' Eleanor said. 'I think there's several gates.'

'At least three.' Tamsin looked up at him confidently. 'We were there yesterday. I'm sure there's three gates.'

'Right,' said the officer. 'Thank you very much for your help, ladies.' With that he got back into the first tank.

'Not at all, don't mention it, old boy...' Tamsin mocked, but Eleanor dug her in the ribs.

'Careful, Tamsin. This may look like a picnic gone wrong, but believe me it's anything but.'

The doorman showed them a safe place to park the scooter and they went into the hotel.

The place was quite transformed from their previous visit there of only a couple of days ago. On Sunday afternoon they had sat around the swimming pool at the back of the hotel. It had still been a bit chilly in the water, but pleasantly warm in the sunshine as they had relaxed drinking beer and coffee with Seretse's friends and looking down at Maseru spread out beneath them.

But today no one was bothering with the pool, and the place was swarming with journalists. Eleanor made her way over to a group which was trying to get some information out of their radio. The guy fiddling with the radio put up his hand and waved for silence: he'd found the BBC Overseas Service news. 'South African troops today entered neighbouring Lesotho to prevent a coup...' Their news figured pretty strongly, although obviously things were happening elsewhere too: Hurricane Georges, which had been making its way steadily across the Caribbean, had hit the Dominican Republic; the floods in Bangladesh were abating, but Dhaka was still half under water.

'Your father and I once went on a bus tour round Dhaka because we were delayed at the airport.'

'Oh yes - I think he told us.'

I do so wish you were here now, darling, taking care of your daughter. Come to that, it would be pretty good to have you here anyway, after all this time. What the hell are you playing at with That Woman? It's so tiring keeping up with you across continents. At least now we've still got our own teeth and hips; will we still be waving at each other from a distance when we're old and withered and looking at sheltered housing schemes? Sending bleak signals to each other across the world.

Eleanor wandered through the hotel to the deserted swimming pool where a journalist was using her mobile to ring the American embassy to see how they were reacting. It seemed they were going to send all their people out in an armed convoy straight away, headed by an armoured tank.

'Not wasting any time, are they?' Tamsin offered Eleanor crisps from a packet she'd bought at the bar. 'I don't suppose the Brits or anyone will be worrying about me for a while...'

'Oh I don't know, Tamsin. I should imagine your father must be pretty worried - he did know you were coming to Lesotho, did he?'

'Yeah, I emailed him. He'll be cool - he ought to know I can look after myself. Anyway, Matt told him I'd be going with you!'

At six o'clock night fell suddenly - there was ten minutes of sunset and then pitch dark. Eleanor asked if there were any rooms free in the hotel, and they were given a small room at the back where Tamsin slept soundly and Eleanor herself fitfully.

In the morning they retrieved the scooter - unharmed, to Eleanor's relief - and made their way down to the town. The scenes in Kingsway were a lot uglier on the second day. The South African army had decided to put a stop to the looting of shops. Amazingly, people were still running out of the stores carrying great piles of whatever they could carry. Eleanor and Tamsin parked well out of the way, and stood on the other side of the street to watch. A BBC journalist and cameraman were there, and they definitely had flak jackets on, Eleanor noticed – not a white coat in sight.

Just across the road a middle-aged woman came running out of a department store with a large pile of blankets and sheets. A soldier rushed up to her and beat her head with a truncheon. For a second the woman stared at him, her mouth wide open – then she collapsed in a heap on the pavement, her legs bent under her, the blankets scattered. The soldier gave her a casual kick as she lay there, then moved on to someone else.

Tamsin gasped and reached for her camera, but Eleanor put out a hand to restrain her: this was not the moment to get on the wrong side of the army. It was great to have Tamsin with her but she was too young to recognise danger. 'We can't get involved, Tamsin,' she said.

'Sorry.'

The fires had spread by now, and a substantial part of Kingsway was in flames. Several sites had already been reduced to burnt-out shells. They turned to look down the road at the Basotho Hat, the building where only a couple of days ago they had bought their souvenirs. It was the national landmark at the entrance to the business district, and today it too was ablaze.

To distract Tamsin, Eleanor suggested they should go and find out what was happening at the palace, and luckily Tamsin agreed. The snipers in the hills were still sporadically active, and as they set off up the road to the palace, a shell whizzed dangerously close to their front wheel. Eleanor leapt off the scooter at once, kicked the parking stick and made a dive for the dusty ground. She lay there for a moment, breathing deeply.

Turning round cautiously, she saw to her astonishment that Tamsin was standing bolt upright facing the hills and photographing them.

'Get down, you idiot!' she yelled, jumping up and lunging at the girl, pulling her to the ground. 'Sorry, Tamsin! Are you OK?' she muttered.

Tamsin grinned. 'Guess I am now!'

As they approached the palace, it was clear that the South African army had taken control. It was a seedy 1970s building in grey concrete with contoured balconies, reminding Eleanor more than anything of the campus of a modern university. Somehow the sight of the great rainbow flag flying there struck her as desperately sad.

The general in command was giving an impromptu press conference over in one of the tennis courts. No tennis had been played there for a good while – the fences were broken and the surface decayed. They left the scooter behind a bush and went over to listen to him.

He was a tall, well-built man reporting success: they had been invited in as a peacekeeping force, he said, to contain the situation, to disarm the rebels and prevent a coup. So far they had secured the radio station, the South African High Commission and other embassies, and would shortly be recapturing the two bases of the Royal Lesotho Defence Force.

A French journalist asked him about casualties.

'Unfortunately you can't do this sort of job without taking a few fatalities.'

'How many?'

'Probably the rebels have lost about fifty or sixty. We've lost eight. And seventeen wounded. Next question?'

Eleanor and Tamsin turned away.

By the swimming pool, which was empty except for a mass of grey sludge at one end, Eleanor stopped an officer and asked if he knew who the snipers were. He said they were rebel members of the Defence Force. 'So where are you ladies from?' he went on.

'We're here on holiday,' Eleanor told him. 'I work in Rome.'

'I'm Welsh,' said Tamsin.

'Not from Cardiff?' To their surprise his face lit up as Tamsin nodded. 'I'll see you there next year, madam! When you've built your Millennium Stadium, we'll be over to defend the World Cup – you wait!'

'Think you've got a hope?' Tamsin retorted. 'What about New Zealand? You won't stand a chance against Jonah Lomu. Or Australia...'

'No, no – what you've got to remember about South Africa, man: in the end, we always win.'

Eleanor gazed at the two of them as if they were out of their minds.

'By the way,' she interrupted, feeling the subject needed changing before she was sucked into a mad parallel universe. 'I ran into an old friend of mine in one of your tanks yesterday, guy from Cape Town. Is he around, do you know?' She gave him Henry's surname and rank.

He frowned. 'Give me a moment, can you?'

They followed him round to the far side of the palace grounds, where the soldiers had put up a small tent. The officer spoke briefly to the man outside, then he came back. He was still frowning.

'I'm very sorry, madam. It seems your friend was one of the soldiers who got hit by a sniper. He died early this morning.'

They stared at him in disbelief.

'I'll be writing to his family, of course,' the officer continued. 'But if you know them maybe you can tell them that you've seen his body? People like to talk to someone who was there...'

Henry was lying on a stretcher inside the tent.

He looked quite peaceful, almost as if he was asleep. It took a moment to work out what had happened to him. Then Eleanor saw the patch of dried blood on the collar of his uniform: the sniper must have caught his neck.

'I'll ... er ...I'll go and see his wife,' she said after a long pause.

There was nothing to say after that, and they made their way back to the hospital in silence to look for Seretse.

They had only been away one day but the place had changed beyond recognition. It had taken a few hits, for one thing. There was a good deal of broken glass, and a few crumbling walls. As they dumped the borrowed scooter back in the shed and took off the white coats, Tamsin pointed to a pile of festering rubbish bags next to some used syringes and old surgical equipment.

Inside, the wards were absolutely full – patients doubled up in the beds, some lying in the corridors. It was hot, and there was an overpowering smell of sweat.

They found Seretse at the back, squatting briefly against a wall with a mug of coffee.

'How's it going?' Eleanor asked him.

He spread his arms out in a gesture of despair. 'We're running out of drugs. There's no food. We can't even feed the children.'

'What can we do to help?' Tamsin demanded. 'Where can we get you what you need?'

Seretse shook his head. 'There's nowhere left in town. All the shops have gone up in flames.'

Eleanor considered. 'Maybe I could get out of the country and fetch some drugs for you, Seretse? Could I take your car?'

'The border's blocked – haven't you heard?' he snapped. 'Everyone who's got any sort of vehicle has piled it up with all their worldly possessions and crammed the whole family in, and is now stuck in a queue on the Caledon bridge.'

'But there must be another way out of Maseru,' Tamsin said. 'Maybe the British are getting people out?'

'Worth a try, I guess.' Seretse took his phone out of his pocket and rang a Second Secretary he knew at the British High Commission. After talking to her for a few minutes, he reported to Eleanor that there would indeed be an unarmed British convoy with space for her and Tamsin if they wished to go.

But Eleanor declined the offer. 'I'd rather try my luck in your car, Seretse. I was looking at your map the day we arrived – couldn't I try going north out on the Peka road? That would give me a much better chance of getting you some supplies and coming back into the country with them. Tamsin can go with the British convoy.'

'No way!' Tamsin declared. 'If you are taking Seretse's car, I'm coming with you.'

Eleanor looked at her. The girl was clearly adamant, and at least that way she'd be able to keep an eye on her. 'Well, OK, then.'

I hope I'm not going to regret this.

Seretse's car had been damaged in the hijacking, but only superficially. When Eleanor tried the engine it started at the seventh attempt. They travelled light, with just a couple of small cases for a change of clothes. Eleanor tried to persuade Tamsin to leave her camera in case...

'In case what?'

'In case you get carried away! We might meet someone who doesn't like South Africans.'

'I'm Welsh.'

'Yeah, right, they're bound to stop and ask to see your passport before th ey shoot you, obviously...'

Once out of Seretse's drive, they turned off the main road and skirted the town successfully. Before long they were out on the Peka road.

It was great to be out in the open country again. Eleanor glanced across at Tamsin, who was enjoying the ride and looking all round with interest. The young girl was good company in a tricky situation; she seemed much older than her eighteen years.

The road across the dry scrubby terrain was pretty good at first. There was a strong wind blowing reddish-beige dust.

Tamsin glanced back. 'What about the snipers?'

'Think we've left them behind. They were concentrating on the town. And the barracks of course.'

It was nearly twenty minutes before they came across the first roadblock.

It didn't amount to much: a handful of Basotho youths, perhaps five or six of them, standing around a makeshift barrier. They were in jeans, and all of them carried guns.

Eleanor slid to a careful halt a good four yards in front of the roadblock and wound down the window.

Tamsin nudged her. 'Look over there, Eleanor!' She pointed some distance behind the men at the burning wreck of a jeep.

'Good morning!' Eleanor called out as pleasantly as she could. 'I'm an Italian journalist.' Almost true. 'We're on our way to Peka Bridge.'

The men glared in silence for a moment. Then one of them grunted, 'OK!' and waved Eleanor on with his rifle. Two of the others walked over to lift the wooden barrier.

Eleanor turned the engine on, but it stalled.

'Keep calm,' Tamsin muttered. 'Just try it again.

She did.

The engine spluttered and died.

One young man took a step forward. 'Try a bit more throttle – it is nearly there,' the lad said. An older man put his hand on the boy's arm to restrain him.

Eleanor nodded tersely. 'Thanks.' This time she started, the beauty, and Eleanor drove slowly – very slowly – under the wooden barrier, waving over her shoulder at the same time.

They picked up speed and after a couple of minutes they turned a corner on the shoulder of the hillside. The roadblock was out of sight.

'Well done, Eleanor!'

After that they passed a couple more small roadblocks, but no one seemed to want to stop them. There were several burnt out wrecks by the roadside.

Tamsin opened a packet of peanuts. 'How far to Peka Bridge?'

'No idea. Could be just around that corner down there for all I know...' Eleanor said, turning her head and opening her mouth for Tamsin to shove a handful of peanuts in while she was driving.

'Looks like we've got through the worst, anyhow,' Tamsin went on.

But the young girl was quite wrong.

As Eleanor skidded round the next corner she came to a halt in front of a much bigger roadblock, with at least a dozen Basotho standing in front of it.

This is getting to be a habit, she thought as she wound down her window and stuck her head out. She was just getting to the 'Italian journalist' bit when Tamsin put her hand on Eleanor's shoulder in warning. Eleanor never found out what Tamsin had seen, because at that moment one of the men came forward and began to shout.

He looked about fourteen. He had a blue and black patterned blanket pinned at his neck, and a black woolly hat. He was holding something under his blanket.

'Fokof!' The lad spoke in Afrikaans, but they got the general drift. 'Jy moet fokof hier!'

'We're not South African! I'm Italian and my friend's English!' Eleanor shouted out of the window.

Then very slowly the boy lifted an automatic rifle out from under his blanket and pointed it straight at Eleanor.

'Welsh, you mean.' Tamsin corrected her, wondering if that was the last thing she was ever going to say.

They heard the safety catch click as the lad released it.

'Voetsêk hier, man, of ek skiet jou vrek!'

Eleanor caught his eye, and in the second before he fired she took in that he had a scar to the left of his mouth and that he had not shaved for a day or two.

She felt a sharp burning in her shoulder. She gasped.

A second shot shattered the windscreen and their laps filled with broken glass and blood. Eleanor felt dizzy.

'Let's get out of here quick, Eleanor!'

Eleanor slid down in the seat, crunching her feet on glass, and put the car into gear again. The engine spluttered.

She felt as if a ton of freshly molten steel had been poured into her shoulder.

Then their amazing car spluttered some more, and suddenly revved up very loudly. There was some rough ground over to the left of the barricade which didn't look too steep, and with enormous effort Eleanor managed to turn the wheel and steer in that direction.

Tamsin grabbed a scarf from the back seat and stretched across Eleanor to search her shoulder for the wound. The scarf was soon soaked, so she tore off her own tee shirt and thrust that on Eleanor's arm in a tight ball.

All the Basotho turned to watch, and Eleanor knew that if any of them had fired again they'd certainly have killed them.

After some hundred yards, they turned a corner out of sight, and Tamsin said, 'Phew! We can stop now and change...'

'Rubbish, we can't stop here! I've got to get us out of Lesotho.' Eleanor accelerated.

'No Eleanor, I mean – I can drive! Pull in and let me take over – you must!'

Eleanor had forgotten about Tamsin passing her driving test. 'Oh. Well, I suppose...' She was beginning to feel light-headed. She brought the car to a halt.

Tamsin fetched another tee shirt from their luggage and tied it very tight indeed around Eleanor's arm to stem the flow of blood. 'All those hours of knotting and first aid with the Guides weren't wasted after all!' She was joking, but her face was white.

After that Eleanor didn't remember too much about the journey. She was dimly aware that Tamsin was doing a fantastic job, belting down the N5 as fast as the old crock would go.

They dug the bullet out of Eleanor's shoulder in Bloemfontein. In the days that followed, there was a woozy haze of distant sounds and smells. Nurses changed her dressing regularly and told her she was doing fine. A couple of doctors who said they knew Seretse came to see her, and assured her they would get supplies through to him in Maseru as soon as possible.

At last Eleanor swam up to the surface and opened her eyes properly: and there was Tamsin, perched on a stool by the bed, looking a lot more anxious than she'd ever seen her before.

'Oh, Tamsin love, are you still here?'

Tamsin broke into a massive grin. 'How're you doing, Eleanor? Ready for a visitor?'

'What? Depends who...'

Tamsin glanced over her shoulder. 'I've just got back from Bloem airport – had to meet someone off the afternoon flight from Cape Town...'

'Did you?'

Then for some reason Tamsin stood up abruptly and slipped out of the room. Eleanor didn't have the strength to ask her where she was going.

Alec dashed in and came to the side of the bed.

Alec? No it can't be Alec, of course it can't – he's thousands of miles away. He's got someone else now... I must be wandering again. Maybe I'm in shock?

He bent down at once and grasped her good shoulder and kissed her.

'What the hell do you think you've been up to, Eleanor my darling? We've all been out of our minds with worry!'

'We? Who's we?' she said weakly. She put her good arm up to stop him going away.

'Well Susanna, obviously, and Matt and Roz. Seretse feels terrible, letting you take his car. Oh and my father was worried too – he sends his greetings. So does Mum. Oh darling, you needn't think I'm ever going to let you out of my sight again, after this!'

She closed her eyes. Maybe...maybe he was right.

Chapter Eighteen

Wales, November 1998

There had been a frost early that morning, but now the bright winter sun was shining on the garden and there was the smell of freshly cut logs in a pile by the wall of the cottage. Alec took a hefty swing at the last of the wood that his father wanted cutting.

'Appreciate you doing this for me.' Norman was sitting on the bench smoking his pipe. 'Seems to take me much longer than it used to, these days; don't know why.'

Alec grinned. 'Glad to be able to help, Dad. There, that's the lot, I think.' He put the axe down carefully and came to join Norman on the bench. 'That should keep the fire going for a few weeks,' he said, pointing at the pile of wood. 'Garden's looking tidy, isn't it?'

'That's mainly the Duchess: she had a great summer this year. Good crop of blackcurrants, too. Busy with the jam, of course; you must take some home with you when you go.'

Alec put his jacket on and leaned back, wiping the sweat from his face.

Norman went on, 'We had a postcard from Tamsin, did Mum tell you? Picture of Table Mountain.'

'Oh yes,' Alec said. 'We noticed it on your mantelpiece yesterday. She's having a great time – working as a political assistant to our old friend Susanna. You know they've got elections next year? Susanna's standing for the ANC, and Tamsin is working in her office. Good experience for her, we both feel.'

'She's a bright girl, your Tamsin. Always thought that.' Norman paused. 'Tell you what – one thing I've been meaning to ask you.'

'Yes?'

'Have you thought any more about making a programme on Monte Cassino?'

'Ah, that. There is a possibility I might get another company interested. Won't be 'til the end of next year, but I think there's a definite chance. Would have to be after we've been back to South Africa, because I'm due to make a programme about the elections there.'

'I see. Next year, you say. The Duchess and I were talking about Monte Cassino the other day.'

'Were you?'

'You know my brother Stanley is buried there?'

Alec was silent for a moment. 'I wish...I wish I'd known about your brother, when I was a kid. He was my uncle, after all – my Uncle Stan. But you never told us. We always thought you were an only child.'

Norman shrugged. 'Terrible waste of life, that battle. Never should have been a battle there at all.'

'I know, Dad.'

'I was thinking, d'you see, that I should like to go down there and find Stanley's grave. While I can. Should have done it years ago, but there you go. The Duchess agrees – we ought to go. Next year, maybe. I wouldn't want to go there in winter!'

'No indeed!'

'If you are making that programme... If it goes ahead, as you say, then I think I should like to take part in it.'

'Dad, that's wonderful!' Alec clapped his hand on Norman's back. 'It's what I've wanted for a long time – you know that.'

The kitchen window opened and Barbara stuck her head out. 'Haven't you finished those logs yet, you two? We've decided it's time for elevenses, and I'm warming up those Danish pastries we bought in Llandod yesterday; I'm dying to try them. Do come along in.'

Alec stood up and picked up a few of the logs to take indoors. 'Coming now, Mum!'

In the sitting-room the fire was burning brightly, giving off a delightful smell of wood smoke. Eleanor was on the sofa with her feet up, a rug spread lightly across her – not that she needed it, but Barbara insisted that this room could get draughty in November.

Alec brought in the logs and dumped them on the pile by the fire. He turned and beamed at Eleanor, raising his left eyebrow. 'How're you getting on, darling?'

She moved up to let him sit on the sofa, and leant her head against his shoulder. 'As you see, I'm living the life of late Imperial luxury. Your mother is spoiling me rotten!'

'Well you've got to be careful, my dear,' Barbara said, putting down the tray of pastries and coffee. 'How is your shoulder now? You said it was aching yesterday.'

'Oh, only a little bit,' Eleanor said hastily. 'It was raining yesterday – I think that makes it ache more. It's fine today.'

'Healing up all right?' Norman asked her.

'Yes, perfectly. The doctors are very pleased with me.'

Alec grinned. 'She's still got a whopping great scar, mind! All the way from here down to...'

'Yes, all right,' Eleanor laughed. 'We don't want the medical details!'

'I'm so glad you're getting some fine weather at last, while you are here,' Barbara said, pouring out the coffee and passing round the Danish pastries. 'We've got some lovely walks nearby. November's beautiful, when all the trees have changed colour.'

'Yes, jolly good idea,' said Norman. 'We ought to take you up the local mountain, if you think you are fit enough?'

'Oh, Norman, I'd love to get out! I seem to have done nothing but lie around for weeks,' Eleanor said.

'We could go this afternoon, if you like?' Alec suggested. 'If we set off straight after lunch, we can easily be back by dark.'

'Yes, let's do that,' Norman said. 'I must show you the view when you get just past the gates on the hill...'

'Er, Norman,' Barbara said quickly. 'I need you this afternoon, remember?'

Norman looked totally blank.

'Yes, don't you recall? We talked about it... Oh, never mind, I'll tell you later. We'd better let Alec and Eleanor go up the mountain on their own this time.'

*

They walked gently along the road to see the river going under the bridge, then turned up the steep lane past the old church.

'This bit needs a bit of puff – one in two, Charlie says – but don't worry, it doesn't last.'

She laughed and linked her arm in his.

188

As the road flattened out, a mangy, smelly old sheep dog came bounding up from a farm and stood panting. Alec patted him. 'What, you still here, old boy? It's good to see you, but we can't stop today, we're going up the mountain.'

They turned off the lane and went up a track to a wide wooden five-barred gate, which Alec held open for her.

'Would you believe, Charlie used to jump right over these gates when my parents first moved up here!'

'I can imagine that!'

'Showing off to Dad as usual.'

As they passed the second gate, they came to some woodland which had turned golden in the autumn.

'What was all that about, this morning? Why wouldn't Barbara let your father come walking with us?'

Alec grinned. 'Unusually for my mother, I think she was being tactful. Giving us a bit of space alone together, after you were in hospital so long.'

'I can't get over Barbara being so nice to me – I always thought she disapproved of me!'

Alec was quiet.

'When you were very young she wanted you to marry Milly, didn't she? And I got in the way.'

'Oh, it's quite different now. She understands about me and Milly – why we've separated. Oddly enough – it hurts me to have to admit this! – but oddly I think my dear brother Charlie may have had something to do with that... Something he said to Mum when she went out to Australia to see him.'

'Really? Good for Charlie!'

He looked at her. 'Anyway, she knows you saved Tammy's life in Lesotho. No one in the family is ever going to forget that.'

'Oh no!' She stopped and turned to him. 'You mustn't think that! It was the other way round. If it hadn't been for Tamsin being so cool and efficient, I would have bled to death right there on the Peka Road. Seriously.'

He gazed at her for a moment, then he hugged her tight. 'Listen, Eleanor, you are never, never, ever going to take such a risk again, not if I can help it. Do you hear?'

She smiled and kissed him. 'I'll do my best...'

They walked on, slowly, and paused at a crag near the top, where they could look down right into the narrow valley, at the village spread out below. Barbara was taking in washing from the lines just beyond the kitchen of the cottage.

'I suppose you and Milly must have come up here to visit them quite often?'

'Oh no – Milly hasn't been for years. She said she wasn't interested in a God-forsaken bit of countryside miles from anywhere. Mum and Dad used to have the children to stay when they were young, especially if I was away, but Milly never came.'

'I see.'

'Milly's led her own life for a good many years now, Eleanor.'

They walked on round the corner and upwards.

'You OK, darling? We can turn round if you like,' Alec said, taking her hand again.

'No, I'm fine – this fresh air is doing me good!' Eleanor answered. 'So you and Milly... You are officially separated now, are you?'

He nodded. 'I guess it was only accepting where we'd been for years. We decided – after that ridiculous business with Cecilia...'

'When your photos first got into the newspapers?'

'I guess she used the situation with Cecilia as an excuse for us to make a break. There's no one left at home – David's loving Atlantic College, you know.'

They came to the flat top of the hill and Alec led the way to a small tarn, which was covered in ice. They stood looking at it. 'Don't think we'll sit down here today! It's a lovely spot in the summer. We'll come up again...' he said.

'So...what about Cecilia, then?' Eleanor said carefully.

'Oh darling.' He spread out his hands. 'It never meant anything to me – can you believe that? I always thought of her as just a colleague who was going through a really tough time, who needed my help.'

'You took her to New York, I read somewhere – or was that just some lie made up by journalists?' She turned and raised her eyebrow at him.

He sighed. 'We did go to New York, yes. Just to see the New Year in. I was so desperately lonely last Christmas, Eleanor. You wouldn't answer any of my emails – I had no idea where in the world you were, who you were with. No one would tell me anything. I had visions of...'

'What?'

'I don't know, I thought you'd given up on me altogether. I thought I might never see you again.'

Eleanor grimaced. 'Funnily enough, I thought much the same about you. Of course I knew Cecilia was in love with you.'

He was silent.

'I saw the way she looked at you, that time last year when I came down to the dig.'

'Is that what you thought? I had no idea...'

'No, you were completely preoccupied.'

'Oh God, is that why you went off to New Zealand and cut me off without a word?'

She hesitated. 'I guess it dawned on me in the end that I didn't want just to be one of the separate compartments in your life: there was Milly the Wife, a nice respectable thing for a public figure like you to keep in Cardiff, and Cecilia the bit on the side in Italy, and me – how did you see me, Alec? Something you could always fall back on if you happened to be in the right continent that year?'

After a pause, he said, 'That's what Charlie said to me when we were in the Grand Canyon. That's why I was so angry with him!'

'He did, did he? I wondered what happened that day! He's a pretty shrewd observer of people sometimes – he's not always given credit for it.'

'But it was never like that – you know it wasn't.'

'Oh I think it was, Alec. I had my own career to think of – I got tired of always being there when it suited you. When it fitted in with your schedule. I stayed on in New Zealand because...well, because I was having fun. Just simple, no-commitments fun. Remember fun?'

He frowned. 'Who with? Patrick?'

'No of course not! Patrick would never have time to go off to New Zealand for weeks on end – he's far too busy.'

'So who...'

'It doesn't matter now – it really doesn't!' She laughed. 'He was a friend of Charlie's, that's all. He built his own boat, and I sailed with him.'

He looked at her. 'I see. We mustn't ever do that again, Eleanor. We must stick together from now on, mustn't we?'

There was a pause.

'If you'll have me, that is?' he said.

'Yes,' she said at last. 'Yes, that's what I want too.'

It was just beginning to get dark when they got back to the cottage, and a wonderful smell of roasting chicken filled the place.

'Come and sit down by the fire, my dear,' Norman urged her, taking her coat. 'You must be exhausted. Alec's walked you off your feet; I knew he would!'

Barbara came in carrying a tray with steaming mugs of tea. 'We can eat in an hour, all right? I thought I would go back to an old recipe – do you remember, Alec, when you were children I sometimes used to make marmalade chicken? It's years since I did that. Charlie used to love it.'

To Barbara's amazement Alec and Eleanor caught each other's eyes and burst out laughing.

Chapter Nineteen

1999

Eleanor sat back on the last remaining armchair, munching a piece of toast dripping with Danish butter.

'How can you eat it so burnt? I'm sure it's bad for you.' Gabriella was busy stacking Eleanor's plates and putting them into a packing case, for they were finally selling Eleanor's flat in Rome. 'Especially in your condition!'

'Oh don't be so ridiculous, Gabby! You of all people... After all the babies you've had in your time! Anyway, I've been eating burnt toast all my life, as you very well know, and it has never done me any harm.'

Gabriella paused and looked at her sister. It was true, Eleanor had been looking remarkably healthy this year. Her cheeks were a warm colour, and she gave off a general air of well-being, a glow of happiness.

'Mum's a bit worried about you,' Gabriella said as she made a start on the kitchen curtains.

'Well she can't talk – she was forty-three when she had me, and look how that turned out...' Eleanor retorted. Gabriella turned to look at her and they both began to laugh, for it was a long-standing joke between them.

'Anyway, I'm coming over to see you in July. I want to make sure you're doing all right, resting properly. Mum insists.'

'July? Yes, OK, we should be back by the middle of June,' Eleanor told her.

'Back? Why, where are you off to now? Can't you stay at home...'

'Alec is making a documentary about our old friend Susanna. You know, I told you – she's standing in the South African elections... Tamsin is working for her.'

'Oh, not more politics! More travel! You never do anything else. Surely this time you don't have to go with him?'

'No I don't have to, but I want to. I'm interested. It's a big thing for Susanna... I'll be fine, don't worry, Gab!'

*

It was indeed a hectic few weeks for Alec and Eleanor that winter in Cape Town. It was only the second multi-racial election in the country's history, and Susanna van der Merwe attracted considerable fame – notoriety in some quarters – as a member of one of the oldest Afrikaner families around. Su was invited to stand on the platform at several rallies. Eleanor would never forget the sight of her old friend, her right arm raised in a clenched fist. The crowd loved it. 'Viva!' they shouted. 'Viva ANC, Viva! Viva Mandela!' Then one day they had actually shouted 'Viva Susanna!' and tears had streamed down Su's face.

In the middle of it all, in early May, Susanna's elderly father died suddenly of a heart attack, brought on – his sons said – by the caustic reports in Rapport about Susanna's campaign. Alec and Eleanor flew up to Pretoria with Susanna for the funeral, a tense family affair.

'Are you sure you're not getting too tired, sweetheart?' Alec put his arm round her as they left the church.

'Stop fussing, Alec! You're getting as bad as my sister. Listen, I'm fine...'

Susanna's mother entertained the funeral guests in the garden of her large home in Waterkloof. Eleanor stood in the winter sunshine, balancing her plate and tea in a delicate bone china cup, when suddenly a major row erupted between Susanna and her oldest brother. At that very second Eleanor had a spasm of gripping pain around her stomach.

Oh no – go away!

Obviously Braxton Hicks again; Eleanor had had false labour pains before, and assumed they were not important.

Look – go away, like now, before anyone sees me.

Eleanor took a step back and began to pant, quietly – which is difficult – so as not to attract attention. But Alec was standing a few feet in front of her, listening intently to Susanna's brother, who was shouting by now: Susanna had killed their father, he raged. How could she let down the whole family and all their tribe?

Others in the family joined in loudly, supporting Susanna's brother. Her mother looked on in silence, deeply distressed, staring in horror at her warring children. Eventually an older man, perhaps an uncle, raised his hands and pleaded with them all to stop, to remember that this was a funeral, a solemn occasion before God, and a time to remember the life of a good and honest citizen of this country.

After an eternity - probably only three or four minutes in fact - the pains subsided and Eleanor relaxed. She looked round - no, nobody had noticed. They had all gone back to where they were before the shouting began, trying to pretend nothing had happened.

'Why the hell didn't you say?' Alec demanded when she told him in their hotel room that night.

'It was fine, honestly. I've had it before.'

'Does it mean anything?' he asked suspiciously.

'Oh no, it's very common.'

'I don't remember anything like this with Tamsin or David.'

She'd got used to talking about Milly's long ago pregnancies; he had been hesitant at first, fearful of upsetting her, but they were part of his life, and she did not want to be excluded from anything in his life - not now, after all those years floating at the edges of each other's existence.

In any case Eleanor now felt very much involved with his children -Tamsin, at least. After they had come through Lesotho together, Tamsin and Eleanor had a bond between them which they both sensed would never be broken.

David was more difficult to get to know. He was in his last year at Atlantic College, and busy planning his own gap year which involved, as far as Alec could gather, going round the world visiting all the friends he had made at college. There was a girlfriend too, but even Tamsin had not heard much about her. 'Dave operates on a need-to-know basis,' Tamsin told them. 'And you, Dad, do not need to know.'

*

The climax of the Alec's filming in South Africa came on election night, June 2nd. The ANC won again, predictably, with a sharp decline in seats for de Klerk's National Party - and much to Eleanor's delight Susanna won her seat. Nelson Mandela had made it clear he was resigning - one term as President was enough at his age, he declared. Thabo Mbeki was going to be the new President, and in amongst all the excitement Susanna was going to Parliament.

Alec tried to interview her outside the count, but it was impossible to hear anything. The whole town had erupted and everyone was out on the streets and in the public parks, singing and dancing with joy, a glorious mix of all the races. Tamsin was there with Susanna.

Eleanor was sure she would never forget this night.

Susanna urged Alec and Eleanor to keep in touch, to come back in the months and years to come and see how the rainbow country was doing; and they promised they would.

*

Back in Cardiff a few days later Eleanor found it very hard to settle. For the first time in her life, she felt bored. The baby was no longer moving about as he had done in the early days, and for some reason the size of the bump was not increasing – it measured thirty-one centimetres on two consecutive occasions.

'What does that mean?' Alec barked at the nurse.

'Steady on, love,' Eleanor said. 'The poor lady is doing her best!'

It could be that the baby had stopped growing altogether, which did not sound good. The nurse suggested listening to the baby's heart. Eleanor almost didn't want to, in case they couldn't hear anything – but it was all right: there was a definite thump-thump there. Alec could hear it too, and his face creased into a smile of relief.

'But why hasn't the bump grown, then?' Eleanor asked.

'It could be that there isn't enough fluid round Baby,' the nurse said, consulting her notes. 'I think we'll have a word with Doctor.'

The doctor thought that there was no immediate cause for alarm. 'But maybe we will need to induce you,' she suggested. 'Not this week, but soon, if fluid is the problem.'

'Is that bad?' Alec asked her.

She hesitated.

'Please tell us,' Eleanor said steadily. 'We'd rather know.'

'Well sometimes too little fluid can lead to brain damage. Don't worry, it's rare – but you ought to get plenty of rest if you can. It's a marvellous excuse!' The doctor laughed. 'You can lie all day on the sofa and get everyone to wait on you! We'll have another look next week.' With that she was off to her next patient.

*

'Good thing I came, then!' Gabriella exclaimed when she had unpacked her bags and cooked the supper. 'You obviously can't take any chances...'

'Oh no don't say it!' Eleanor interrupted, her hand in the air.

'What?'

'You were just going to say at my age, weren't you? Pur-lease! We can do without that...'

Alec grinned. 'She's got a point, though, hasn't she, love? Wouldn't hurt to rest for a bit. We could get you some magazines?'

Luckily Eleanor knew he was teasing.

'No! I want to do something, Alec – anything! Something new... Deep sea diving? Roz says Matt is into that big time, remember?'

Gabriella was completely dumbstruck by this suggestion, but Alec laughed, sharing Eleanor's quirky sense of humour. 'Tamsin's due back any day now – that should be enough excitement for everyone, never mind deep sea diving,' he said to Eleanor.

Then he turned to Gabriella. 'Sorry, you've no idea what we are on about! Let me take you down to South Africa, Gabby – we are in the sea off Betty's Bay, and my cousin Matt has just disturbed a great white shark...'

Gabriella gasped. 'No!'

'Matt is separated from the other divers, and he's gone down at least four metres on his own. Suddenly there's this huge fish staring at him! What can he do?'

Gabriella's eyes grew large as she waited.

'He stares back, but he can't move at all – he can't swim or even breathe out because the bubbles would show and the shark would have him for elevenses. So he holds his breath and gently treads water,' Alec went on.

'So what happened?' asked Gabriella after a pause.

'Oh, the shark just swam off in the end.'

'Oh I see. Is that all?' Alec was a nice man, Gabriella thought, but sometimes the conversations he had with Eleanor were completely crazy.

'Sorry, Gabby!' Eleanor said.

In the end Eleanor was persuaded to stay indoors for a few days, resting, on condition that Gabriella cooked her favourite Italian specialities every day. She demanded tira misu, which was one of her sister's finest desserts, and she ate three helpings, even though she knew from experience that it would give her terrible indigestion; but then practically everything did, these days.

Braxton Hicks came back later on the evening of the tira misu. At least she assumed it was Braxton Hicks, but it didn't stop this time, and eventually she had to admit that it might be a good idea to get over to Llandough hospital just in case.

*

Tamsin was the first visitor next afternoon – she arrived breathless, clutching a teddy bear with a rather fancy green jacket that she'd been keeping for several months, and also some flowers she'd bought at the entrance to the hospital.

'Oh he's wonderful!' she said. 'So tiny! Can I...'

'Well I'm not sure...' Alec hesitated.

'Oh go on,' Eleanor told her. 'You're dying to pick him up! Of course you can. He's your brother, after all...'

Tamsin bent down and put her hands round the baby as gently as she could, and lifted him up.

'He was a good size in the end – seven pounds three – after all that panic about him not growing,' Eleanor said.

'What panic?' Tamsin demanded.

Alec and Eleanor glanced at each other. 'Sorry, Tammy, we didn't want to worry you with all that,' her father said. 'We knew you'd be back soon anyway.'

Tamsin glared at him. 'Another time, Dad... You could have told me.' She peered at the small bundle in her arms. 'Oh, he's got Dad's eyebrows! I've never seen them on anyone so little before. Hallo, Will, aren't you wonderful?'

Eleanor smiled.

He's real. He's solid. He's going to go on now, existing, demanding, changing our lives.

Eleanor turned to Tamsin. 'I think he looks like you, Tammy. Round his mouth, and his nose, definitely.'

'Oh, do you think so?' Tamsin beamed at them.

She glanced round the ward, and her eye caught the enormous vase of flowers on the windowsill. 'Who are they from? Exotic, or what?'

Her father laughed. 'Can't you guess, Tammy? From your Uncle Charlie of course! Never knowingly understated. He got Interflora in Australia to deliver the most extravagant bunch they could find in the whole of the principality...'

*

It was six weeks later. The afternoon sun shone on the olive trees around the cemetery, and high above, the mountain dominated the town of Cassino as it always had. Barbara was wheeling the baby in his pram around the garden, careful to keep the linen shade in place above him; he had in any case been smothered in baby sun cream of factor something like a hundred. She was singing gently to him: Guide Me O Thou Great Jehovah, out of tune.

'I haven't heard you sing for years, Mum!' Alec said, coming up behind her.

'Oh, there you are,' she said. 'I haven't had the opportunity. I used to sing to you when you were in your pram, you know.'

He laughed. 'I don't remember that!'

'I always sing to babies, but I tend to give up if there's anyone over the age of two present. William seems to like it, just for now.'

Alec bent down and inspected his son. 'How're you doing, little boy?'

William stirred in his sleep and grunted.

'He's going to want another feed shortly,' Alec said. 'How long has he been asleep?'

'Oh, a good hour, I should think. Have they found Stanley's grave?'

'Yes, it's over there on the far side, beyond that row of trees, look,' he told her. 'Why don't you have a sit down on that bench, Mum?'

'Oh no – Will needs pushing: he'll wake up and start crying if I stop! How did you get on this morning, with filming your father?'

'Very well, Mum! Didn't he tell you?'

'He wouldn't say a thing about it.'

'And you didn't ask him?'

She looked at Alec. 'I do have some discretion, you know.'

'I know!' He put his arm round her. 'He was amazing. We went right out onto the hillside where the fighting was, and he just talked about it. What it was like. The cold, the wet. Why it went on for so long. How he saw people killed... So much detail! It was as though he'd forgotten we'd got a camera crew following us, he just wanted to explain what happened. Mum...'

'Yes?'

'Did you know about Stanley, when you first met Dad? Did you know he'd had a twin brother?'

Barbara stopped and adjusted the sheet around the baby as he slept.

'Yes. Yes he told me the night we first met.'

'Did he?' Alec was surprised.

'It was one of the first things he told me about himself. Oh we met at a party – I'm sure you remember that old story – and we just talked and talked. Forgot all about the party. Yes he did mention Stanley, but I got the impression he didn't normally talk about him. And he didn't want it talked about again – that I did know. We never had any photos of Stanley.'

William stirred again, and this time began to wake up and fret.

Barbara glanced at her watch. 'Come on – time to find your Mummy, young man. You're getting hungry!'

Over on the far side of the cemetery Eleanor was standing in front of a headstone towards the end of a row. They had identified Stanley's name, and she had put a small bunch of flowers in front of it. Norman stood in silence beside her, his thoughts private, not to be disturbed.

How arbitrary life is! What unlikely set of events so long ago brought these two young Englishmen here to Italy to this particular spot, to fight so unnecessarily, so uselessly? And what if it had been Norman and not his twin brother who had trodden on that landmine? Then there'd have been no Alec, no William... And I would have been somewhere altogether different from here, living quite a different life.

Eleanor turned and saw Barbara and Alec approaching briskly with the pram. Must be nearly time for Will's feed.

Norman said, 'Thank you, my dear. Thank you for bringing me here.'

'I'm so glad you felt able to come, Norman.'

'Yes. Yes, so am I. And look, here comes the Duchess with your little one. You've got work to do now, I think.'

Eleanor smiled. 'There was something I wanted to tell you, Norman. I hope you don't mind...'

'What's that?'

'You know we're calling him William because...well, because we both like the name. But we've given him a couple of middle names too. Svend, after my father. And we wanted Stanley. I hope that's all right with you?'

His face lit up. 'Stanley, eh? Yes I should think Stanley would do nicely.'

ACKNOWLEDGEMENTS

I am forever grateful to my husband Robin Attfield, who has accompanied me over the years to nearly all the places you will find in this novel, often while he was lecturing in philosophy or giving conference papers. I'm also grateful for our wider families in Denmark and India for their friendship and support. The cottage in Powys, mid-Wales, was shamelessly stolen from our old friends Margaret and Robin Fawcett. For the Afrikaans spoken during the armed invasion of Lesotho I am indebted to Johan Hattingh and his son Diederik of Stellenbosch, South Africa. My daughter Jo was caught up in that conflict when she had recently gone to teach Maths in Lesotho and she sent me a large and extremely useful collection of cuttings about it from the local press afterwards. I am grateful for the support of our Scottish Country Dancing class, many of whom have read my books and offered welcome encouragement – next time I produce a collection of short stories, one of them will have to involve Scottish dancing, I promise! My daughter Kate not only illustrates my work but has always provided thoughtful and inspired criticism which I could not do without.

I have used the modern spelling Kolkata, although at the time this story takes place it was still called Calcutta. Matt's Uncle's name, Som, is pronounced Shome. M'shoeshoe Airport is pronounced M'shwayshway. In Ukraine in 1990 I stayed with a family in a town they called Lugansk, which I now understand is the Russian spelling; I am told that the Ukrainian spelling changes the 'g' to an 'h' so I have used the spelling Luhansk in this novel.

About the author

Leela Dutt is an outsider, an only child brought up in Golders Green by an Indian father and a Danish mother. She has travelled all her life since the day her mother had to tuck the toddler under her arm while she struggled up a steep metal ladder on the side of a warship in order to be taken to Denmark to see the family just after the war.

Leela lives in Cardiff with her husband the philosopher Robin Attfield; they have seven grandchildren, of whom six survive, and one great-granddaughter. After history at Oxford she was briefly a teacher, a shop assistant and a journalist. She then took a degree in computing, and set up and ran a database about housing research for Cardiff University, before joining the Big Issue Cymru as a proof-reader and reviewer.

For full details see the website attfieldduttbooks.co.uk, which covers Robin's philosophy publications as well as all Leela's writing.

More from 186 Publishing

THE TESTING OF ROSE ALLEYN – Vivien Freeman
Vivien Freeman's intelligent and heartwarming exploration of the choices facing a young woman in the late Victorian era

WELCOME TO MARMOT (Population 32) – Chris Mason
Following a mail truck after he gets seriously lost in rural Washington state, Kevin Calenda finds himself in a tiny, remote town that has no phone service, no Internet, no regular mail service (the mail truck is private), and a population of 32. But it does have paved roads, a Town Hall that could service a city of 30,000, a vegetarian cafe, a tasteful bar, a resident artist, and a Montessori school. And right outside the grand Town Hall is a six-foot statue of a marmot.

Visit www.186publishing.co.uk to find more books

Lightning Source UK Ltd.
Milton Keynes UK
UKHW020925031222
413263UK00015B/748